A HOUSE MADE OF GLASS

ROGER BAKER

First published in 2020

All rights reserved. No part of this book may be reproduced or used in any manner without written permission of the copyright owner except for the use of quotations in a book review.

© Roger Baker, 2020

The right of Roger Baker to be identified as author of this work has been asserted in accordance with Section 77 of the Copyright, Designs and Patents Act 1988.

ISBN 978-1-78972-828-6 (paperback)
ISBN 978-1-78972-827-9 (eBook)

*To my parents, who gave me, together
with so much more, a love of books.*

I

1

I had never thought to own such a house. It was altogether too grand. The scope and location of its site set within a wide loop of the river, the beauty of its gardens, the huge living and working spaces it offered, the flair and daring of the design itself: any one of these would have placed it beyond the reach of my resources. Style more than anything else would have ruled against it. Where I looked back to forms and materials of an earlier age, this was a structure that trumpeted its modernity to the world. It was unlike any building I had known, demanding to be viewed against the best of the old and setting a path for a new generation of architects to follow.

Every known canon of taste and economics decreed that this house and I were not meant for each other. Yet, against all the laws of probability, it was mine. I could lay claim to every inch of its land. I could exercise rights of ownership over every stick and stone of its fabric, right down to its very last nail or screw. Legal rituals had been observed; documents had been processed. The house did indeed belong to me. I still held in my hand the key that had unlocked the front door. Given time I could have produced title deeds. They would show beyond question that the house was mine.

That would have been the easy part. In questions of ownership something further is required beyond the furnishing of proofs and that something was missing. The exact nature of that missing factor is not easily explained. I can only describe it by saying that something did not feel right, for this was precisely what I felt on taking possession of my new property.

The feeling did not relate to anything concrete. Its origins were intangible, lying within the realms of mind rather than of matter. Its roots fed deep within the layered memories of the subconscious. There, legal niceties were arrayed against other thoughts and emotions. They told a different story. I had not built this house. Nor had I planned for it or acquired it by any of the usual methods. There had been none of the longing and striving that characterize most achievements. I had felt none of the desires, made none of the sacrifices that cleave cherished possessions to one's very soul. I cannot honestly say that I had ever wanted it. A piece of paper had been handed to me. That was all. Title in the strict legal sense had passed to me; ownership in its truest sense had not. I was left with this feeling of being a stranger in my own house.

The feeling persisted as I made my new owner's tour of inspection. It surfaced when I parked in the arc of the driveway and remained as I inserted the key in the lock. If anything, it increased in strength as I made my inspection room by room of a house I had known, it seemed, in another life.

There was an instant reminder when I opened the front door. The hall was still furnished. Only the withered brown stalks of rosebuds in the bowl on the table and the heap of letters on the floor suggested that the house had been unoccupied for some weeks. It was much the same in each of the family rooms upstairs. Everywhere there was the evidence of its former life. Living-room, dining-room, bedrooms: all had been left fully furnished.

I did not stay long in the dayrooms, but made for the

master-bedroom. The bed was made-up ready for use, but when I slid open the wardrobes I found myself gazing at empty shelves and bare clothes hangers. By the time I had made my way into what had been the main drawing office, I was no longer surprised to find the drawing tables and even the new computerized work station still in place, nor that all evidence of commercial activity had been removed. I remembered Philippa and the sacks of drawings at the time of my last visit. I had thought then that her actions went beyond the call of mere duty.

Curious, I sat down before Rollo's computer and switched on. The hard disk had been wiped clean, but a floppy disk left in the 'A' drive had been missed. It contained a single file bearing the name 'Xanadu'. The drawings showed designs for small chalet constructions and the detailed drawing for a larger pavilion which I had glimpsed once before. There was also the ground-plan of a large house showing before and after treatment for the remodelling of one of its wings. The plan was incomplete, but I needed no labels to guide me. I knew Eastonbury too intimately not to recognize it at once.

I switched off the machine and sat before it for a while. Xanadu. The words of the Keats poem we had learned at school came back to me. Xanadu, the site of Kubla Khan's pleasure dome on the banks of the sacred river Alph. I smiled to myself at the aptness of the name Rollo had chosen for the project. I smiled too at the unplanned irony. Just as with the poem, this project was doomed to remain uncompleted.

Save for the rosebuds in the hall, that single floppy disc was the only evidence of human activity I found in the house. Everything else had been methodically cleared out. Sudden as Rollo's departure had been, it had not been precipitate. There had been no frantic moonlight flit. All the evidence suggested a methodical clearance of any personal effects that could not have been effected at short notice.

The realization that all that had happened in those final days had been a sham left me feeling deflated. Everything had been premeditated. It was impossible to avoid that conclusion. Yet now I had been given the house and seemingly all its contents. I made my way back to the entrance hall more puzzled than ever of what to make of it all.

It was certainly no ordinary house I had acquired. Future generations might even call it a great one. Even now, after my earlier visits over the past few months, my heart still leapt at the sight of the atrium soaring with all the audacity of the high gothic to that incredible crystal crown. That power to stir the imagination was still there, but there was a strangely different feel to it now. The house was dead. All its vents were closed. The water had been switched off so that the stone of the cascade looked grey and lifeless. Only the surface of the pool was alive, reflecting the sunlight that poured in from above. Around it the palms stood motionless as if waiting on the mood of their owner.

Well, I was now that owner. It was within my power to summon them to life. The controls were simple enough for a child to operate. A faint hum indicated that the house was responding to my instructions. A barely noticeable movement of palm fronds betrayed the passage of the first currents of air through the opened vents. Then an irregular pattering quickly developed into a continuous subdued roar as a curtain of water slid over the edge of the concealed reservoir high above the balcony to fall first into the high pool and then on down the series of cascades to the main pool set in the floor of the atrium. I pressed more switches and the hidden spotlights bathed the wall of falling water in a luminous blue-green light. I had seen it all in operation before, but now for the first time I had witnessed this dramatic surging into life. I stood as filled with awe as Livingstone must have been at Victoria.

The balconies had been designed to give the best views of the cascades, so I moved upstairs and settled on one of the long leather settees. I sat for some time lulled by the sound of the falling water. My thoughts turned again to my ownership of all that I now saw. It was strange. I was alone in this house, yet I could not feel alone. His presence was everywhere. This had been his home, his creation. I had been not even the merest onlooker, for all this had been wrought after we had become estranged and I was many miles away attempting to build a new life free of his influence.

He had been such a dominant feature of my life for so many years that it was hard to accept now that I had seen the last of him. Yet I had to accept it. There had been an air of finality in his last letter and there was also the matter of this house. That had been the most surprising development of all. What had been his motives? Was it merely some last-minute decision or had it been planned. I would probably never know. His moves had always been hard to fathom and his mind was so quick and intuitive that often I had seen him make instant responses to some chance happening that had all the appearance of resulting from long and careful thought. What was without question was that the bequest of so rich a property was a deeply uncharacteristic act.

This house had had a mesmerizing effect on me from the time I had first seen it lighting up the night sky. How else could I explain my renewed involvement with him when all sense and experience should have told me to stay well away. How else could I explain my acceptance of the largesse he had offered. Now I had been presented with this new crystal chalice. Was this too to prove charged with that same treacherous mix of poison and fine wine. Would this new vessel prove as unsafe to drink from as the last. Perhaps somewhere in the past, I reflected, lay the answer to that question.

2

We made a strange group that first morning, alike as penguins, scattered beneath the line of lime trees that bordered the yard. I had arrived much too early. Night-time mist still hung in wraiths giving a chill to the morning air which sharpened the shivers of apprehension I felt gnawing inside. I had taken up station beneath one of the trees and stood patiently, feeling alone and insignificant. Around me a straggle of other boys had slowly assembled. We were all made conspicuous as newcomers by the newness of our uniforms and the gleaming empty satchels hung with maternal exactness across our chests. Alone among the boys in the yard we wore our caps.

Beyond the trees the yard filled with teeming life. Like us, all were uniformed and yet seemed set apart. They were already part of this new world we were joining. They were familiar with its rituals fashioned over four hundred years. They did not feel intimidated by the numbers or the size of the buildings. They already belonged. As yet unclaimed, we did not.

An electric bell shrilled. Boys moved away, draining from the yard like water draining from a bath. No adult had appeared. No one had issued instructions. Still we waited beneath the trees, our uncertainty increased by the order and purpose we had witnessed. At last at the edge of the group there was agitation. A figure trailing an academic gown barked instructions and finally we were led away to the great hall to become part of this strange new world.

Chance alone could have conspired to place Blake and Bradley in third and fourth places on the list flourished by the gowned figure who had collected us from the hall and led us to the room in the annexe that was to be our base for the next year. So it was that, as I responded to the bellowing of my name and the arm waved generally in the direction of the back of the room, I found myself sharing an old double desk with Rollo Blake.

The thought that all eyes were upon me was enough to keep my head bowed down and I crept to my appointed place with all the courage of a mouse. I remained seated with head bowed while seating allocations continued. It was some time before a lull in proceedings enabled me to steal a first shy look at my new fellow. I was aware of a shock of dark wavy hair and a handsome smiling face. He had obviously been waiting for my attention, for he immediately squirmed sideways in the bench seat in order to thrust a hand towards me.

"If we are to be friends", he whispered, "we had best introduce ourselves. I'm Roland Blake, but you can call me Rollo."

It had not crossed my mind at that stage that we were to be friends, but the proffered hand demanded a response.

"Paul Bradley."

I made the simple hesitant statement of my name and we solemnly shook hands within the narrow confines of the desk.

"I shall call you Brad", he continued.

I wanted to reply that I was perfectly happy with the name my parents had given me and to which I had answered for eleven years. Yet there was something about his self-assurance that melted any objections. Instead I grinned foolishly and so Brad I became and have remained to this day to all outside my family.

In the lunch hour, it was Rollo who gave the lead in exploring our new surroundings. Looking back, I can see now how shy and unassertive I was then. Rollo, by contrast, had a ready supply of ideas that he intended to pursue. I was all too happy to follow his lead and he seemed to like it that way.

It surprised me at first that Rollo should continue to spend his time in my company, for he was soon well known throughout the school. He was taller than the average boy of his age and was accepted as an equal by boys several years older. He might be seen in the thick of the fray when the lunch hour football game was at its most frenzied, or lording it on the fives court where the gable end of the old barn provided the playing wall. My own acquaintance ran only to a few boys from my own form and without him I would never have plucked up enough courage to join such playground activities. As the weeks progressed, I found that I had come to depend on his company. He in turn, whatever he had been involved in, would unhesitatingly seek me out with a full report of his doings. In this, as in so many other aspects of his life, he was a source of surprise. For all his numerous acquaintance, no one else was admitted to the rank of friendship. It seemed that I was his single close friend.

What was it that produced our friendship; that is something I have never really understood. Nor could I understand then why he needed any confidant at all. To my youthful eyes he seemed to be quite self-contained. Whatever may have been his reason, I gradually came to realise that I was Rollo's chosen one and that, however uncritical might have been his original choice, from there on I was assured of his friendship and its many benefits.

School milk was a good example. At primary school, I had always taken school milk. It was a surprise to find no organised system for this at my new grammar school. A few crates were left each morning by the caretaker in the Old

Barn, available on a first-come-first-served basis. Equally surprising was the amount of bullying that continued unchecked. For new boys, it was a case of – if you want it, you must run the gauntlet. I received a hard lesson in this during that first week. Our morning lesson had overrun into break-time. Only a few bottles remained in the last crate when I made my way to the barn. They were being guarded by a pair of Fourth Years. One of them sent me sprawling on the brick floor as I bent over the crate. I can picture it very clearly. I was fighting back tears of impotence and rage, when suddenly I was aware that Rollo had jumped forward.

"Leave my friend alone!"

His cry was delivered simultaneously with a punch to the nose of the bigger of my assailants. For a moment, I thought that they would fall upon him, but the initiative was his and they backed off. Rollo pulled me to my feet and with a glare at my tormentors, took a bottle from the crate and handed it to me. It was my first taste of the benefits of Rollo's friendship.

That was the first revelation of a wilder, more impulsive side to Rollo's nature. There was at times a reckless bravado about his actions which I found daunting. Initially, he laughed at my timidity and poked gentle fun at me if we were alone together. Despite this, I began to grow a little uneasy. Beneath his good humour I could sense a growing impatience with my lack of daring. I knew that a time would come when my adulation would not be enough. He would expect me to make greater efforts to follow in his wake.

I remember clearly the day the gauntlet was thrown down. A railway line ran through a wide, deep cutting near the school. We had fallen into the habit of spending the lunch hour watching the passing trains from the footbridge that spanned the cutting. That day, what had begun as a routine train-spotting foray, suddenly changed. During a lull in traffic Rollo became bored and began to cast around for something to do.

It began innocently enough. He climbed up to stand on one of the flat-topped hand-rails of stout timbers no wider than his shoe and took a few tentative steps.

"Come on, Brad," he urged. You take the other side."

There was no backing out. I climbed reluctantly onto the rail and stood swaying unsteadily. I looked across at Rollo, but he was already ahead of me.

"Come on", he called again, "I'll race you to the other side."

With that he was gone. Without so much as a wobble he skipped swiftly across the entire width of the cutting and turned to check if I had responded.

I felt a rising shame. While he had made the complete crossing, I was still coming to terms with the fear that gripped me. I was strongly aware that the ground beneath me sloped away down to the trackside and that I would then be exposed to a drop of over thirty feet. I made a mental note that if I felt that I was overbalancing I must jump into the safety of the footway. Then slowly step by step I began the crossing.

I think that both of us realised the significance of it all. For me it had become a test of my courage. I simply felt that I had to show that I was worthy of his friendship. I was grimly determined to make the crossing in his wake, perhaps not in the confident, dancing manner that he had displayed, but slowly and deliberately in my own dogged way. For his part Rollo stopped yelling his exhortations. He stood on the far bank watching my progress, aware of the mountains of doubt and fear that I had to overcome.

Slowly, one fearful foot after another, I made my way out over the first of the four tracks gleaming hard below. Too late, I realised that the lull in traffic that Rollo had seized on was at an end. So intent had I been on my footwork, that I had not noticed the goods train moving purposefully up the gradient, the engine at its head pumping out huge plumes of smoke. The train would pass directly beneath me and I had the choice of staying put or of jumping down and beginning the nerve-wracking process all over again. I chose the former and stood quite still, ignoring the wild gesticulations of the engine crew. The bridge trembled. I felt the heat of the exhaust fumes as the engine passed beneath me and then I was alone in a world of billowing grey smoke.

It seemed an age before the smoke drifted away and I could see Rollo again. I felt strangely composed and completed the remainder of the crossing in little or no time. I jumped down triumphantly alongside him. Nothing was said, but I sensed that an important milestone had been passed.

Amid the flurry of afternoon classes and the demands of homework the exploit was quickly forgotten. It came as something of a shock the following morning when the Deputy Headmaster rose at the end of assembly to announce that complaints had been made to the school. Boys wearing the school's uniform had been seen carrying out dangerous practices at the railway cutting. As a result, the area adjacent to the railway line had been placed out of bounds. The boys concerned were to report to the Headmaster immediately. Although it was not spelled out, the consequences of such an interview were obvious to everyone.

I had frozen in my seat as the announcement was made. It seemed to me that guilt was printed across my face and that all eyes were upon me. I stole a glance across at Rollo sitting alongside me. He was checking the homework timetable at the back of his school diary with studied unconcern.

As we filed out from assembly, I detached myself from the other members of my form and headed for the Headmaster's study. Rollo had guessed my intentions and tugged me back by the sleeve.

"You're not going to own up, are you?" he demanded. "They're only fishing. They don't know it was us. No one knows."

"Yes, but I know," I replied. "Don't worry. I shan't say anything about you."

He looked at me searchingly, but he could see that I had made my decision.

"You're a fool," he said, and walked away leaving me to face the headmaster alone.

It was typical of Rollo's restless nature that other interests were soon found to occupy the lunch hour. It was as if the railway cutting had yielded all its excitements for we never again visited it. Nor was our feat of walking across on the handrail ever referred to. Our friendship settled into a new, deeper stage in which I felt that I was more on equal terms with him. More significantly, for the first time it moved outside the narrow confines of school life.

We were sitting with our backs to a wall enjoying the spring sunshine when he casually broached the subject.

"It's my birthday next week. Would you like to come to tea?"

"Yes. I'd love to. Who else is coming?"

"Oh. No one else. It will be special." He paused. "So. After school on Thursday."

He was in one of his enigmatic moods and it was clear that he had no intention of saying anything further on that subject. Instead he scrambled to his feet.

"It's time to move. We'll be late for Maths."

He had said little about his home or family, so I had no idea what to expect. My mother ensured that on the appointed day I was wearing a clean shirt and advised me to be sure to wash my hands before leaving school. I saw little of Rollo during the day and he was coolness itself when we met up after lessons. He led me directly towards the town centre and to my growing astonishment approached a rather elegant lady who was standing beneath the clock that graced the market square. She was wearing a dark suit which she had topped out with a fox-fur tippet. She was about to consult her wristwatch when she became aware of our approach. She beamed with pleasure.

"Ah! There you are darling. I was hoping you would not be late."

Rollo's good timekeeping was rewarded with an arms length embrace and a peck on the cheek. He was obviously used to such public displays of affection, for he bore her embrace without any hint of embarrassment and then turned to me.

"Mummy, I would like you to meet Brad."

The beaming smile was turned on me.

"Brad, it's so nice to meet you. Rollo has told me all about you."

I took the gloved hand she proffered and mumbled something suitable in response. This was not what I had been expecting. As a little boy, I had been invited to birthday parties. I had worn party hats and been filled with jelly and cakes. Something similar is what I imagined Rollo's birthday tea would be, but this was turning out to be altogether different. I was still coming to terms with the turn of events when they led me to a building I knew, but had never before entered. Brownings was the town's leading tea shop, a long-established business that clung to a past in which waitresses, dressed like Victorian parlour maids, fluttered from table to table bearing delicate silver trays. The tea room was at first floor level and we mounted the stairway from the street in silence. Mrs Blake paused briefly for Rollo to open the door for her and then swept to a table at the window which overlooked the square. She took a seat directly facing the window and indicated that Rollo and I should sit on either side of her. One of the parlour maids placed a leather-bound menu before each of us, stepped back and waited. Mrs Blake smiled at Rollo as she carefully removed her fox fur.

"Would you like to order dear?"

I looked at Rollo with some surprise, but he seemed quite at ease with the request.

"What would you like Brad?"

I studied the menu dutifully until my eyes rested on something familiar.

"I'd like an ice cream".

"Then you shall have one."

He turned to the hovering waitress with all the assurance of a man twenty years his senior.

"Tea for three, poached pears with fresh cream for two and a single ice cream ... oh, and would you bring a tray of cakes."

Mrs Blake smiled approvingly and patted Rollo's arm.

"I do love poached pears."

She must have noticed my bemused look, for she next addressed me.

"You see Brad, my husband died some years ago. It is so difficult being a single woman again. Rollo has had to become the man of the family. I think he does it awfully well."

I wanted to see how he reacted to this, but his mother was already directing her next thoughts towards me.

"And what does your family do Brad?"

"My father owns a nursery on the edge of town."

"A garden nursery? Oh! how lovely. I absolutely adore flowers. It must be a real joy to have them around you every day. Do you intend to follow your father in his business?"

I choked back the urge to say that I loathed the whole nursery business with the never-ending demands of the plants and the meagre return they brought in. Instead I shrugged deprecatingly.

"I don't really know yet what I want to do."

"Of course. It is early days yet. But do take my advice. Choose something interesting and preferably something that will earn lots of money."

I found Rollo's mother fascinating. I had no way of knowing whether her interest was genuine or feigned, but it was the first time I had been treated as something other than a child and the experience was not unpleasant. I began to relax and enjoy the ambience of the deep pile carpet, damask table cloths, silverware and hovering parlour maids.

It was some weeks later that I eventually visited Rollo's home. The house was a rather forbidding Victorian villa that lay just off the centre of town. I remember the apprehension I felt as I approached a front door inset with Gothic revival stained glass and tugged the wrought iron bell pull.

Mrs Blake answered the door and greeted me with the same ease as she had shown at the tea room.

"Oh hello, Brad. Rollo is out running an errand for me at the moment. Would you like to come in and wait for him? He should not be many minutes."

As I stepped into the hall my attention was caught by the display of large coloured photographs which adorned the walls. The one I had first noticed showed dramatic mountain scenery.

"That is the Andes."

She had noticed my interest and came to stand beside me. She waved her hand in the direction of the other photographs.

"They were all taken in South America. My husband was a mining engineer. We travelled all over. Did Rollo tell you that he was born out there?"

I made my way round the hall examining each of the pictures. They were a mixture of mountain views and vast mineral excavations. There was a single picture of a hillside villa. Bright sunshine lit up the stuccoed walls and the garden terraces were a blaze of colour.

"That's our house in Santiago. We lived there several years."

"It's a lovely house."

"Yes, it is. I was very happy there . . . but, I wanted Rollo to be educated in England. So, here we are."

Rollo returned home at this point and we went upstairs to his room.

"Was Mummy showing you her pictures?"

"Yes. I liked the house in Santiago. It must have been hard for her to have to sell it."

"Oh, it wasn't sold. It's still ours. Mine I should say. Dad left it to me. I may go back to South America one day. I have dual nationality."

"You own a house in Chile?"

"Mm. I own other bits of land there and in Peru and Brazil, and there are blocks of shares in mining companies. It is all held in trust for me. The bank pays me an allowance every six months, but I can't touch the capital until I'm twenty-five."

I did not press him further. He did not think his wealth in any way unusual and seemed more anxious to show me the illustration of the racing bicycle he was planning to purchase with his next allowance. Even so he had revealed much more of himself than he had ever done before. I began to understand the source of his worldliness and self-assurance. His had been a different life to the world of greenhouses and pot plants that I had always known.

It was, perhaps, that visit to the Blake's house that first awakened my interest in the art of building. Long afterwards I could remember the details of the villa quite clearly. At that stage I had no fixed idea of becoming an architect; that was to develop in the later years of my youth. Initially it was simply one more feature in a world that was slowly coming into focus. I had noticed for the first time how one building differed from another and how each bore the stamp of the age in which they were built. The discovery was strangely exciting and I began to seek out more information on this absorbing new mystery.

All of this lay in the future. In the meantime, Rollo and I continued to enjoy our years of innocence. He had purchased the cycle he had pointed out in the catalogue with such enthusiasm. Together he and I began to explore the local countryside, he on his new lightweight racer and I on the more traditional bicycle that my father had once used. The possession of the faster, lighter machine gave Rollo the advantage his competitive nature required. We would begin by riding out to a favourite spot. Then, with frequent stops to look for bird's nests or some other such boyish activity, we would explore further in whichever direction fancy took us. Invariably, once we turned for home, the return ride would become a pursuit, which Rollo, with the advantage of greater strength and the better machine, always won.

As I remember them, these were the good years when we were as one with each other and seemingly with the whole world. During the long days of the school holidays we would spend all day together. We seemed to live on our bicycles as they gave us the mobility to move away from the orbit of home and parents. A favourite haunt was a spot a little way out of town which we called the rapids. The river here narrowed and cascaded to a lower level over a series of rocky ledges. In winter, or after heavy rain, the waters would rush over these in dark, swirling eddies. We enjoyed throwing heavy branches into the water upstream and then, mounting our bikes, to follow their progress from the riverside path until they reached the calmer water where the river made a wide horseshoe bend around a long meadow. In summer, the river was much shallower and it was possible to wade across at this point or swim in the natural pool that formed above the first of the ledges. Winter or summer this place attracted as no other and as we outgrew boyish games we would ride out there just to sit and watch the movement of the waters.

In time, more serious interests emerged from our cycle rambles. During one of our explorations my fancy had been taken by a village church and I resolved to make drawings of it. Unwittingly, for the first time I had suggested a joint activity. Rollo took readily to the idea and the following day we returned armed with drawing paper and pencils.

It was a beautiful July day. We had a picnic tea and the whole afternoon and early evening to ourselves. The church was an interesting mixture of several building periods and sat atop a small rise with its churchyard sprawling down one side of the slope into a narrow valley. We stood our bikes against the churchyard wall and looked for a suitable place to work. For once we did not sit together. I took up a position on the grass near the driveway and began to draw the porch and its medieval oak door. Rollo had wandered around for a while before settling among the gravestones some way down the slope. We both became engrossed in our work, a rare thing for Rollo, who usually found it hard to stay with one idea for very long. It was only when, much later, Rollo called out that he was feeling hungry, that we realised how far the sun had moved round.

We ate tea at the foot of the tower and viewed each other's efforts. I had made detailed studies of the porch, the top of the tower and the tracery of a window in the south wall. I handed them to him without comment. He looked at them intently.

"Wow, Brad. These are really good. I didn't know you could draw like this."

I caught echoes of his mother in his enthusing, but I think his appreciation was genuine, for the style of our drawing was quite different. While I made drawings, which were precise in detail and shading, he looked for broad general impressions. He had made a number of sketches that took in the whole sweep of the church and its surrounding village.

"What do you think?"

Typically, he could not wait for me to give my verdict unprompted. I studied each drawing in turn appreciating what he had created with just a few deft strokes. I finally settled on one sketch that looked past the church to the old vicarage alongside.

"I like them all," I said, "but this one in particular. You've really caught the feel of the place."

"You can have it."

"Are you sure?"

I could not understand how he could so readily part with

something he had only just created. I have kept all the drawings I have made over the years in a series of notebooks and folio cases. To Rollo it was different. He always looked to the morrow and had little interest in what was past. In any case he was always more interested in the effect his work had on others. This sketch was the by-product of a pleasant afternoon in the sun, once completed he had no further use for it.

"Of course. Keep it."

I handed the drawing back to him.

"You've not signed it."

"What?"

"I would like you to sign it for me."

"All right. But why? Are you planning to keep it?"

I nodded my head and he signed his name with a flourish. I still have it. Even when the bitterness between us was at its most intense I could not bring myself to throw it away.

For once we did not race home, but rode alongside each other. A month or so earlier we had completed our O-level examinations. Already boyish interests were being pushed into the background by thoughts of the world that lay beyond school. That afternoon had given a first indication of what our roles in that world might be.

That first afternoon of sketching was to prove a turning point. For the first time, I was no longer trailing in Rollo's wake. I had found an interest that I wanted to pursue and which I could practice at any time that suited me. I purchased my first sketchbook and began to fill it with drawings, often several to a page, of any one of a hundred and one architectural features that caught my eye. Where possible I would read up on my subjects and squeeze detailed annotations between the drawings. In this way, I began to build up an encyclopaedic knowledge on this subject.

Rollo and I saw less of each other now. We were following

different programmes of sixth-form study and his looks and physique made him popular with girls in our age group. We still cycled out together during holiday periods, but some of our former harmony was missing. Increasingly we eschewed our old riverside haunts and our rides became reconnaissance expeditions during which we looked for interesting buildings. Once a subject had been found I would happily spend an hour or two sketching all the details I wanted to record. Rollo found this increasingly irritating. The smaller houses and barns that sometimes interested me held little appeal for him. He would kick his heels in an exaggeratedly bored fashion whenever I called a halt to examine something. Only larger buildings caught his attention and here his work was much more rapid than mine. He was interested only in the overall design. He had the gift of encapsulating the essence of a building in a few brief lines and the sketches he made were simple rough impressions. Often, he would not bother to make any drawing at all, preferring to commit any impressions to memory.

I remember him being particularly irritable one day. We had ridden out to examine an old tithe barn in a distant village. Once there he had found little to interest him. While I settled down to sketch a section of the roof timbers he walked around looking thoroughly bored. Finally, he came to look over my shoulder.

"Why are you bothering with this," he asked. "It's only boring old gothic."

"This type of roof truss is not very common."

"Maybe so; but why all the detail?"

"I think it's important," I replied. "I like to understand the intricacies of the design."

"What's the point? This is bog-standard for the middle ages. It's just a church without a tower. You can see hundreds like it. Whoever built this was just repeating an old familiar design."

"So! What if he was?"

"An architect should not be complacent. He should always be looking for new methods, new materials."

It was obvious that his comments were not just a reaction to the barn. These were feelings that had been building up for some time. I laid down my pencil and took up the challenge.

"Good architecture is about detail. A building is made up of dozens of detailed features which must meld with each other."

"That's bullshit. Real architecture is about vision. You have to see the whole structure first and how it fits its role and location. The detail comes afterwards. If there is no vision it's not architecture - just building."

I was surprised by the vehemence of his comments. This was something he obviously felt strongly about and his ambitions for the future were on display for the first time. I was not in any way cowed by his sudden onslaught and looked him steadily in the eye.

"I disagree with you. You can't write a building off just because the design has been used before. This is a good, well-proven design. It was built to last, serves its purpose and is pleasing to look at. What more can you ask of a building?"

Even as I spoke I realised that this was an argument that would carry little weight with him, for it was not buildings as such that interested him, but the admiration and glory of the architect.

"Well if that is all that interests you ..." He left his sentence unfinished and turned away. "I'm going back. I have things to do."

"Hang on. I have finished here."

We rode back together in silence. It was the closest we had come to quarrelling and we were both conscious of the gap that had opened between us. We were developing in different ways which would prise apart the close camaraderie of boyhood and we were unsure of how to handle it.

. . .

Matters were now coming to a head at home over what I should do when I left school. It had always been my parents' wish that I should receive the best possible education. They had been tremendously proud when I donned my grammar school uniform for the first time and had never counted the cost of the sacrifices I knew they made on my behalf. Now I found them strangely divided over the next step.

I brought matters to a head one evening as we finished dinner.

"I have to make a decision soon about next year."

I tried to sound as casual as I could, but I knew that this was a topic that was on all our minds. We had talked around it for many weeks and 'next year' was understood by all to mean whether or not I should apply myself to further study after A-levels. The decision could no longer be delayed. Most of my sixth-form friends had already embarked on university applications.

"Have you thought any more about what you want to do?"

Mom as usual took the lead. She had always been the strongest advocate of the benefits of a good education, but she was aware that the decision facing me would affect the rest of my life and she had little knowledge of Higher Education to guide her. Intuitively she had centred on the real issue - what I wanted.

"Yes. I'm pretty well decided. I would like to go away to college."

"And what would you study?"

"Architecture."

There was a pause. If I had said that I wanted to study law or medicine they would probably have been perfectly happy. Yet both of them seemed unhappy with my statement.

"Are you sure Paul?"

My mother looked me in the eye. Her gaze was unwavering.

"Are you sure that is what you want? How would you earn a living?"

"There would be all sorts of work I could do. I might even end up lecturing or teaching"

I had been prepared for that question and knew the mention of teaching would mollify her for it had often been suggested as a good safe job. I was not to get off so easily. Dad now took over the cross-examination.

"Would you be any good at that? I mean I know you like looking at buildings, but surely there would be calculations and that sort of thing. Would your maths be up to it?"

"I'm not intending to be a civil engineer."

He sighed and I knew what was coming next.

"You don't have to go to college. It's not the only option open to you."

"I know that Dad. You have told me often enough."

He had himself left school at fourteen and gone to work with the council's parks department. Now he had his own business and was proud of what he had achieved. I think too, perhaps, he was afraid that going away to college might change me in some way.

You can always join me in the business. It's getting too big for me to handle by myself, and it will all be yours one day."

"No Dad. It's not what I want."

He had long cherished the idea that he was founding a family business which would grow with each generation and I knew that my answer would spell the end of that dream.

I think Mom felt his pain.

"Your Dad and I only want what is best for you."

"I know that Mom, so let me make my own decision. I want to study architecture. It's the one thing that really interests me."

I thought that this would resolve the issue. I was unprepared for what followed. They exchanged a look. Then Dad drew a deep breath and finally said what must have been on his mind all along.

"Are you sure this is your own idea? You have not let Roland influence you have you?

"No, he has not," I exclaimed angrily. "What has made you ask that?'

In truth, I knew exactly why he had asked. His feelings towards Rollo had always been ambivalent at best.

My school-friend had made his first appearance at the nursery a few weeks after the birthday tea at Brownings and had soon become a regular visitor. He seemed to like the informality of our home life for he would often turn up when not expected. My mother had taken to him quite readily and he to her. I think the secret was that she ignored his superficial manly charm and treated him as she would any boy of his age. It must have been a rare treat for him not to have any demands made upon him.

His relationship with my father was more complex. Dad was quiet and hard-working. He was a man of simple beliefs and must have found Rollo's worldliness difficult to accept in one so young. As a result, there was always a degree of suspicion on both sides and Rollo was never fully relaxed with him in the way in which he was with my mother. It did not help matters that Dad always addressed him as Roland and never by the sobriquet he preferred.

Initially both my parents were wary of this new friendship.

"He seems a nice-enough young lad," my mother had said after his first visit, her words of approval somehow sounding like a reproof, "and very well-mannered."

As usual, Dad was blunt and to the point.

"Do you know anything about him?"

"What's the matter? Don't you like my friend?"

"I have not said that I don't like him. As your mother says, he seems a nice-enough young lad."

"But what?" I knew Dad well enough to know that there would be a 'but'.

"It's just that he is not the sort of lad I expected you to pal up with. That's all. Just make sure he doesn't lead you into anything."

I had turned away to hide the tears of disappointment that welled up. Deep down I knew that he was right. The problem was, Rollo was not anyone's sort. He was a one-off.

They had warmed to him more after I had told them of the school milk incident, but Dad's wariness of him had never fully disappeared. Looking back, I realised that the strong lead he took when we were together was plain for all to see and my reports of his South American property and the trust fund must have given them much to think about. All too clearly, I could now see how they must have viewed our outings of recent months. I had always been fulsome in my praise of Rollo's gifts and had brought home a number of his sketches which I had proudly displayed to them. It had never occurred to me to sing my own praises and display my own work.

Mom had risen to collect the dishes for washing up.

"No." I said. "Leave those for a minute. There is something I would like you to see."

I ran up to my room and returned with my sketchbooks. I handed one to each of them.

"There!" I said. "That is what I do when Rollo and I go off together."

Mom had seen odd drawings of mine before, but it was the first time Dad had really seen my work.

He slowly leafed through the book taking in the detail of the drawings and my copious annotations. I could see that he was impressed.

"And you have done all this?"

"Yes." I pointed to the other sketchbooks. "And all of these. You see it's not Rollo leading me. If anything, it has been the other way around. It was me that got him interested in architecture."

Dad handed the book back to me.

"All right. If it's what you want, you had best give it a go."

I went ahead with the tedious business of making applications. Rollo had already gone ahead with his and had immediately been offered a place. My own success was harder to come by. Of the four colleges I approached, two extended interviews and it was many weeks before one wrote offering a provisional place. I smiled ruefully when the letter informing me of this arrived. It appeared that fate had again taken a hand. In all probability Rollo and I would be studying at the same college.

<h1 style="text-align:center">3</h1>

That first term in Bristol was the most miserable period I had experienced. It was like being a young boy starting school all over again. Everything was strange and new. This time, however, I was not treated as a child with all arrangements made for me. On the contrary, there seemed to me to be a noticeable lack of information about anything. I was a young man and I was expected to look after myself. In time, I came to enjoy the challenge of growing up, but at the beginning it came as quite a shock to be suddenly cast adrift in a strange city without the props of home and family.

Home for the time being was to be the responsibility of Mrs White. Her house was an old town villa that stood uneasily between the respectability of Redland and the seediness of Cotham. Student lore spoke of digs that ranged from homes-from-home to visitations of hell, and even with a wistful longing of the attractive young widow who shared her bed with her student lodgers. None of these extremes was to be my lot. Mrs White was a no-nonsense lady in her late forties who took in students to boost the family income. Her policy was to do exactly what was necessary to meet the requirements of the lodging officer and no more.

I found that I was to share what had formerly been the

large front sitting-room with a university student named Mike Davies. We saw little of the White family, for we had our own small bathroom and took our meals separately in a small parlour adjacent to our room. Meals were always at set times and Mrs White would become very annoyed if we were late or upset her arrangements in any way. She did not cook on Saturdays, but served a dinner of pie and chips from the local take-away at 1 pm. It was then that she liked us to pay our rent for the week in cash.

Mike seemed to attract her wrath more often than me. He was an engineering student and had to work long hours in the university laboratories. Meeting the conflicting demands on his time of his tutors on one hand and Mrs White on the other was a continual problem. He asked if the evening meal might be served later, but the lady's timetable appeared to be carved in the same stone as Moses' commandments, and so his struggle continued.

It was only made possible by the motorbike which he rode like a madman between one and the other. It was the motorbike that was the usual cause of any friction. He was accused of bringing oil into her house and she made a point of inspecting her tablecloths for tell-tale oil marks when she served our meals. Chiefly I think that what really bothered her was that the machine was parked every evening by the front gate.

Gradually, I adapted to my new style of life. Before I had left home, Dad had taken me to his bank and opened an account for me. I had added my first term's grant cheque and now, for the first time in my life, I had means of my own. The sum involved was small, but to me it seemed like a fortune.

It was a few days before I met up with Rollo. We had talked of travelling down together, but had finally decided to travel separately. Dad had driven me down in his little van with my cases and bike crammed in the back. Rollo had travelled by train accompanied by his mother. She had been insistent on a personal inspection of his accommodation. We had arranged to meet on the morning of enrolment. In the event there was only time to exchange a few words with him before he rushed off. I had his address and he had asked me to call on him at the week-end.

He had been allocated a place in one of the college's own residential halls. The address turned out to be a three-storied house that served as an annexe to a larger building around the corner of the street. The front door stood open as I approached. The beat of jazz music filtered down from somewhere above. I rang the doorbell and a man emerged from a room adjacent to the front door.

"Yes. Who do you want?" He asked.

"Roland Blake." I replied.

"Rollo! Someone for you"

He yelled up the stairway and disappeared back into his own room without waiting for a reply. Upstairs the jazz ceased and I heard Rollo's voice answer.

He came clattering downstairs moments later. He was dressed more casually than he used to and there was a flushed look to his face.

"You found it then."

He led me up two flights of stairs.

"Not bad eh. I share the top floor with two other blokes."

We crossed the small landing into what was evidently a communal sitting room. A fair-haired youth in a black roll-neck sweater lounged on a settee beneath the window. He looked up as we entered.

"Brad, meet Chris and Greg. Brad and I were at school together."

Chris nodded from the settee and went back to lounging. Greg was reloading the record player and did not bother to look up.

I looked around the room. On the occasional table stood an empty wine bottle and three used glasses. Rollo followed my look.

"We can go to my room if you like. It will be quieter."

We crossed the landing to a room at the back of the house. It was simply furnished and I sat on the bed while Rollo showed me the books he had bought.

"Did you bring your bike? I asked.

"No. I don't suppose I shall need it. I am taking driving lessons. There's a place just off the Centre that offers a reduced rate to students. That's where I was going on enrolment day."

I thought how different was this Rollo from the sixth-former of a few weeks ago. In the old days, we would have gone together. I said nothing.

"I'll be getting a car once I have passed my test. Something sporty. That's what the girls like."

We were interrupted by Chris and Greg coming to the door. They talked agitatedly with Rollo in the doorway for a few moments and then I heard them going downstairs.

"They're going to the offie. We're throwing a party tonight."

"Here?" I said. "Can you do that?"

"Of course," he replied carelessly. "We can do pretty well whatever we like. Jimmy - that's the bloke who let you in - is supposed to keep an eye on us. He's a post-grad student so he lives here rent-free. He's a good bloke. He doesn't bother us at all."

My face must have registered some of the surprise I felt for he turned on me angrily.

"Oh, come on Brad. Don't be such a puritan. We are not at home now."

I do not know whether he had been inclined to invite me before this outburst, but in the event, he did not. In a way, I was relieved for I had already raided the college library and had a week-end of reading and note-making planned. I stayed with Rollo for another twenty minutes or so. His mind was clearly on other things for he repeatedly glanced at his watch and wondered aloud what was keeping Chris and Greg. In the end, I decided to leave them to it.

Rollo followed me downstairs. He seemed anxious to go to the off-licence in search of his friends. We walked together to the end of his street. At the corner, he gave me a sorrowing look.

"Loosen up Brad. We're here to have fun."

We parted company there. The afternoon had not turned out as I had anticipated. It was a beautifully mild October afternoon, so I went in search of Brunel's suspension bridge, determined to salvage something from the day.

When classes commenced on Monday morning Rollo made a point of sitting next to me. During the break, he guided me to the cafeteria for coffee. He toyed with his spoon for a while. There was something he needed to say.

"I hope you didn't mind about Saturday," he finally said.

"What about Saturday?"

"My not inviting you to the party. I didn't think that it was your scene ... in any case it was mainly to get to know the other blokes in the annexe. We all got drunk."

"I didn't mind. Honestly." I smiled at him.

"It's useful being in hall. You get to know a lot of people quickly."

This was a new Rollo that I would see much more of in the future. He was determined to make a splash in his chosen career and was already networking.

At first, I had thought that I would be cast aside, but it was not to be so. He was not so unfeeling. I was his oldest friend. He would come to me when there was something he wanted to discuss or when he simply needed a sounding board to bounce ideas against. For the rest, he quickly built up a circle of friends who amused themselves by throwing parties whenever possible.

I was useful to him in one particular way. He found taking notes tedious and on occasions missed lectures on mornings after a particularly late night. Before exams or when an assignment was due he would ask me to run through things with him or borrow my notes. In turn, I often turned to him for help. The technical aspects of the foundation course stretched my abilities as a mathematician to the limit and Rollo was a ready source of help. On these occasions, it was quite like old times.

It was to be short-lived. From the second year onwards much of our time at college was spent on specialist options. Rollo had naturally chosen to concentrate on design and materials and spent many hours in the design studio where his work was already attracting attention. My own chosen path lay in the fields of architectural history and the conservation of historic buildings. Without realising it, we were developing lives of our own. We still met up from time to time, but not on any regular basis.

We had made one expedition together. He was anxious to see the suspension bridge at close quarters and I willingly led him to the place which from that first Saturday had become a favourite. In those early months, when I had felt low or unhappy, the picturesque serenity of the Avon gorge and Brunel's superb span had given me the spiritual uplift I needed.

I remember saying all this to Rollo as we made our way through the centre of old Clifton.

"Can you see what I mean?" I said as we approached the bridge. "Isn't it beautiful up here?"

My words were wasted on Rollo. He was looking at something quite different. He walked about for a while silently appraising the scene. Finally, he made his pronouncement.

"It would appear to join nothing to nowhere," he said, "and it is too narrow for practical use. But what a statement! Brunel will always be remembered for this. That is what I want."

• • •

The loss of Rollo's company was not the great event it once might have been. I had come to terms with the need to stand on my own feet and had begun to enjoy some of the pleasures that city life had to offer. I had also become aware of the constraints of living as a lodger and had given notice to quit at the end of term.

I was set on finding a place of my own. There was no doubt in my mind where this place would be. Clifton had cast a spell over me. Living there would entail travelling across the city each day, but I found it easy to ignore such handicaps. I could not contemplate living anywhere else.

My budget only allowed me to run to the expense of a bed-sit, but there were always one or two advertised in the local paper. Eventually I found an advert for a room in the old village and went to inspect it. The house formed part of a regency terrace that had seen better days. My heart sank a little when I took in the peeling paintwork and general drabness. However, I was cheered by the friendliness of the balding man who answered the door and led me upstairs. The room was large with double sash windows that let in plenty of light. A neat kitchenette had been set in an alcove with a curtain that could be drawn across when it was not in use. It offered much more space than I had to share at present at Mrs. White's.

"What's the rent?" I asked as I checked the outlook from the window.

"Three pounds a week. That's not counting electricity. There is a meter for that."

Even to my unpractised eye it seemed unreasonably cheap. I was still turning this and other factors over in my mind when another younger man came into the room. He made only the faintest swishing sound as he entered, for he wore felt carpet slippers that seemed too large for him. He was over six feet tall, his build accentuated by the untidy sweater he wore and the shambling way in which he walked.

The landlord looked up as he entered.

"Hello," he said. "I'm just showing the room to someone."

The newcomer merely grunted and shuffled across to the kitchenette. He looked in several cupboards and then left in the same silent way as he had entered.

"My son." The landlord explained. "He suffered brain damage at birth. Everyone here spoils him. He likes biscuits."

I made a play of looking over the room a while longer and then left with the promise that I would think it over. I was in two minds. I had burnt my boats with Mrs White and would have to arrange something before long. The room was just what I wanted and was very cheap, but I wondered how I would handle a retarded thirty-year-old who came around cadging biscuits. I decided to get away from Bristol for the week-end.

The significance of the role that coincidence plays in our lives is something which has always puzzled me. Had I not gone home that week-end, I would not have renewed my acquaintanceship with Steven Armitage and things might have turned out very differently, but that was much later.

He was standing forlornly on the platform when I arrived to catch my train back to Bristol on Monday morning. It had been almost a year since I had last seen him. Steve had followed my path through school a year below me, and it was not until we were both in the upper school that I had really got to know him. We had been paired together in the team of stage hands who built the sets and carried out the backstage work for school plays. That was the sort of situation where you get to know someone's real character. He was good with his hands, always in good humour and thoroughly reliable. We had worked well together and a tenuous bond had formed.

My first thought on seeing him had been simply that it would be nice to talk over old times with him on the train.

When I greeted him, I was surprised to see how ill-at-ease he looked. He returned my greeting with palpable relief.

"This is well-met," he said. "Thank God for a familiar face."

"How far are you going?" I asked.

"Bristol. I'm starting work there at the beginning of next month. I have to sort out somewhere to live."

He explained that he had joined an accountancy group, the name meant nothing to me, and would be based in Bristol. He would be studying for the Chartered Institute examinations at the same time.

"The exams are killers," he said. "There will not be time for much else. I shan't mind that. It's things like today that get me. I haven't a clue what I'm doing."

"Don't worry," I assured him. "The natives are friendly. You'll survive ... Look, I've nothing on today. I'll give you a hand"

I was deliberately flippant. I recognised the signs that he was feeling much as I had done a year earlier.

Our train arrived and we found seats in an empty compartment near the front. He quickly returned to the subject that was uppermost in his mind.

"What's it like? Living with a strange family I mean?"

I regaled him with tales of life with Mrs White and her tussles with Mike and his motorbike. He listened attentively.

"You don't think it's a good idea to go into lodgings then," he ventured.

"Some are OK. It's pot-luck what you end up with. All I know is that I would prefer to be able to eat what I want, when I want and to be able to come and go as I please."

"Yes. I can see what you mean."

"I was looking at a place on Friday. Went home for the week-end to think it over. I shall have to do something soon. I've already handed in my notice."

Steve perked up. His hangdog look was suddenly gone.

"You mean you don't have anywhere yourself at the moment?"

"No. Not after next week."

"Why don't we go shares? What would it cost? I mean you wouldn't mind, would you?" The words came pouring out.

"Yes." I said. "Why not."

It all worked out surprisingly easily. That afternoon we looked over a furnished flat in Royal York Crescent and the following week we moved in. The flat was small, but we had a bedroom each and, a real luxury, our own bathroom. Looking back, I realise what little thought we had given to the matter. We had the happy optimism of youth and had taken it for granted that we would rub along together well.

4

Life fell into an easy regularity from that point. It was the beginning of the spring semester before anything happened to change that pattern. There were a number of new faces present for the module on the History of Interior Design that began that second spring. A number of the newcomers were girls. They stood out in what had hitherto been a male environment. I was to become acquainted with one of them much sooner than I would have expected.

I had turned up late for the first lecture. When I entered the lecture room the only light came from a slide projector which Ollie Jenkins was already using to illustrate his talk. I made for an empty table which I could just make out in the dimness. There was a crash as my feet caught on something and I went tumbling into the first row of tables. The light from the projector went out. Roars of laughter broke out from the rest of the group as I groped about on my hands and knees for the end of the cable I had evidently tripped over. Eventually I found it and replaced it in the power socket. The projector lamp blazed again. Ollie, I knew of old, would have to make some quip. It duly came.

"Well, whoever you are, it's nice of you to drop in."

My ordeal was not yet over. I lurched hurriedly into the

seat I had targeted. Fortunately, everyone was still laughing at Ollie's response, so few heard the second smaller clatter as I dislodged a small drawing case from my neighbour's desk. I bent to retrieve it at the same time as its owner and we bumped heads. I pulled back at once to my own station conscious of the long hair that brushed against my face. For some reason that I did not fully understand, I suddenly felt my face reddening. I was thankful for the half-light which concealed the worst of my embarrassment.

When the lights came on at the end of the session. I stole a glance at my neighbour. I could see little other than a curtain of long fair hair, for the girl was already on her feet collecting her papers together. She straightened and threw her hair back over her shoulders with a toss of her head. I was conscious of a handsome face and then she was turning towards me. To my surprise she spoke as she squeezed past.

"Do you always make such spectacular entrances?"

"I was a bit clumsy. Sorry."

"I was referring to your arrival."

I searched for something to say in response, but she was already past me and heading for the door.

I did not see her again until the following week. This time I timed my arrival with precision. As I had hoped, she was already there and sitting in the same seat. I slipped into the seat alongside her with all the nonchalance I could muster. She had seen my approach, but feigned surprise.

"Oh! You startled me. I didn't hear you falling in."

I laughed with her.

"I suppose I deserved that."

We were interrupted by the entrance of Ollie. I just had time to say what I had been planning.

"You ran off last week before I had chance to say anything. Would you like to have coffee with me afterwards?" I gave her a hopeful look.

"I'll think about it." She spoke quietly, for Ollie had already begun.

To my relief she agreed to have coffee with me. My experience with girls had been very limited before this. I had anticipated all manner of difficulties, but in the event, I found her very easy to talk to.

"I was surprised to see girls in the lecture room."

"Why so? Fifty per cent of the population is female."

"I know that." I coloured slightly. "It's just that there are not many of you here."

"Oh, we are not from here," she continued airily. "We are Art & Design students. We do a hybrid course. We just come here for the interesting bits."

"So, Architectural Design isn't interesting?"

"That's not what I said. Don't twist things. We do the most interesting bits from either college. I mean, who would want to study concrete."

"Not everyone here studies concrete."

"I know that. I was only using concrete as an example of something most girls would find mind-numbingly boring."

"Most boys too," I added and we laughed.

"So," she continued, "what do you study when you are not falling over?"

"Architectural History mainly and Conservation."

"Mm. Interesting. What else do you do?"

"I sketch."

"Nothing else?"

"Isn't that enough?"

"It will do for the time-being." She looked at her watch. "Golly just look at the time. I must dash."

I suddenly realised it would be another week before I would have the chance to speak to her again and desperation gave me courage.

"I also like going to the cinema. *Breakfast at Tiffany's* is on at the Whiteladies. Would you like to see it?"

"Can't afford it."

"I'll pay."

She tossed her hair back in her characteristic way before

giving me a steady look.

"All right. When shall we go?"

"Tomorrow evening?"

"OK. Tomorrow evening. I'll see you at seven o'clock outside the cinema."

When Steve returned from his office the following evening I was putting the final touches to my preparations. This was something he had not witnessed before. Our usual weekday practice was to get in a couple of hours of studying and then slip out late evening for a quiet beer.

"Going out?" He enquired, throwing his briefcase on the settee.

I looked at him with a self-satisfied smile. "Yes," I said. "I've got a date."

"Have you now." He gave me an arch look. "And who is the lucky girl?"

"Oh, just a girl," I said as I headed for the door. "See you later."

I hoped that I had created a suitable aura of mystery for it had suddenly struck me that I knew virtually nothing about her.

A steady trickle of people passed into the cinema while I stood outside. I had last minute doubts that she would turn up. Then suddenly she was standing in front of me. She was wearing one of the pale blue macs that were the fashion that year. Her long fair hair hung down over its shoulders.

"Well," she said. "Shall we go in?"

"There is something I would like to know first."

"What's that?"

"Your name. I don't know your name."

A smile played briefly round her lips.

"It's Jo. Jo Westgarth."

"I'm Paul Bradbury. My family call me Paul. My friends call me Brad. Take your pick."

"Brad." She tried it for size. "Mm. Suits you."

We walked into the foyer.

"What is Jo short for?" I asked.

"Promise not to laugh. My full name is Joscelyn Lucinda Westgarth. Would you believe it?"

"I knew a Joscelyn at primary school."

"Poor girl! Well, meet another."

I was still smiling as I paid for the tickets. The evening had got off to a better start than I had dared hope for.

A light drizzle was falling when we emerged some hours later. Bristol in its customary fashion was already shutting down for the night. She shared a flat with two other girls in Redland, so I offered to see her home.

"It was nice of you to pay for me. I'm always broke."

"Don't you get a grant?"

"Yes, but only ten pounds a year. Dad earns too much. In theory, he's supposed to pay me the difference to bring it up to a full grant. The trouble is he never does. So, I'm always short."

"I expected to pay. I mean it's customary on a first date, isn't it?"

We walked for a while in reflective silence.

"Have you ever felt like the girl in the film?" she eventually asked.

"In what way?"

"It's difficult to explain. There are days when I get this urge to just go away somewhere."

"Anywhere in mind?"

"No. There is nothing specific. Just this feeling that I would like to break away. You know, just go. Don't you ever feel like that?"

"Not really. There are places I want to see, usually because of some building like the Parthenon, but I'd be going there with that in mind."

"Mine is not like that. I don't know where I want to go or what for."

"Maybe you are searching for something."

"Are you happy with yourself?" She looked at me thoughtfully. I considered for a moment before replying.

"Yes, I think so. I am not sure what I am going to do when I have finished the course, but I am happy with what I am doing, so I suppose it will be something to do with architecture."

"You're lucky. Perhaps I would feel differently if I had some great aim instead of this craving for something I don't understand."

She was silent for a moment or two and then assumed an aged grandmotherly voice.

"It's your age, dear. It will all sort itself out."

We both laughed and the mood was broken.

It was not long after this that she stopped before a pair of stuccoed gate pillars which had lost their gate.

"This is where I live."

There was a pause while I wondered what might be expected of me.

"It was a lovely film," she continued. "Thank you for taking me. Good night."

I felt the briefest of kisses touch my cheek and before I could react she had run up the short path and was passing into the house.

"Good night," I called gently after her.

I did not walk straight home. The light rain had passed over and a pale moon shone down on the quiet streets. I strolled home by a roundabout route enjoying the night-time faces of the buildings.

That evening marked the beginning of a new life. Until this time, I had been content to be an observer of the patterns of life. Now, as spring began to burgeon, I found myself cast for the first time as a player. It felt good to be in tune with the rhythms of nature and I threw myself into its vernal celebrations with Jo as my willing guide and accomplice.

• • •

After that first evening we began to meet irregularly. There was no set pattern to our dating, perhaps that was why I found those evenings so enjoyable. They never seemed to last long enough and left me counting the hours to the next. The long Easter vacation produced changes that we were not aware of at the time. That would only become evident with hindsight. By the end of the vacation we were both aware of the change, for we met much more frequently and now spent whole days in each other's company.

Steve had watched these developments with little comment. His initial surprise had given way to an amused detachment. I had encouraged this by continuing to cloak our doings in an aura of mystery and he played along with this. The deepening of the relationship over Easter had made this old joke somewhat threadbare and I eventually agreed to bring Jo to meet him.

The move into the flat had produced one unexpected development. We had given little thought then to the actual mechanics of catering for ourselves. It was easy enough in any case to eat out during the week. Weekends, however, presented a different challenge. Steve's answer to this was to buy a cookbook and to begin to develop his own culinary skills. After a disastrous first foray, he had become quite a passable hand in the kitchen, although I would never venture anything more than a shrugged "Not bad." The opportunity to show off his new-found skills was irresistible to him and after much impassioned pleading it was decided that we would invite Jo to Sunday lunch.

I met her half-way and we walked back to the flat together in the spring sunshine. I had left Steve busy with the final preparations. In my absence, he had obviously taken matters to heart for when we entered he was wearing a tea towel round his waist held in place with his dressing gown cord.

"Steve, this is Jo," I announced unceremoniously. "As you see he is the chef. That's why he is wearing the pinny."

She flashed him a smile and thrust out a hand. To my

surprise he wiped his hands on his makeshift apron before accepting her proffered hand. Then he raised it to his lips with a murmured, "Mademoiselle Jo, enchante."

"You poser!" I howled with derision.

"Au contraire," he countered, "all ze best chefs are French."

Jo had already moved away. She was standing by the window taking in the view over the rooftops to the harbour and the hard ridge of Dundry with its proud church beyond. She turned to me as I went across to join her.

"Isn't this lovely," she said. "You have the sun too."

"Is that important?" I asked.

"I think I was made for somewhere sunny. I seem to wither away during the winter."

There was a clattering of saucepans from the kitchen and a muttered expletive. All was well, however, for this was quickly followed by an announcement from the chef that lunch was ready.

Seating presented a difficulty, the living-room boasting only a small table and two chairs. We solved this by pulling up the settee and using its broad arm as the extra seat. Steve was determined that we should have the two dining chairs as he insisted that we were his guests.

He had taken no chances with the menu. He had opted for a simple roast chicken with a rice pudding to follow. He had even bought a bottle of cheap white wine. It mattered not that this was the archetypal Sunday lunch, nor that the plates were old and chipped and the glasses did not match. To us it was like a banquet. We were all in rare good humour and happy for Steve to enjoy his triumph.

"It is too nice to stay indoors," Jo said as we cleared the table. "Let's go for a walk."

"Good idea. You coming Steve?"

"No. I have lots of reading to do. In any case you don't want me around."

Jo would have none of this and immediately linked her arm in his.

"Nonsense! We would love you to come with us, wouldn't we Brad."

I immediately gave my support and we were soon heading for the Downs.

We followed the path from the bridge that runs along the edge of the gorge. We stood for a while looking down at the toy cars making their way along the Avonmouth road far below. As we moved on Jo turned to us.

"Were you two close friends at school?" she asked.

"Not really." It was Steve who answered. "Brad was a year ahead of me. In any case," he added turning to me, "you were always so thick with Rollo then."

"Who is Rollo?"

"Just an old friend."

I tried to fend off the inevitable question as guardedly as possible, but Steve would not leave it at that.

"He was Brad's alter ego at school. They did everything together."

We had all stopped again. For some reason, I felt angry.

"I thought we had come out for a walk," I growled and moved off. The other two quickly followed and nothing more was said.

Later that evening Jo returned to the subject. Steve had shut himself in his room to study and we were sitting together on the settee.

"Tell me about Rollo." She said.

I shrugged. "There's not much to tell."

"Tell me anyway."

I told her about how he had befriended me and all the things we had done together. I even told her about his mother and his property in South America.

Jo listened to it all without comment until I had finished.

"He sounds interesting. What's he doing now?"

"Same as me. He's here in Bristol, only he concentrates on architectural design."

She looked puzzled.

"Don't you get on with each other any more?"

I found her question hard to answer.

"We get on in a way." I finally offered. "We've not quarrelled. We just don't see much of each other now."

"Why is that?"

"We seem to want different things from life. He does his thing and I do mine."

"I think I'd like to meet him."

"Maybe we shall run into him." I said.

I replied casually, but her words left me with a strange feeling of uneasiness which I could not explain. It was still there when I went to bed that night.

Easter had long gone before the fine weather returned again, but this time it settled into the dry warmth of summer. Classes had finished and I was left to my own devices to prepare for sessional exams.

I was seeing Jo almost daily now. She spent a lot of time at the flat, preferring its quietness, while Steve was at work, to her own cramped living quarters. Neither of us could concentrate while the other was around so we kept apart in order to get on with our revision. I would prop myself up on my bed with my books and notepads while Jo used the living-room. She found the window much to her liking and would move one of the easy chairs across to it. I often wondered how much work she did, for whenever I came through to the kitchen to make coffee, I would usually find her, knees pulled up to her chin, gazing out of the window deep in thought.

It was at this time that Steve was sent out on fieldwork to assist with his first company audit. He was away for three weeks. It was strange to be without his cheerful company, but at the same time it came as a welcome relief. Relations with Jo were entering a new phase. We had both outgrown our initial shyness and reserve. With this new easiness with each other came a growing awareness of the physical attraction we both felt.

It seems strange now, but we were too modest to seek the privacy of my room. Instead we conducted our courtship rituals in the living-room, much as if we were at home with our parents. There was always the concern that Steve would walk in at a key moment. So, we held back and felt always on edge. Nothing was ever said and I often wondered if he could sense the tension that was developing between us.

That first day of Steve's absence passed much as usual. The afternoon was hot and oppressive. By nightfall it became obvious that a storm was developing. We were both ill-at-ease and little was said. As the skies darkened, the first flashes of lightning began to split the gloom. We stood at the window watching the rain that began to lash down. It was the time that I would normally walk Jo home.

"What are we going to do?" She voiced the thought on both our minds.

"Stay here. There is no point in going home in this."

My words sounded so matter of fact. I looked directly at her as I spoke to reinforce their hidden meaning. She returned my look briefly before lowering her eyes. Her look said it all. There was no need for her whispered "OK."

I remember taking her by the hand and leading her into my bedroom. I felt very callow and my heart seemed to be pounding in the base of my throat. We undressed quietly with much fumbling. I think my hands were shaking. Then we stood naked and uncertain. I had seen pictures of girls in magazines that had circulated in school, but this had not prepared me for the natural splendour of the female body. She was very beautiful and I felt suddenly humbled.

Despite the closeness of the atmosphere she shivered slightly. I took her in my arms and was surprised to find that she was cold. It seemed the most natural thing in the world to draw her into bed and pull the covers over us. We huddled together for a while regaining our warmth. Then, while the storm raged outside, we left the innocence of childhood and the uncertainties of youth far behind us, leading each other gently into another world.

Afterwards we lay together, conscious of the touch of each other's body, saying nothing and not moving. I felt totally awed by the experience. The feeling of peace and well-being was so all-consuming that I could not help feeling that surely life had nothing better to offer than this. I lay like this long after Jo had gone to sleep. I wanted to wake her then, for it had suddenly become very important to know if she loved me.

The following morning dawned clear and bright. Jo was already up and dressed when I woke up.

"I've had a bath. Is that alright?"

I smiled at her from the bed. That morning she could have asked for anything and I would have cheerfully given it to her, but she asked for nothing else. Nor did she appear to want to talk about the previous night and that subject was studiously avoided. It was apparently to be just another day.

"Are you working this morning?" she asked later over breakfast.

"I suppose so."

"What about this afternoon? Any ideas?"

"Yes." I said. I don't know why, but the idea had come to me out of the blue. "Let's go swimming and afterwards we can go across to Brandon Hill and lie in the sun."

We spent an hour buying swimming costumes in the Clifton stores. We also bought fruit and some buns for a rudimentary picnic before descending the long hill to the Jacobs Wells baths.

It was the first time I had been there. I was used to the swimming baths at home, with their communal changing rooms and the unregulated pandemonium of the pool during school holidays. Here everything was different. Changing cubicles were ranged down either side of the pool, one side for males the other for females. There was none of the usual fuss with baskets or lockers, bathers simply left their clothes in their cubicle and stepped out directly to the side of the pool. Most significant of all, there was little noise. The only sounds were the lapping of water and the gentle swishing made by the handful of swimmers. It all seemed very calm and genteel.

I was already in the pool when Jo emerged from her cubicle. She had pinned her hair into a bun. It was the first time that I had seen her with her hair up. It somehow seemed to give her an added elegance.

She swam with a practised ease which made me realise how limited were my own skills. The events of the previous night were still with me. I very much wanted to impress and slip and glide around her like a porpoise. Instead I found myself floundering and gasping for breath after very few strokes. I was conscious of what a poor figure I cut.

It was still only mid-afternoon when we emerged from the baths. A straggle of vehicles rolled down the hill from the Triangle and we waited to cross to the lower slopes of the park on Brandon Hill. An open sports car was at the rear of the group. As it approached, the driver waved vigorously and stopped at the roadside. I had recognised him immediately. It was Rollo. I had not set eyes on him for weeks.

He had filled out in the time we had been in Bristol. He now looked very strong and fit. His skin had always tanned easily. Now he was taking full advantage of the sunshine, for he wore only a pair of shorts. His skin was the colour of old copper. As he sat waiting for us to cross to him, a satisfied smile played briefly across his face.

"Brad!" He yelled. "Where have you been hiding?"

I was busy looking over the car.

"You got one then."

"Yep. Bought it in the spring. Wouldn't be without it now.

Adds a whole new dimension to life."

I could not help noticing that, although his comments were addressed to me, his eyes were fixed on Jo.

"Who is your friend? Aren't you going to introduce me?" He asked.

"Of course. Jo this is Rollo."

"Hi." She gave him one of her special smiles. "I had already guessed who you were."

"Really!" He looked very pleased. "Has my fame spread so far already?"

"Not yet. Brad has told me a lot about you. It was easy to recognise you from that."

Rollo beamed at her.

Jo ran a hand through her hair.

"We've been swimming. I must look a mess."

Rollo was still beaming.

"Where are you two going?" He finally asked.

"We were thinking of finding somewhere quiet to sunbathe." I replied, thinking at the same time that half a minute either way and he would have missed us.

"I can think of something better than that. Jump in. I'll take you for a spin."

This was the Rollo I knew of old, just taking over with no concern for anyone else. I wanted to tell him what he could do with his car.

"Another time." I began to say and looked to Jo to lead her off into the park. To my surprise she was already opening the passenger door.

"That'll be grand." She said slipping into the seat alongside Rollo. "Come on Brad. Jump in."

"You'll have to use the dickey seat." Added Rollo cheerfully.

Biting back my words I climbed into the cramped back seat with as good a grace as I could muster.

We sped off over the Avon and into the Somerset countryside. Rollo drove with great panache. All the time, he and Jo were chatting away like old friends. I tried to sit forward and join in the conversation, but my seat did not enjoy the same degree of shelter as theirs. My words seemed to whirl away in the slipstream.

We drove down to Blagdon. Rollo parked the car and we walked along the lakeside. For a time, Jo walked next to me and we held hands, but Rollo was in full flow and her attention was on him.

I remember one passage well. We had stopped to sit and eat our picnic. Rollo was looking at a tongue of land that reached out into the lake. He pointed to it with the banana he had just been handed.

"Now that's the sort of site an architect dreams of." He said. "It's perfect. You could put a house there which would really complement it. Something with plenty of glass to reflect the water."

"Mm. And every room could have a view of the lake." Jo took up his theme.

"Exactly. There would be wide sliding doors leading out to terraces..."

"Leading down to gardens which merged with the lakeside."

She had become quite excited and there was a look on her face I had not seen before.

"Of course, it's no use discussing such projects with Brad," Rollo continued airily. "He doesn't have the feel for anything to do with design."

They both laughed merrily at this and I began to wish that I was miles away. Only Rollo, I thought bitterly, could make me feel like a gooseberry when I was out with my own girlfriend.

It was early evening when we drove back to Bristol. Rollo pulled up outside the swimming baths where we had met him. I climbed out of the dickey seat. Jo had opened the passenger door as if to join me on the pavement, but then appeared to be in two minds.

"It's hardly worth coming back to the flat," she said. "My hair is a real mess and I shall have to spend some time on it. You don't mind do you Brad?"

She turned to Rollo.

"Could you drop me off at the top of the hill?"

"I'll take you all the way home," Rollo replied. "What about you Brad? Do you want to get back in?"

"No," I said. "I can walk from here."

I don't think he heard me. Within seconds the car was accelerating away up the hill. They both waved as they turned the corner out of sight. As they disappeared I reflected that I had not arranged when to see Jo.

I waited until the following afternoon before walking across to her flat using the route we normally took. I did not meet her along the way, nor did I have any more luck at the house. One of her flat-mates told me that she had been out since late morning.

It was the following day before I managed to meet up with her.

"I'm sorry about yesterday Brad," She said. "I needed some time to myself. I went shopping."

"That's all right," I replied. I felt that something was far from all right, but I was not sure what else to say. I changed the subject instead.

"What shall we do today? Do you want to see a film or go for a Chinese?"

"I can't see you tonight," she said. "I'm going to the theatre."

I did not reply, but I think my face must have said it all.

"What happened the other night - the night of the storm. That was a one-off. I don't want you to get the wrong idea. I like you enormously, but I don't love you."

She had obviously found this hard to say, for she then softened.

"We are still friends. We can still do things together."

I must have mumbled something and walked away, but my mind had become numb from the shock of learning that my feelings for Jo ran well ahead of hers for me.

There was not long to get used to this new state of affairs. Before I had met Jo, I had taken the option of studying abroad at one of the European centres the college was linked to. I was scheduled to spend the autumn and winter in Florence. I had wondered how to break this to her. Now I was not sure whether I should be happy or sad about it.

In the event my time in Italy went well. It was my first trip abroad. I found everything very strange at first, but without noticing I soon settled into a new way of life. It was mind-blowing to be living and working amid the glories of the Renaissance and in Tomaso Gedda, my tutor, I found a kindred spirit who took me under his wing and treated me as his adopted son.

Jo had promised to write while I was away. I wrote long letters to her telling her of everything I saw and was doing. She kept her promise and wrote to me, quite frequently at first. As the days shortened with the coming of winter there were long pauses before she replied to my letters. Then strangely after New Year there was silence.

I returned to Bristol at the end of February. That first evening I went across to the Redland house. There were new tenants in the flat, but they gave me the forwarding address Jo had left. I did not look any further that night.

The following morning, I sought out the address I had been given. It was a flat in an unpretentious house on the Pembroke Road. The bell at the outer door did not work, so I went in and knocked on the flat door. I had to knock a second time before I heard sounds of movement. The door was opened partially and I found myself looking at Rollo's bleary-eyed face.

II

5

All that week I had been going early to the office. My current project was proving more difficult than anticipated and I was determined to meet the deadline. Even so, that morning Henry Hutchings was ahead of me. He came into the room I used as I was sorting through the papers I had taken home with me the night before. He was a small man, very neat and precise in all that he did. It was typical of him to come to speak to me before I settled into the day's work.

"Ah! Paul! I guessed you would be in early." He said from the doorway. "Could you come through to my office. There is something I have to discuss with you."

I followed him to his office feeling puzzled. Normally his greeting would have been warm and friendly, but there was a formal ring to his manner this morning. He had something on his mind and it was obviously something of importance, for, unusually, James Harding the other partner was already sitting there.

I did not much like James. He was a tall lean man whose face always bore a dissatisfied look. This morning he was looking particularly sour. I do not think he much cared for me either, not that that bothered me. I worked as Henry's assistant. Henry and I got on well together. His standards were high, but he had a way of getting the best out of people without demanding it. Perhaps it was the friendly twinkle that was never long absent from his eyes. For the past three years we had operated a flexible arrangement that allowed me to lecture on two afternoons and evenings each week. In return, I took work home at week-ends. It was an arrangement that suited everyone. He often claimed with a laugh that I worked harder at home than in the office. There was no twinkle in his eye this morning. He seemed to be decidedly ill-at-ease.

Henry settled behind his desk.

"Sit down, Paul."

He indicated a chair in front of the desk. It had been like this when I was first interviewed for the position. It seemed that this was to be another formal interview.

"How long have you been with us?" he began. "Is it six or seven years now?"

"Eight, actually."

"Eight." He shook his head in disbelief. "Tempus fugit."

"This must seem rather formal to you." James Harding took over. "So, we would like to make it clear from the outset that we have no complaint with your work. Far from it! Your inputs have been of an extremely high standard and the lecturing you do has not created any problems."

I began to feel my stomach tighten. I had long ago learned that when someone begins a conversation with words of praise they usually end up saying something unpleasant.

"What we are leading up to," Henry had taken over again, "is that there will be changes here. As you know, my wife has been unwell for some time. I have, therefore, decided to retire. We intend to move abroad - somewhere warm for her. James has agreed to buy out my share of the business."

A light began to dawn. At last I could see what all this was leading up to.

"As you well know, James' professional interests are

different from mine. There will be no new conservation projects taken on."

He paused and gave me a long sorrowful look.

"I'm sorry Paul. There is no easy way to say this. There will be no more work for you here once the current projects are completed."

"I understand." I said.

"All of this will be put in writing. We intend to pay you three months salary from the date you finally leave. There should not be any difficulty for a man of your abilities to find a new position and I will be more than happy to supply you with any references you may need."

I thanked him and took my leave. I stole a glance at James Hardy as I left. He looked more dissatisfied than ever.

I walked back to my own office feeling strangely shaken. Deep down I had known for some time that it was time for me to strike out in a new direction. I told myself that I would wait for the right moment. Now that change was being forced on me the prospect did not look so inviting.

By the end of the week my feelings were much more positive. That was when I rang Tomaso in Florence.

"Paulo!" He boomed down the line. "I am wanting to call you for a long time. When are you coming to visit us in Firenze?"

I explained to him about my new-found freedom.

"Good!" He said. "This will be a good thing. Now you will have much time. You can spend a long time with us. Maria thinks you are too small. She will feed you like me."

I could picture his huge frame shaking with laughter as he spoke.

"I'm coming to work." I replied. "But I shall need to see Rome, Milan, Venice. Lots of places. I shall have the time to make a proper study."

"That is good." He bellowed. "We shall work together some of the time. Leave everything to me."

We had been working together for several years on a

major study of Renaissance interiors. Progress had been slow, as I had only two weeks each year to spend time in Italy. I knew he was pleased at the prospect of completing all the ground work. I was feeling very relaxed at the prospect of a prolonged stay in what I had come to think of as my second home.

Early the following week the letter arrived. I had time to give it only a cursory glance as I left for the office. It had been forwarded by my parents. The nursery address had been heavily crossed out. Even so I instantly recognised the handwriting. I slipped it into my pocket and there it lay all day. It was much later that evening that I remembered it.

I placed it on the table beside my plate and looked at it while I ate supper. I continued to look at it for some time after I had finished eating, uncertain as to whether or not I wished to read it. In the end, I slipped my finger under the flap of the envelope and tore it open.

The letter consisted of a single page, little more than a note. His untidy scrawl looked incongruous on the expensive headed notepaper. It expressed the hope that life was treating me well and then went on to say that he was developing a new project which involved the restoration of a listed building and he needed someone with my skills. If I was interested would I get in touch with him. No more than that. It was so typically Rollo. Yet the work he was describing was so untypical. I re-read the letter several times trying to glean more from it. There were no further clues. My first scanning had gained all there was to learn.

It is difficult to describe the impact this brief note had on me. It had been over eight years since I had last seen him. At that time, I had no wish to see him again. As soon as I had finished my course I had moved to London. It had been a deliberate attempt to distance myself from Bristol and all its associations. It had been painful at first and I deeply regretted having to part company with Steve. During those final terms, he had proved a true friend and we still kept closely in touch. I remembered his comment when I had told him about Rollo and Jo.

"Rollo Blake is a self-centred bastard." He said. "Everyone else has always known that. It's just that you were blind to it."

He was wrong. I had always known it. It was part of what made Rollo what he was. I had always been happy to accept it until that last time. That had been an example of self-centredness that even I had found impossible to accept. So why, I asked myself that night as I lay turning things over in my mind, should a short note out of the blue from him, after years of non-contact, cause such an upheaval. I lay awake for some time trying to find an answer to that question.

Back at work the following morning it was soon pushed to one side. Henry and I were busy tying up all the loose ends we could identify. James seemed to be always hovering around, anxious that he should not be left with any problems. When the final day came I think we were both relieved to be going.

I shook hands with Henry after I had cleared my desk.

"In time," he said, "I think you will come to feel that this came at the right time for you. Think of it as an opportunity and do what you really want to do."

He was right of course. Later that was how I came to see it, but at that point, other than completing the drawings and research for the book, I did not know what I wanted. In a sense in going to Italy I was putting off making any decisions. Perhaps I was waiting for something to happen. Perhaps something had already begun to happen, for I had not thrown Rollo's letter away.

When I handed in my keys to James and quit the office for the last time I felt curiously light-hearted. Working with Henry had always been interesting and on occasions fun. He was a good man and with him I had gained enormously in practical experience. Yet, somehow, he had never touched the inner me. I found that I could walk away with no real sense of regret.

A few days later I was back in my old room in Tomaso's flat. He was roaring in his usual high-spirited way while Maria fussed over me like a second mother. Ahead of me lay several weeks of the most enjoyable work that could be imagined. England, Hutchinson & Hardy and Rollo's letter were all soon forgotten.

I look back on that summer as my dream time. Tomaso and I had roughed out an itinerary that took me all over the northern half of the country. I travelled alone much of the time for we both wanted me to see everything through my own eyes. I even found time to visit some of the smaller hill towns and feast on their marvellous townscapes and hidden treasures. For weeks on end the same hot Mediterranean sun beat down. I ate simple meals at country inns and bought fruit at roadside stalls. I was bronzed and fitter than I had ever been when I finally returned to London.

It was a very different homecoming. It was raining and everything seemed grey and cold after Italy. Worse was to follow. Steve had been acting as my poste restante, but there was, as always, the clutter of unwanted commercial mail. Among it lay a letter from home. I read it with an empty horror. After that I did not bother unpacking. I simply grabbed my bags and headed for Paddington.

It was a strange journey. It was as if the whole railway system was in sympathy with my own disjointed spirits. Everywhere it was convulsing with change. Sidings had been torn up, the rails and sleepers left in neat stacks. Comfortable looking structures that had once seemed part of the landscape stood empty and unwanted. Already vandals had been at work, for scarcely a pane of glass was left intact.

It was as if all this was to prepare me for the sights that greeted me as I paid off my taxi at the nursery gates. I was shocked by the look of dereliction. In the old days Dad had used the road frontage as a showcase for his business. At this time of year, the lawns would have looked as trim as billiard tables and the borders would be rioting with colour. Now all was uncared for and overgrown. At the side of the house there was more evidence of neglect. Clumps of coarse grass were growing through the tarmac drive and a rambler rose swung drunkenly from a broken trellis. It seemed wrong to see everything so drab and unkempt.

There was no one in the house when I let myself in. It is always strange to go back to one's childhood home. Nothing ever appears as we remember it. At least, on the times before this when I had returned, it was a home. Now it seemed lifeless.

The back door stood ajar. I went outside and followed the path across the lawn to the work area. There was the same air of neglect as I had noted at the front of the house. The nursery beds had obviously not been worked, for they were choked with weeds and dead plants from an earlier season. Neither of the two old greenhouses appeared to be in use. They had not received their customary coat of varnish and the woodwork looked old and grey. I peered in through the glass of the first one. The staging had an untidy clutter of pots and dead plants. The second was much the same. Further across there were signs that the newer house, that had been installed after I had moved to London, was in use. The vents along the south face were open and the door had been slid back. I stepped quietly inside.

When I was growing up I had never liked the greenhouses. It was not so much the constant injunctions to watch the glass when I was playing; it was the interiors I most disliked. They had a feel and smell that marked them as alien places. In those early years, I was not allowed to touch anything. Unsurprisingly I grew to hate the neat regimentation of everything. It was as if the plants themselves lay watching, waiting to betray me.

He was at the end of the greenhouse, pricking out seedlings and setting them in small pots. He worked with the easy rhythms of long practice. He was unaware of my presence and I stood watching him for a while. Then I moved my position and a box scraped against a pile of pots. He swung round at the noise and I found myself in the confrontation I had been dreading and which I would have given anything to avoid.

He had aged measurably since I had last seen him. I could only guess how much of it was recent grief. The face that confronted me was lined and hollowed, the eyes strangely dull. It was the face of a man driven to the limits of despair. Guilt welled up almost choking me as I looked at him. What traces of surprise showed on my face I could not say, but on his there were none.

"You have found time to come at last." He said flatly.

"I only found your letter this morning. I came straight away."

"It makes no difference now. She's gone beyond our calling." He gave a helpless shrug of his shoulders and turned back to his work.

"I'm sorry Dad. I didn't know."

"Where the hell were you? She was asking for you." His voice was harsh with bitterness.

"I was in Italy."

He made no answer.

"I'd like to stay for a day or two."

"You know where your room is."

He spoke without turning. He obviously did not want to talk and I sensed that he was fighting to suppress his emotions. The almost fierce thrusts of the fingers forcing compost around each seedling told me everything. I left him to his work and went back to the house.

. . .

The sun was already high when I awoke the following morning. I lay for a time slowly drawing together the threads of consciousness. It took me a while to realise that I was in my old room at home. I found myself listening for the old familiar sounds, but the house was strangely silent. I remembered too late that this was now a different home and cursed myself for my stupidity.

There was no sign of Dad downstairs, although in the kitchen there was evidence that he had breakfasted. I assumed that he was already at work outside and looked for something to eat. Things were much as I remembered them. He had not let the inside of the house slip as much as the outside. Yet it was not the same. The kitchen had been Mom's domain and without her it was empty. Not for the first time I felt regret for the decision that had taken me to Italy.

I wondered how Dad had managed during those last weeks. For the first time I could remember, I felt a real sympathy for him. He had said little the previous evening beyond giving a bare outline of events. There was so much I needed to know; questions that I needed to ask. How was I to ask them? He had always been an independent man, one not used to showing his feelings openly. Now he was suffering and the mix of his emotions was likely to be highly volatile. He would need careful handling. The thought hung over me like a pall. The more I thought about it the stronger grew the realisation that I first needed to get my own emotions sorted out. A visit to the churchyard was the obvious starting point.

The church was typical of the neo-gothic the Victorians built for their sprawling new suburbs. Alongside it a modern church hall had been squeezed in looking very stiff and angular beside the older style. The vicar was emerging from the hall as I opened the gate to the churchyard. Robert Jenkins had been the incumbent in the days when I had sung in the church choir and for as far back as I could remember. He must have been approaching retirement by now.

He did not recognise me at first, but after peering at me for a moment, a flicker of recognition crossed his face.

"Why it's ...."

"Paul Bradley." I helped him find the name.

"Paul! Yes of course. You see what time does to one. How are you my boy?"

He took my hand. His handshake was much stronger than his memory.

"Of course, you have come to pay your respects to your mother. She will be missed. She was a fine woman." He sighed deeply.

"Come. I will show you the place. We found a good spot for her by the beech in the south-west corner. It catches the evening sunshine beautifully. We like to look after our regulars." He gave a guilty smile at this admission of such material considerations.

"This is the one."

I looked down dumbly at the barren mound of earth.

"Would you like me to say a prayer with you?"

I nodded and we prayed together at the graveside. Then he slipped away and left me to my thoughts.

Afterwards I sat on the grassy mound below the beech tree. It had been a favourite place when I was a boy. I do not know how long I sat there. Perhaps it was the atmosphere of the place: perhaps it was the effect of that simple act of prayer with the Reverend Jenkins. All that I know is that for the first time for months I could think clearly.

Of one thing, I was certain. I would leave London. It had never really been my scene and my work could be done away from the bustle and expense of the capital. The value of the leasehold flat I had purchased there had appreciated dramatically. Its sale would allow me to establish myself in a new base.

I walked home feeling totally at peace. Knowing from past experience how fate has a way of lifting us before dashing us down, I ought to have known that it would not last, but at that point I did not think that. I honestly believed that I had witnessed the dawning of a new day that marked the beginning of a new stage in my life. The dawn was a false one; the new era was short-lived. The period that was beginning was one of trauma and anguish. Many months would pass before I found that promised day.

6

"For instance, take those buildings over there. What do you see?"

I had put that question to Steve during one of our many walks around Bristol in the old days. We had stopped to look across the harbour to the old warehouses, already well-advanced in decay, that stood on the other side. He thought for a while before answering, sensing that there was a hidden catch to the question. Finally, he gave up and gave the answer I expected, only he gave it with a grin that told me that he knew that I was setting him up.

"Dock buildings. Warehouses."

"Exactly! So why are they derelict?"

"Because the docks are no longer used." He looked at me quizzically, waiting for the punchline. "What are you trying to say?"

"Only that there is no reason for them to be derelict. They are perfectly good structures."

"Yes, but if the port is no longer used why would anyone want them?"

I smiled in triumph.

"That's exactly it. You have just pin-pointed the problem. People get stuck in a mindset about buildings. They pin usage labels on them like warehouse or church and that seems to be as far as they see."

"What are you saying? Those buildings are not warehouses?"

He looked genuinely puzzled and I smiled at his discomfort.

"Try looking at it this way. They are structures which have been used as warehouses. What else could they be used for?"

He looked again thoughtfully for a minute or two. Then he exclaimed.

"I get it. Take that one on the end with the regular windows. It could just as easily be an office block or a hotel."

He seemed enormously pleased with this discovery.

I smiled at the remembrance of that afternoon walk in student days, for the new address that Steve had given me was leading me to that same harbour-side area. I found it easily enough, a small brick building from the Regency period. The brickwork had been grimed with more than a century of smoking chimneys, but the windows and door were new and in proper period style. So too was the door-knocker which made a satisfyingly heavy thud when I used it in preference to the discreet bell push.

A worried-looking Steve answered the door.

"Oh, it's you. I might have known. Come on in."

The worried look changed quickly to the usual grin when he saw me. He looked thicker around the waist than when I had last seen him.

"How are the money-grubbers?" I asked, repeating a long-standing jibe.

"Can't complain." He gave his old familiar lazy grin. "In fact, I'm grubbing quite well. Setting up on my own was the best thing I ever did." He waved his hand about the entrance hall.

"This was a good buy too. I remembered what you said. Bought the lease when prices were at rock bottom. Got parking spaces in the yard behind. They're like gold dust. The whole area is on the up now."

He led the way upstairs.

"I use the ground floor as offices and I've converted this floor into a flat. Not bad, is it?" He noticed the suitcase I was still holding. "I'll put that in your room. What are your plans?"

I gave him a brief account of my situation and the general resolve I had made. His response was pure Steve.

"Why not join me here? There's a whole floor above this that I'm not using and a spare office downstairs. It's all modernised. I was thinking of letting it."

"How much?"

"We can talk about that when you're established. In the meantime, make yourself at home. I'll make some coffee."

I looked around the living-room while he was busy in the kitchen. Unsurprisingly his tastes were traditional. The many pictures, however, were originals.

"I like the watercolours."

Steve grinned as he bore in the coffee.

"A client. We have an arrangement." He settled himself on a settee. "So! How was your father?"

I remembered that they had been in regular contact ever since I had persuaded Dad to place the nursery accounts with Steve's fledgling practice.

"It's difficult to say. He looks very old. At least he's working again."

"Things are not too good. Did you know?"

"I could see the place was run down if that is what you mean."

He nodded. "It's worse than that. He's not moved with the times. He was losing trade before your mother's illness."

"How bad?"

"Uh! Uh!" He shook his head. "Privileged information, even to you, old son."

This was the first time that I had seen Steve in sober-minded professional mode and I think that it was this, as much as what he said, that worried me. He read the concern on my face and was quick to re-assure me.

"Nothing to worry about. He has stacks of asset value. It is simply that if he is serious about staying in the nursery business he needs to make a big outlay. Given the circumstances, his age and the sort of competition that is building up, I think his best play would be to sell up. The site would fetch a good price as development land."

"Have you told him that?"

"Yes. Twelve months ago. That was before... Anyway, I thought that I had best mention how the land lies. Try to steer him in the right direction if you get the chance."

I laughed ironically.

"Me! You must be joking. I would be the last person he would want to hear that from. He's not forgiven me for turning my back on the business."

"Right! I'll work on him myself." Then, as suddenly as it had appeared, his professional face dissolved and the familiar grin re-appeared. "Moving to more pressing matters, on hearing of the return of the prodigal, I booked a fatted calf for the evening. I'll show you where everything is before we hit town."

Later that evening over dinner I mentioned Rollo's letter. Steve's eyebrows raised.

"You are honoured, old son. He's made quite a name for himself in the area."

"Nationally too." I ventured. "Wasn't he featured in one of the Sunday Colour Supplements?"

"Oh yes. And House and Garden, or rather that house of his was. You should see it. The external walls are entirely of glass. It created a sensation when it was built. He has not looked back since. He moves in very exalted circles now and charges astronomical fees."

I nodded in agreement. "I think that was always his game plan."

Steve ran his finger round the rim of the glass debating inwardly whether or not to probe. He finally decided it was safe to go ahead.

"What did he have to say?"

"I don't know exactly. Something vague about needing my expertise on a new project and an invite to a party he's throwing."

"Will you go?" He looked at me quizzically. I knew what he was thinking.

"I don't know. The jury is still out."

"Could be interesting." He pursed his lips. "But I would watch him. He is a slick operator."

I grinned ruefully back at him. "You're forgetting I have already had a good lesson on that subject."

I sensed a hesitancy on Steve's part as if there was something he wanted to say. Instead he grinned.

"What were you going to say?" I asked.

"Go." He said. "It is time you faced up to Rollo."

All reason told me to ignore the invitation. Sense told me to continue to turn my back and keep him out of my life, as I had done for the last eight years. But what is sense, and what chance has reason, when there are other voices calling out in the names of mystery and curiosity and excitement. Did ancient mariners feel this way, I thought, when they ignored the sounds of waves crashing against rocks and heard only the siren calls of the mermaids. The closer time moved to the date of Rollo's party, the more insistent those siren calls became.

I gave in to them on the final morning. Once the decision had been made I was surprised to find a new emotion had taken their place. That evening, as I was preparing myself, I realised that I was looking forward to seeing him again. Even more, though I would never have admitted as much, I was excited by the prospect of seeing the house he had created.

Rollo's letter had given me brief directions into the Somerset countryside. It had ended laconically, "You can't miss it." He was right; one could not miss it. It was already dark as I neared the place. Ahead of me a pale glow lit up the sky. I knew instinctively that it was the house. I found a place to pull in and climbed a hedgebank for a better view. The house lay below me in a shallow valley. All details were obscure, but the house itself was unmistakable. It simply blazed with light like a giant beacon.

That first sight of The Cascades was something that I will always remember. It printed itself on my memory with an urgency that I knew would never be expunged. I think that sight finally settled any lingering doubts I may have had. I stood there looking at it for some time. I had always recognised the flair and originality that Rollo brought to his work, but all I had seen to date were preliminary sketches. This was different. This was real. He had created something that fused site, shape, materials and perhaps most importantly the imagination. Had he also created a functional house. I was impatient to examine it more closely and hurriedly scrambled down from my perch.

Cars filled every available space in the village and I had to park some distance away. As I neared, the unmistakable sounds of partying filled the air. The house looked stunning close up. There was a lower floor with evidence of stone buttresses, but this was all in shadow, for on all sides the upper floor jetted out from it. It was this upper section which caught the interest in the most dramatic way. Rising upwards above one's head were walls of continuous glass that seemed to float on shadows. Above this and seen only as one approached was a fantastic crystal crown. All was a golden blaze, for every light in the house was switched on. The effect was magical. It was as if a giant lantern had been suspended in the darkness.

For some inexplicable reason, I felt strangely proud that it was my boyhood friend who had created this magic. At the end of the drive I stood again taking in the effect. A pair of guests passed by me up the driveway as I stood and I followed in their wake. The great glass doors of the front entrance were thrown wide open. Beyond the curtained entrance hall, a further pair of doors stood open. I hesitated at this second doorway like a country bumpkin visiting the big city for the first time, for the sights that greeted me were staggering.

The purpose of the crystal crown was immediately obvious. It was the way he had devised of lighting the magnificent atrium

that rose through all floors of the house. Around it balconied galleries looked down on the lower floor. Every wall was festooned with tropical plants so that the galleries seemed to be built in the air like so many tree houses. Most amazing of all was the waterfall. It fell in a flowing sheet of water that changed colour like some liquid chameleon. The main fall dropped vertically for most of the height of the atrium before the water, swirling and bubbling down through a series of pools, entered a large tropical oasis in the centre of the floor.

A trio played at the side of the waterfall, their amplifiers battling against the roar of the water and the strident chatter of the assembly. I noted older faces among the guests as well as the younger ones I had expected. A few of the latter danced in the centre of the floor, performing dances that seemed outlandishly strange to my untutored eye. Most stood in small groups talking animatedly or moved around this seeming tropical paradise. There must have been several-hundred people present, but the house seemed to swallow them effortlessly.

It was only when I had finished rubber-necking that I realised Rollo was directly in front of me. He was in the process of welcoming the couple I had followed in. I watched him greet his male guest with a jovial handshake. It was as he kissed his female partner that our eyes met over the lady's shoulder. He showed no reaction, but completed his greeting and chatted with them for a few moments before they moved into the atrium. Then we were face to face.

We stood motionless facing each other for a moment. He looked much as I had seen him on the day we had been driven to Blagdon. His hair was perhaps a little shorter, but it retained its old dark lustre. His handsome features were dressed with the same deep coppery tan. For the evening, he had donned an expensive-looking pair of slacks and a rich sea-green silk shirt with long voluminous sleeves of the type I always associated with the eighteenth-century buccaneers portrayed by Hollywood. He looked more like a film star than a professional architect, but had I said as much to him he would have laughed and said that both were branches of show business. In fact, neither of us said anything. We simply stood and looked at each other.

Rollo finally broke the impasse. A broad smile spread across his face and he stepped towards me.

"Brad. It's good to see you again. Why did you not say you were coming?"

"I didn't decide until the last minute." I admitted ruefully then grinned back. "It's OK, isn't it?"

"Oh, I think we can squeeze another one in. You know you're always welcome."

I offered him the bottle of wine I had brought.

"Is that for me? There was no need. Caterers are handling all that."

He looked at the label. "Chateauneuf du Pape! This is far too good for this crowd. We can drink it together some other time."

He glanced towards the door. More people had entered behind me. "Look," he said, "I shall not have much chance this evening to speak to you. Come to lunch on Tuesday.

Come early. Say eleven-thirty. We can discuss business then. Now, lets find someone to look after you."

He settled on a dark-haired young woman in a dazzling red dress.

"Philippa! Come and meet Brad. Show him around for me, there's a sweetie."

"Hi." She flashed a smile that was as dazzling as the dress. I guessed that it was for Rollo's benefit rather than mine. As she drew me away I could hear Rollo greeting the newcomers.

"First of all, let's find you a drink."

A waiter glided past with a tray of drinks. Philippa beckoned him to her and took a glass for me.

"Oh dear! I seem to have got ordinary wine. There's champagne doing the rounds somewhere." She cooed.

"Still wine is fine. I much prefer it."

She turned to me with a look of something akin to astonishment on her face.

"Do you not like champagne?"

"Not really. I have always thought the bubbles a clever way to sell bad wine."

"You're just a philistine. I adore it . . . especially the bubbles."

I shrugged a smiling acceptance of her point and realised that I was still holding the bottle of Chateauneuf.

"Where can I put this? Rollo wants to keep it for private consumption."

"You can take it upstairs. Come I'll show you."

She led me to one of the stairways that flanked the entrance. She walked with an assured elegance that bespoke familiarity with the house.

"It's a brilliant design don't you think? He was working on it when I first joined him."

"Are you an architect then?"

"Oh, no. I'm Rollo's PA."

She was so obviously pleased by my mistake that I did not want to spoil things by asking what exactly was a PA.

"And what is your line of work Brad?"

"I specialise in building conservation."

"How lovely!"

She tried to sound appreciative, but it was obvious that she measured anyone in the architectural field on the Rollo Blake scale of achievement. By the time we had reached the top of the staircase she had returned to singing his praises.

"Look." She said, "Isn't this fabulous. Home and office either side of the atrium. We are based in the other wing. Domestic accommodation is this side. There's a wine store in the kitchen."

She led me along the gallery past tables of food staffed by white-clad catering assistants. She greeted a number of the guests as we passed. Whatever a PA did, I mused, she was well connected.

She paused momentarily in a hallway that led off the main gallery.

"Rollo's wife is in the kitchen. I'll introduce you."

I had already caught a glimpse of the figure drawing a glass of water from a tap.

"There's no need. We're old friends. Thanks for the guide."

I eased past, leaving her standing nonplussed in the hallway. My stomach seemed strangely tight.

"It is Mrs Blake, isn't it?"

The figure swung round.

"Oh Brad! You startled me."

A small tired smile flitted briefly across her face.

"I was just taking something for a headache."

It was so ordinary a remark I could have forgotten that it had been eight years since I had last seen her. She had fixed her hair up in a way that reminded me of that last afternoon we had spent together in the swimming pool. The difference was that then it had been pinned into a loose bun, whereas now it was fashioned into a perfect coil surrounded by a pearl clasp that matched the pearls she wore at her throat and ears.

On both occasions, the effect of raising her hair had been to emphasise the classic beauty of her face. That beauty was still there, but as her smile passed, her face looked thin and tired.

"Well! What do we say?"

"I don't know." She smiled again as she spoke. "I wasn't prepared for this."

"Nor I."

"You knew Rollo had married?"

"No. Steve has never said anything. I just assumed so. But then, it had never occurred to me ..." The sentence petered out.

"That he would make an honest woman of me? There I have said it for you."

"I wasn't going to say that." I said gently.

"But you must have thought it, and I wouldn't blame you for that."

"Maybe. It was not the best of times."

A look of concern crossed her face.

"Brad, I didn't want to hurt you, but you weren't there and Rollo ..."

"Rollo was Rollo. You don't have to say any more. I know he had more to offer than I did."

"No. Not more. Something different. Don't think it was easy for either of us."

"I thought it would be best all-round if I went away." I shuffled uneasily as I spoke.

"Yes. I think perhaps you were right."

We looked steadily at each other for a moment. Then her face brightened.

"Anyway! That was a long time ago and it is lovely to see you again. How are you?"

"I'm fine. How are you?"

"Oh, you know. Still living. At least I shall be when I have finished taking these."

She popped another pill in her mouth and took another drink of water from the tumbler.

"There! Those will kick in soon. You have no idea of the stress this sort of do creates."

"Is this the first time?"

"Oh no! We throw these parties twice a year. New Year and summer. Rollo says they are good for business. It seems to work.

People keep coming and money keeps pouring in. Which reminds me, we had better re-join the throng."

She led the way out into the gallery. A middle-aged couple passed, the lady small and birdlike touched Jo's arm as she passed.

"Lovely party Jo. We are just going to have supper."

"I'm so glad you could come Helen. The supper tables are at the end of the gallery. I'm sure I have ordered far too much of everything, so I am relying on you Walter."

The lady's partner, with a girth that suggested that this was not the first time that he had been called to the aid of a hostess in distress, continued his portly way towards the promised supper without pausing.

"Don't worry my dear." He promised as he passed. "I'll try not to let you down."

"Nor will he." Jo whispered to me as they passed out of earshot. "Ghastly man. No conversation. Just stuffs himself wherever he goes."

"So why invite him?"

He's a city councillor. He sits on the Planning Committee. As I said, it is all good for business."

"You've changed."

"Have I?" Her hands rose subconsciously to touch her pearls. "I suppose I have, but then, you surely did not expect me to stay a student for ever."

We paused at one of the balconies and looked down at the atrium floor. The trio was playing a tango. Amid the stiff posturings of the dancers, a dazzling red dress moved in sensual rhythm with a sea-green silk shirt. The dance came to an end and we turned away.

"What exactly is a PA?" I asked.

"I see that you've met Philippa."

I nodded.

"A few years ago, she would have been called a Private Secretary. Now they style themselves Personal Assistants."

"Oh! She gave the impression that she was some sort of partner."

"Yes. I can well imagine that. She's very ambitious."

She looked at me and smiled.

"This is not a particularly good evening to meet. You can see the house in all its glory, but I think it looks better on a normal day. We could also hear each other speak then."

"Rollo has asked me to lunch on Tuesday. Is that all right with you?"

"Oh, I shall not be eating with you. It's a business lunch for Rollo and some of his cronies. Why does he want you here for that?"

"He said something in his letter about a project he wants me to join him in. Does that mean anything to you?"

She shook her head.

"Not really. He has so many projects these days and I'm not involved overmuch in the practice."

We had reached the top of a stairway. She turned to me with a rueful look.

"It has been lovely seeing you again Brad and I would love to go on talking to you, but now I really must see to my other guests."

"I'll look out for you on Tuesday."

"I shall be busy slaving in the kitchen."

She gave my hand a quick squeeze and turned away down the staircase. I watched her descend and engage in conversation with a group at the foot of the stairs.

Later that evening, as I drove home, my thoughts returned to the way she had descended the staircase. She had been beautiful as a girl, but now womanhood had added a measure of calm and elegance to her beauty. I was pleased in a way that Rollo had married her. It somehow made the events surrounding my return from Italy easier to accept.

I had caught glimpses of them during the evening. They had performed the roles of gracious host and hostess impeccably, moving among their guests with an easy assurance and had rounded off the evening by dancing the last waltz together. Everything had seemed so opulent and ordered. It was a rich and exotic world that Rollo had fashioned with himself and Jo as its gilded centre. Yet, the more I reflected on it, the more this tiny doubt nagged at the back of my mind.

Something did not add up. Rollo had seemed his old self, but there was something about Jo that did not seem right. On the surface, she seemed calm and controlled. Beneath this I sensed a tension that could not be explained by my unexpected appearance. Of only one thing could I be certain. I had looked at her face as we had stood on the balcony watching the tango being danced. She had been most definitely biting her lip.

7

Lunch with Rollo. The thought returned to me again and again. He had suggested it and I had agreed, or at least I had not disagreed. He had made a point of saying come early. He was expecting me. These thoughts ran through my head like a litany as I drove to meet him on Tuesday morning. I was not completely certain when I set out if I would keep the appointment. That unacknowledged promise was the key. Without that I doubt if I would have ever returned to the house. All weekend the issue had burned at the back of my mind like a bad conscience. It was an unsettling experience for it repeatedly asked questions that I would have preferred not to answer, questions that I had left Bristol all those years earlier to avoid answering.

I think that I had long forgiven Rollo. We went back too far together: the relationship was too deep for any other response. The question that kept recurring was on a different slant. It asked what sort of relationship this was. It had always aroused a strange mishmash of reactions. It was not the classic love-hate relationship. That described feelings that were too strong; that suggested emotions at the extremes of human behaviour. My feelings towards Rollo had always been more complex. Admiration and disapproval, affection and annoyance, these were the ingredients that came closest to describing what I felt. That is, they had until the night of the party. Now a new feeling had entered the frame. It had come to me suddenly as I had seen him at the centre of his world. I realised then that, for the first time, I was envious of him.

It took some time to face up to this realisation, for envy is a bitter draught to swallow. In earlier days, I had always been happy to share his joys and triumphs, to bathe in his reflected glory. My plant was slower growing and had required careful nurturing. Now it too needed its place in the sun. It seemed unfair, I reflected, that the fates could have been so prodigal in settling Rollo's gifts, and worse that he could appear so careless of such an endowment. I was reminded of the day we had crossed the railway footbridge on the handrail. It was as if we were crossing that bridge once more. Just as he had then skipped so effortlessly across, was he not doing now the very same thing. I had followed slowly and timidly then. Now I seemed to face the same challenge. His achievements were held up to me in a way that called my own lacklustre efforts into question. I could still hear him calling back to me across that railway cutting. "Come on Brad."

Is that what all this was about? I had pondered that question long into the night and much of the next two days. In one sense, I knew what my response must be. There was an inevitability about it. Our lives were too intertwined. I would again have to cross that bridge.

But then there was that other voice urging me to stay well away. The arguments that this voice spoke made sense, and yet I did not trust them. Was this the voice of that envy whose arising had so surprised me or was it something else. Hurt perhaps; wounded pride. Maybe it was neither of these. Maybe it was something else. Maybe it was Jo.

I remembered the stab of the shock that had hit me in the pit of the stomach when I recognised her figure in the kitchen at The Cascades. Meeting her again had been so unexpected.

Its effect had been unsettling. It had left me feeling confused and uncertain. I was angry with Steve for not telling me and yet at the same time I was thrilled at seeing her again. Dared I admit that much.

Then somehow all the conflicting feelings about Jo and about Rollo somehow merged into one, and the whole tangled issue began to churn round in my mind. It all seemed to be interlinked. Was this the basis of my new-found envy. I pictured how she had descended the stairway after she had left me and the memory brought a rueful smile to my face. I realised that it was then that envy had first reared its head.

This mix of ideas was still running through my head when I turned into Rollo's driveway and pulled in alongside a huge Mercedes. The house looked different in daylight as all structures do, but it was strikingly so in this case after the magic of the night of the party. It now seemed a very aloof structure and I realised that this was a trick of the glass. Far from creating a giant goldfish bowl, the glass acted like a mirror reflecting all that lay around it, but revealing nothing of what passed inside.

I was still studying this effect when a figure emerged from the front door. It was that of a large man with a well-built body that had long run to fat. He walked with the heavy deliberate tread that big men develop. The effect seemed incongruous viewed against the ill-fitting suit of bold check he wore and the almost fluorescent brightness of the broad orange tie at his neck.

He stopped and turned to look up at the house with me as if we were old friends.

"Well Brother." He opened. "I'll bet you aint 'alf glad you're not a window cleaner."

"Yes. It would be a bit like painting the Forth Bridge. I was interested in the way the glass reflects the surroundings."

"Yeah. It's clever. I'll grant you that. For myself I prefer a nice bit of stonework."

"Oh. I like it." I replied. "I think it creates a superb effect."

"Maybe Brother, but it was a bugger to build. Especially that crown thing on the top. There's only prayer and a touch of mastic holding it up."

"You saw it being built then?"

"In a manner of speaking. My boys did the work. Made a pretty good job of it all in all."

He was still chuckling to himself as he climbed into the Mercedes.

Rollo was standing at the door watching us. The flamboyance of his party attire had gone and I was surprised to see him in sober business shirt and tie.

"I see that you have already made friends with Oliver."

"I must have. He called me Brother."

"He calls everyone Brother."

"Who is he anyway?"

"Oliver Meadowes. He's a builder. Biggest in the area."

I gather he built the house for you."

"Yes. Not an easy assignment, as he never tires of telling me. We'll see him later. He'll be joining us for lunch."

"Is he one of the cronies Jo mentioned?"

"He's useful. He gets things done."

He paused for a moment.

"Look Brad, about Jo..."

I stopped him going any further.

"There's nothing to say. All's fair and all that, and you married her."

"Good! Come and see the rest of the house."

I followed him into the atrium. The waterfall flowed in gentler fashion and without the special lighting. Jo had said that she preferred the house when it was quiet and I could see what she meant. It was all very peaceful.

Rollo divined my thoughts.

"Quite a change isn't it". He grinned and waved a hand indicating the whole scene. "I designed all this with large-scale parties in mind. It works quite well, doesn't it? It also has the added virtue of impressing the pants off prospective clients."

He led me off upstairs.

"The water is drawn directly from the river and held in a header tank. I had to pull a few strings to get permission for that."

He grinned again and I felt strangely happy. It was like the old Rollo of long ago.

One complete wing of the house was given over to his business interests. Philippa was working in an open area with more exotic plants that served as office and reception room. She gleamed as we passed through. Rollo's own office overlooked the front of the house. It was sumptuously fitted out with deep leather chairs and at one side the latest in drawing tables.

"Nice." I said appreciatively.

"Good enough." He shrugged disparagingly. "The equipment is a bit dated. Computer Aided Design is the coming thing. I shall be replacing all of this soon."

We had passed into the main drawing office. Two young men were bent over drawing desks.

"I do very little now. These chaps do all the work. There are usually four of them."

I looked at him archly. Somehow, I could not swallow such a claim. It seemed much more likely that the team were employed to carry out all the more tedious aspects of the work leaving Rollo free to discuss concepts and produce the overall design. I knew that scene. I had served my time as a foot soldier.

A small client dining room overlooking the gardens and river completed the business accommodation. We looked in briefly. The table had already been laid for lunch. A vase of flowers stood at its centre.

"This is Jo's province. She does a super job. She has become quite the hostess."

He looked at me as I took in the details of the place-settings.

"Well! Are you impressed?"

"It's quite a set-up."

"Business is booming. I may have to move out if we get any bigger. Pity. I like this arrangement and it has certain tax advantages."

We moved on. He had all his old restless energy. He showed me the waterfall controls and explained the venting and heating systems.

"It's pretty much the same as the big stores use." He commented airily.

We walked out through the sliding doors at the rear of the atrium. Terracing and ornamental lawns led down to the river. At the end of the formal garden a path looped through groves of saplings around the edge of what must once have been a huge meadow. I was intrigued to see that it had been laid out as a small golf course complete with fairways, greens and bunkers.

"Do you play?"

"No. You know what I'm like with any ball game."

"Pity. I love it. I was out here practising after breakfast."

A golf club and a net of balls lay at a tee adjacent to the path. Rollo crossed to them, selected a ball and placed it on the ground. Then taking up the club, he made a couple of practice swings through the air. Finally, he drove the ball in a high arc towards the distant green.

"This is a short hole. It makes a good practice range. I come out here when I want to think or need a breather."

I watched him hit several more balls with that same easy swing before broaching the subject that had intrigued me since I had received his letter.

"What's this project you wrote about?"

He addressed another ball and played his shot with studied deliberation before turning to me with a lazy smile.

"I was about to come to that."

The club was tossed aside and we walked a little way along the path.

"There is a period house near here that I'm negotiating to acquire. Not my normal line, but interesting. It could prove quite profitable too. That is if it ever comes off. The old girl that owns it is proving a bit difficult. She does not seem to trust me and wants some form of undertaking that the house will be restored to its old glory. You know the sort - long on family history, short on cash.

"So where do I come in?"

"You are that undertaking. You're an expert in architectural restoration. I want you to complete the negotiations with her and then handle the restoration itself. That should keep her happy."

I thought about the idea for a moment or two before replying.

"Yes. I could do that. What period is the house?"

"Mid-eighteenth century, but not in good shape."

"What about finance?"

"I supply that and my good name. You supply the expertise."

He paused and looked at me.

"Net of all expenses I hope to clear two hundred thousand. What would you say to twenty-five per cent of that?"

I must have been in some state of shock from the size of the figures he had just tossed at me for I heard myself replying - fifty."

Rollo did not turn a hair. He just looked at me steadily.

"Thirty."

It did not register with me that he had just upped his offer by who knows, perhaps another ten thousand. It was more like schoolboy haggling. I smiled as I shook my head.

"Forty."

"No. He said. "One third is as far as I will go."

"OK. It's a deal."

We were both laughing, as for the second time in our lives, we solemnly shook hands.

"You surprised me." He admitted. "I thought you would jump at twenty-five. Anyway, I'll get Philippa to draw up an agreement. Always get things in writing. It can save a lot of fuss."

Then, almost as soon as the deal was struck, the subject was dropped. Instead we returned to golf, a subject which obviously deeply engrossed him. We made a leisurely tour of the golf course before returning to the house. Rollo reeled off the yardage of each hole and went on at great length about the siting of each pin and the deviousness of all the hazards. I listened to him with one half of my brain. The other half was busy digesting all the prospects that had suddenly opened up before me.

Philippa was waiting for us on the terrace.

"Francis and Richard are here. I've given them a sherry."

"Good. Where are they?"

"Upstairs. Watching the waterfall."

"Right. Time for lunch. Come on Brad. I will introduce you to some of my associates."

I reflected on his use of the word associates as I followed him into the house. Jo had called them his cronies. Crony or associate, there was a hint of unsavouriness to both words. For the first time, I began to wonder what I was letting myself in for.

The new arrivals were chatting at one of the balcony rails.

"Francis. Richard. Good to see you both."

Rollo shook hands with each in turn.

"I would like you to meet Paul Bradley, a very old friend of mine. Paul this is Francis Fielding and Richard Crowley."

There was something about the way Rollo seemed to address his remarks directly to Fielding the taller and older of the two that I found curious. Everything about the man was immaculate from the silk tie and tailored suit to the hair brushed back from the temples. It was an appearance that suggested wealth. As Rollo introduced us he extended a manicured hand. It was soft to the touch and the grasp a perfunctory gesture with no strength to it.

"Nice to meet you Paul."

He smiled as he spoke, but like his handclasp, his smile was brief and superficial.

"Rollo tells me that you have recently returned from Italy."

"Yes. I was there for several weeks."

"Business or pleasure?"

"A mixture of both."

"Really. Then you are a very lucky man."

Further conversation was cut short by the return of Meadowes to bring the party to full strength. He barrelled his way into the atrium below us, his voice booming out his customary acknowledgement of the brotherhood of man. Rollo had obviously been waiting for him, for, no sooner had he joined us, his broad face red from the exertion of climbing the stairs,than we were shepherded into the dining room I had seen earlier. Jo had been busy while Rollo and I had been outside. A side table had been laid out buffet-style and two bottles of Chablis stood in buckets of ice.

Rollo immediately drew me into conversation.

"So. How was Italy?"

"Fine." I replied. "As you can see I built up a good tan."

"You did not say what your business was?" Fielding was looking at me attentively.

"I was researching material for a book."

"And will that be a work of fact or fiction?" Fielding maintained his steady gaze.

"It's a work on Renaissance interiors."

"Mm. Interesting."

Fielding turned his to his plate, but Meadowes now took over.

"What's all that about then?"

It will look at how the interiors of buildings changed with

the move from the old medieval styles to the new classical ones."

"Is there a market for that sort of thing?"

"Not a huge one." I replied ruefully. "Mainly libraries or historians and restorers like myself."

Fielding nodded wisely, but Meadowes had not finished with me.

"Will your book have any pictures? I mean I would have thought a book like that would be a bit dry without any pictures."

"You're quite right." I said. "And yes, it will have lots of illustrations. Quite a lot of them will be my own drawings."

"Brad produces the most marvellous detailed sketches." Rollo added. "They are better than any photograph."

"You are obviously a man of talent."

Fielding smiled across the table. It was a thin smile that gave the impression that it was intended as a sign to the others rather than to convey real warmth. Rollo immediately responded by broadening the conversation.

"Do I take it that you are not a great reader Oliver?" He asked Meadowes good humouredly.

"Don't find much time for it. If I do, then it would be something like a detective story."

"And would that be with or without pictures?"

Meadowes took the dig well and joined in the laughter with Rollo. Fielding gave a dry chuckle, but it was noticeable that Crowley did not react. Conversation after this settled into other channels. They spoke mainly of city politics and local developments of which I knew nothing.

I took the opportunity to study my new acquaintance. They seemed an ill-assorted trio. Meadowes had piled his plate high with cold meats and potato salad. He was determinedly reducing the mound before him, transferring large forkfuls to his mouth and consuming them with relish. All the time he maintained a flow of conversation. By contrast, Crowley seemed ill-at-ease and made no attempt to speak. He kept his head bowed, satisfying himself with an occasional glance around him, as a bird might when taking food from the ground.

It was to Fielding that I found my gaze returning. There was something about him that fascinated and repelled at the same time. He ate sparingly, carefully cutting his food into small pieces which he positioned precisely in his mouth before chewing. Between each mouthful he dabbed carefully with his napkin at the corners of his lips. After his opening questions to me he said little, contenting himself with making the occasional comment. It was noticeable that when he did speak the others listened carefully and no one chose to disagree with him.

The lunch party broke up a little after two. I bade goodbye to the other visitors and Rollo walked with me to my car.

"I hope you don't think that I'm throwing you out." He said. "We had this business meeting scheduled, so I thought that it would be a good opportunity for you to see the house."

"Don't worry about it." I replied. "Everything was fine."

We reached the car.

"Give my love to Jo, and thank her for a wonderful lunch."

"I'll do that."

He paused as he turned away.

"I'll give you a bell when I have been in contact with Miss Tyzack about the old house. We can take it from there. Ciaou."

I watched him walk back into the house. I felt puzzled. Something did not add up. It seemed to me that the invitation had not been as casual as Rollo had tried to make out. As lunch had progressed, I had gained the distinct impression that I was under scrutiny. What that signified and the nature of Rollo's dealings with this strange trio I could not imagine. In fact, I did not even try. My thoughts were already turning to the possibilities that the deal we had struck earlier that morning was opening up.

8

The following day anti-climax set in. The euphoria I had felt after the lunch with Rollo had dissipated leaving in its stead a feeling of empty anticipation. Things were out of my control and I had to wait on the doings of others.

Two weeks elapsed before I heard from Rollo again. He rang early one morning as I was preparing to go out.

"We need to talk", he said. Come over this afternoon. Make it about four. I have a client to deal with after lunch."

Typically, he did not bother to ask whether or not I had any prior engagements. He simply assumed that I would fit in with whatever he arranged as I had always done in the past.

His call was welcome nonetheless. The long wait was proving irksome. During the first week, I occupied myself making my temporary quarters in Steve's upper floor more comfortable and in completing a small commission James Harding had referred to me. After that I was driven to roaming the dock area with my sketch pad. I had sketched extensively there back in student days, but after ten years much had changed and there were now some interesting juxtapositions of old and new.

I tried my hand too at a much larger street scene with Steve's office as the centrepiece. It was one of the few large-scale drawings I had attempted and I was pleased enough with the result to carefully colourwash it and have it framed. I presented it to Steve after dinner one evening. To my surprise he seemed quite touched by my small offering and insisted on hanging it immediately in his office.

Sketching was an anodyne pastime. I could relax while doing it, yet at the same time my thoughts were free to roam. Increasingly that week they turned towards Rollo's project. I was itching to get started in a way I had not felt before. All the time there was this feeling that fate was beckoning me to a rendezvous that would be of great significance. I was aware of this huge sense of anticipation. Exactly what I was anticipating and just what developments fate had in store for me I had no idea. The rest of that day seemed abnormally long after I had taken Rollo's call.

The front door to The Cascades lay open when I arrived. A notice directed visitors upstairs by the left-hand stairway. Philippa was working at the reception desk. Her face was concentrated in a deep frown as I crossed from the head of the stairs. She looked up as I approached.

"Hello', she said. She had ceased frowning, but her face was quite expressionless. "Rollo's expecting you. Go on through."

Her face had resumed its frown of disapproval even before she had finished speaking. Clearly my name had not been added to her Christmas card list. I mused on the possible reasons for this as I passed into Rollo's office.

He was sitting at a table adjacent to his desk. Before him the complex skeleton of what looked like a sports pavilion filled the wide screen of a computer work station. He swung round as I made my entrance.

"Brad. Come and take a look at this."

"What am I supposed to be looking at?" I asked.

"Oh! Not the design. This is something I knocked up for practice. No. Look at my new hardware. I told you I was planning to move into computer aided design."

He looked at me expectantly. There was an old light in his eyes.

"Well? What do you think? Isn't it beautiful? There's masses of computing power. It can design in three dimensions. There is also the option of tilting and rotating the design on the screen. That way you can see the inside or the underside of whatever you are designing. I haven't learnt how to do that yet, but I'm getting there."

He was like a schoolboy again, anxious to show off his latest acquisition.

"Well? Do you like it? One of these would be good for your restoration work, especially the colour version. And it also solves the problem of storing all the sheets of drawings."

Despite his obvious enthusiasm I found it hard to get excited over a piece of machinery.

"It looks good, but I think I'll stick to drawing the old way."

He grinned at my response.

"You've not changed. Still the same old Brad."

I could have laid much the same charge at his door, but I refrained and made some comment about drawing being what I was good at.

"All the same," he continued, "this is a good tool. I plan to have a network of them linking up both offices. It will increase our productivity enormously."

I was not really listening to him. I was more interested in snatching a last look at the skeletal building on the monitor as he shut the machine down. It seemed a very detailed design for a practice effort and he had made a point of carefully saving it before switching off.

"Grab a chair and bring it round here."

He moved back to his desk as he spoke. He took an Ordnance Survey map from a drawer and spread it out on the open surface.

"Things have moved a little since we spoke last," he said.

"I think it just needs one more push and we are home and dry. That is what I want you to do."

He leaned over the desk and pored over the map for a moment or two. Then he stabbed it with his finger.

"Here it is, Eastonbury Court. Remember the old days when we cycled out on sketching trips. This is just the sort of place we used to like to find."

I flicked open my notepad and made a note of its position while Rollo continued talking.

"As you can see, it lies in its own valley and a stream runs through the grounds. Very attractive: A lovely site. The house itself is a strange mix of styles. Not my scene at all really."

There it was again, that same question about this project that had been nagging at me since the subject had first been broached. Now Rollo himself was saying as much. If it was not his scene, why was he involving himself in it.

"So why are you interested in it?"

I looked him square in the face as I pitched the question. He looked guarded for a moment before he replied.

"I can't say too much at this stage, other than that I am taking it on as a favour to someone very influential. Can we leave it at that for the moment?"

His reluctance to tell me more surprised me. It did not add up. The restoration of an historic building does not make money. Quite the reverse, it eats it. What can make money is the use that property is put to afterwards. What eventual use did Rollo's client have in mind, and why all the secrecy. I had a feeling that somehow the design on the computer had something to do with it and for some reason, when he had spoken of the client being someone very influential, Francis Fielding had sprung to mind.

"You will have to trust me on this Brad. Just remember that it is going to be quite lucrative."

"Is money all that matters?" I asked, continuing to look him directly in the face.

"It is important. Don't you think so?"

"Up to a point," I replied, "but I don't make it my God. At the end of the day it's the architecture that comes first in my book."

Rollo leaned back in his chair. His face bore an amused grin.

"When are you going to join the real world. This is life, not high art. Art is something academics rabbit on about. In the real world, you make a name for yourself by being bold and different. Then when you have done that you make lots of money and enjoy yourself. That is what I did when I designed this place. I used glass in a new and adventurous way and added a few gimmicks like the waterfall. A new generation will do something else. Right now, there is probably some young student dreaming of designing a structure like a huge plastic bubble. When he does it, then it will be goodbye to Rollo Blake. There is nothing so dead as an old fashion. Don't take life so seriously. It's all a game. We are here to play and have fun."

"I'm not like you," I replied calmly. "I don't have your design flair for one thing and I'm not hell-bent on making a fortune. I believe very strongly that it is important to preserve the best of the past for future generations. That is what concerns me with this project. I can't see where I fit in."

He studied me for a moment. Then he folded up the map and put it back in the desk drawer.

"Right, what can I tell you," he said. "The house was requisitioned during the war and suffered some internal damage. It has also not been maintained since then. Other than that, it's a bit of an unknown quantity. The present owner is a Miss Letitia Tyzack."

The name seemed to amuse him, for he broke into a broad smile as he pronounced it.

"Straight up," he said. "It's like something out of a Trollope novel. Actually, she is quite a nice old girl, but she has this thing about her family. She is proving quite stubborn about selling. God knows why. She is broke and the place has had no money spent on it since the war. It's like a time warp. Anyway, you will see that for yourself."

He gave me a long steady look.

"So! I would like you to go along and talk to the old girl. She insists on the place being restored as a condition of selling to us. That's where you come in. You are a restoration expert. I want you to convince her that we are in earnest about restoring the house to its former glory. When you have done that, I would like you to carry out a full structural survey. There are one or two obvious defects. The rest I think is largely superficial. Once those two steps are in place, I can carry out the final negotiations. Clear?"

I nodded.

"Assuming we get the place," I said, "you realize that there is restoration and there is restoration. Which hat are you wearing, 'Cheap and Cheerful' or 'National Trust'?"

"Not quite National Trust," he replied, "but something close. The work will have to be done well."

I breathed a sigh of relief at those words.

"Good. That's what I wanted to hear. I would've walked away if I had thought that the work was not going to be done properly."

Rollo was grinning again.

"Do you think I don't know you? Anyway, don't worry about that for the moment. Swinging the old lady round is the first objective. On your way out, have a word with Philippa. Give her all the details about yourself that she needs. She will write to Miss Tyzack and arrange an appointment for you. Now I must dash. I have to meet a client on site at four-thirty."

The call came while I was out. Steve's secretary had made a note for me. A meeting had been arranged with Miss Tyzack at Eastonbury Court at 3pm on Friday. She said that the caller was Rollo's PA, but for brevity and enigmatic content it could not have been bettered by the man himself. I did not bother chasing it up.

The Eastonbury estate lay only a few miles from Rollo's house. I had not given much thought to it since the day of the lunch party. In my subconscious I must have pictured another Blenheim or Castle Howard, for I was unprepared for what I found. The entrance was situated at a break in a long strip of woodland that bordered the road. Set some yards back from the road, half-hidden by foliage, sad-looking lions sat atop a pair of decaying stone gateposts, as if guarding the cattle grid set between them. Juddering across I found myself at the head of a shallow coombe that widened as it fell away between flanking woods.

This was no driveway in the grand manner, but had more the feel of a country lane as it dipped and curved with the contours of the ground between an avenue of irregularly spaced oak trees. On either side sheep grazed. Half-a-mile or so further on after clearing the shoulder of a hill the drive ended at a bank of rhododendrons. Another pair of the same sad-looking lions marked the entrance to a gravelled forecourt with a mellow stone flower trough at its centre. Behind it lay the house. It gave off a forlorn unused air, for the outer door of the front entrance was closed and there were no hangings at the windows.

I was still taking in the main details of the layout when I heard the sound of another car approaching. A hard-topped sports car swung in past the lions and came to rest alongside mine. It was driven, not by Rollo as I had expected, but by Jo. She joined me looking up at the house.

"Rollo got tied up. He asked me to stand in for him."

"Does he often do this?"

"No. This is the first time. But then it's not the normal sort of meeting. He's already had detailed discussions."

"That's fine. To be honest I was not sure whether or not I was doing this solo."

We looked directly at each other briefly. It felt good to

have her around again and I think I must have smiled for a quick grin flashed across her drawn face.

"Are you sure we have the right place?"

"Positive." Jo looked at me quizzically. "Well. What do you think?"

"It's interesting." I reflected as I spoke.

"What is that supposed to mean?"

"Just that. It's an interesting mixture of styles. The main house in front of us is Palladian as expected, but I think that was added to an earlier house that was set back against the woods. Look at the brickwork of those chimneys."

"It has a nice feel to it. It's almost homely."

"Yes. That is not a bad description. Including the outbuildings, I can see details from five distinct building periods, yet somehow they all seem to blend."

I was conscious of Jo looking at me.

"It is strange how different your approach is from Rollo's. He never pays any attention to the details. If he were here now he would simply study the setting and decide whether or not it had been used to best advantage." She broke off. "Why are you smiling?"

"I was thinking of when we were at school and first began to study buildings. We would ride out somewhere on our bikes with our sketchpads. I would spend hours making drawings of features such as doorways or chimneys, but Rollo seemed to capture the very essence of the building with a few simple pencil strokes."

"That is more or less what he does now," she said. "The boys convert his ideas into finished drawings."

"Lucky man!"

"No! Not lucky Brad. He simply knows what he wants and goes for it."

Her mood had changed abruptly. I sensed she was no longer thinking solely of Rollo's architectural practice, for I had detected a hint of bitterness in her last comment.

"Let's see if we can find Miss Tyzack." She moved across

to the house as she spoke and I followed her up the steps to the simple portico that formed the main entrance. She pulled on the ornate bell-pull alongside the door. A bell clanged in the recesses of the house and we waited. No one answered our summons. Jo tried the pull again. Again, we heard the clang of a bell and again we waited for a response.

I looked at the nearest window.

"It does not seem to be lived in," I offered. "Perhaps we should look around.

On either side of the forecourt, archways gave entrance to ranges of outbuildings. I chose the one nearest the driveway, intrigued by a building which had a timber-framed base, but which had a classical upper storey complete with bell turret directly above the arched opening. It led into a yard paved with flagstones. Around two sides, what had obviously been an earlier structure had been remodelled as a coach house. A flight of stone steps led up to the upper floor which had the regular sash windows of the classical period. The lower level was open-sided. An old pony trap with a broken shaft lay in one corner. In the other wing a Morris Minor estate car was parked. I inspected its windscreen.

"The tax disc is up-to-date," I announced. "There must be someone here."

"Let's try the other side."

We both heard it as we re-crossed the forecourt. It was the unmistakeable sound of a garden fork striking a stone. A wide double door closed the archway on this side, but the smaller inset door was unbolted. Stepping through we found ourselves in a large walled kitchen garden. In the corner nearest the house an elderly woman was digging.

"Miss Tyzack?" Jo called across to her.

She straightened and ran the back of a hand across her forehead.

"Yes." She replied guardedly. "What do you want?"

Jo smiled to reassure her.

"We represent Rollo Blake the architect. We have an

appointment to see you. I'm Jo Blake and this is his associate Paul Bradley."

Recognition flooded across the older woman's face.

"Oh heavens! Is it today? This is just typical of me. I don't know where I am from one day to the next."

She came across to us, a slender figure with wispy grey hair that had become disarranged from her exertions. She was dressed in a print dress and a pair of walking socks rolled down to the ankles above a pair walking boots. The hand which she offered to us after carefully wiping it on her dress, was thin and hard and bore the tell-tale marks of age.

"Do forgive me. As you see I am not dressed to receive visitors."

"We can come back another day when it is more convenient," Jo offered.

"No, no! It would not be right to drag you out here a second time. If you would not mind looking round the house by yourselves for a while, I will make myself presentable."

Jo and I looked at each other. I spoke for us both.

"Yes. That will be fine."

She led us along a brick path to a door and stopped at the stone doorstep to take off her boots.

"This part of the house was the kitchen wing. It is the only part I use now. The rest of the house is in a sorry state, but you will see that for yourselves."

We were left free to wander at will. As Miss Tyzack had admitted, the house was indeed a sorry sight. Much damage had been done at some stage and this had been compounded by years of neglect. It was apparent that in places partition walls had been erected in the main rooms, for sections of the cornices had been cut away. Their removal had been none too gentle either to judge by the gaping holes in the plaster work. Not all the partitions had been removed and this and the absence of all internal doors radically altered the symmetry of the original design. Most glaring of all the lowest sections of the marble staircase balustrading had been removed. Each room told the same story and yet, despite the damage and neglect, despite the absence of any furnishing, there was still an indefinable appeal.

Jo had wandered ahead of me. I was studying the detail of a particularly fine ceiling that none too elegantly had been coated with whitewash when she called to me.

"Brad! Do come and see."

I followed the direction of her voice and found her in a large room at the rear of the house. She stood in a pool of light thrown by the afternoon sun on the dusty floor.

"Look!"

She drew me to one of the pair of large windows. It looked out over a stone-flagged terrace and beyond to the great lawn that sloped gently down to a small stream spanned by a simple double-arched bridge. Strategically sited clumps of trees completed the vista.

"Isn't it beautiful?"

She looked at me as she spoke. There was a light shining in her eyes and for a moment she looked like a girl I had once known.

When we finally made our way upstairs, we found it in much the same state as with the ground floor, but with one added horror. In the south-west corner rainwater had penetrated. The outer walls of two bedrooms were discoloured with a sickening mix of mildew and fungal growths. To judge by the state of the mess, the problem had been there for some time.

"How bad is that?" Jo asked. There was concern across her face.

"Not quite as bad as it looks. The plaster will have to be stripped off and replaced. A section of the roof may need replacing too."

We were still viewing the damage in the second room when Miss Tyzack rejoined us. She had obviously been very busy during the time away from us. Her gardening dress had been replaced with a blouse and tailored skirt. In place of the walking boots she now wore an elegant low-heeled shoe. To complete the transformation, her hair had been brushed back into a neat bun.

"I'm afraid we are not quite ready for the House and Gardens photographer." She smiled ruefully.

"What has been happening here?" The question came from Jo, her face showing a mixture of puzzlement and concern.

"What here in this room, or throughout the house?"

"Both, I suppose."

"Well this is the effect of rain damage, is it not Mr Bradley?"

I nodded my agreement.

"It is the same answer to both questions. No money. It is as simple as that."

"But the house was not always like this surely?"

"Oh! Heavens no! It was requisitioned during the war. Most of the big houses were. It became a hospital for wounded officers, which was a better use than many were put to. Of course, once the military got their hands on it, they could do pretty much what they liked. There were lots of partition walls put up to make offices and extra toilets, and the dining room was converted into an operating theatre."

"That would explain the white painted ceiling." I exclaimed.

"Oh, you have noticed that, but there again that is your job." Regret had crossed her face. "Such a pity. It was the most beautiful ceiling in the house. Oh, the colours!"

She broke off suddenly.

"I don't know why we are talking here next to this mess. We can talk much more comfortably sitting down with a cup of tea. That is if you have seen everything."

She led us back downstairs. As we reached the bottom of the staircase she indicated the missing sections of balustrade.

"This was done apparently to make it easier to move stretcher cases up and down stairs. We made complaints when the house was handed back, but we were told that nothing had been removed from the house. Goodness knows what they did with the missing pieces."

Miss Tyzack led us back towards the kitchen wing and up a short stairway leading from a hallway adjacent to the kitchen. We were ushered into a small sitting room.

"Do sit down. I have everything ready. I shall not be a moment."

We sat on an old but surprisingly comfortable settee and took stock while she hurried out to her kitchen. She returned a few minutes later bearing a tea tray.

"This used to be the housekeeper's flat." She announced as she began pouring tea. "We were allowed to stay on in this bit. I have stayed here ever since."

"Didn't you mind giving up your home to strangers?" Jo asked.

"We had no choice." Miss Tyzack chuckled. "But, no we did not mind really. It was a national emergency and it's hard to believe now, but at that time everyone pulled together."

"Was your father still alive then?" I spoke for the first time.

"No. Daddy died in 1938. Perhaps it was just as well. He would have hated to have seen what happened to the house. He loved it so much. We all did."

"You say we ..." Jo queried.

"Yes. I had two brothers, Tom and Henry. I was the youngest. Henry was a fighter pilot. He was killed during the Battle of Britain. Tom was the eldest. He inherited the estate after Daddy, but he died during the awful winter in 1951. He was in the army. He was wounded in the chest in Normandy. He never got back to full health afterwards. His death certificate said that he died of pneumonia ... so there were heavy death duties to pay. That is why I was never able to carry out any restoration work."

"And you never married?"

Miss Tyzack paused.

"No. I was engaged during the war. Richard, was in the same regiment as Tom. That is how we met. He was killed a month after Tom was wounded."

"Oh! I am sorry. That was very thoughtless of me." Jo looked mortified.

Miss Tyzack gave her a wan smile. You were not to know my dear, and it was all a long time ago."

She spoke the words softly with only a tinge of sadness to their bravery, but there was a far-away look on her face. It seemed that in this too, as in so many of the other aspects of her life we had seen during our short visit, time had not moved on. The compassionate look on Jo's face suggested that she had picked up the same message. I was intrigued by the discovery of a side to her character that she had not displayed during our student years.

"And you have lived here alone all this time?"

A wide smile crossed Miss Tyzack's face.

"Bless you my dear. No. I have Nanny Adams. She was my nanny when I was a little girl. Then when Mummy died, Daddy asked her to stay on."

"Was that when you were still a little girl?"

"Yes. I can't remember her. I was very young. She died in a riding accident. We always had lots of horses. At any rate Nanny stayed on and became a surrogate mother. I am very, very fond of her."

She smiled fondly and the smile developed into a chuckle.

"She is old now of course, so the boot is on the other foot. I look after her and tell her what to do. She sleeps every afternoon. That is when I like to get out and do a bit of gardening. I grow all our vegetables and flowers."

"We noticed the lovely plant trough in the forecourt."

"Yes, I like to do things to try to lift the old place, but there are limits. Daddy used to have five gardeners ... Still I must not bore you with all this maudlin talk of the past."

"You must not think that." Jo protested. "It's all fascinating. I felt that there was something special about the house when we looked round and you have been bringing it to life."

"Well I'm sure we could spend all afternoon talking about it, but I think Mr Bradley would find that very boring."

I assured her that I had not been at all bored. It was not just politeness. I had enjoyed sitting back and not only listening to their conversation, but watching the animation that all too briefly had erased the strained look from Jo's face. I was also conscious that I was here on behalf of Rollo and that he would be more concerned with making progress on the purchase of Eastonbury Court than an account of the travails of its present owner.

I think Miss Tyzack must have read my thoughts for she now turned to me.

"It is very kind of you to indulge an old lady, but I think it is time we got down to business. After all that is what you are here for. Now tell me about yourself Mr Bradley."

I was caught off guard by the change of mood and the directness of her question. I found it difficult to frame an answer.

"There is not a lot to say really. I specialize in the restoration of period buildings. I worked for several years after qualifying with an architectural practice in London that specialized in restoration work. I set up my own practice earlier this year."

Miss Tyzack gave me a searching look. "I am sure you are being too modest." Interestingly she turned to Jo for support to her assertion. It was not long in forthcoming.

"He is being extremely modest. My husband has known him for many years. He is highly regarded in his field in both academic and professional circles."

Miss Tyzack beamed.

"And what is your position with Mr Blake?"

"I have been retained to produce a survey on the house and, in the event of his purchasing the estate, to undertake a full restoration."

"Good!" She spoke emphatically. "As you know Mrs Blake that was my only reservation when I discussed matters with your husband. One cannot dictate what a new owner should do with the property, but I would not sell it to anyone who did not respect its past. You have set my mind at rest on that matter so I can see no reason why the sale should not go ahead."

She rose to her feet and shook hands with us in turn.

"Obviously you will need to spend more time here to carry out your survey Mr Bradley. I go shopping every Tuesday, otherwise I am always here. There is no need for you to make an appointment. Just turn up whenever you like."

She escorted us downstairs and back out through the kitchen garden.

"Where will you go when you leave here?" Jo asked her.

"Oh, I have that all planned." Miss Tyzack chuckled again. "I shall take Nanny to the seaside. We should be able to find a comfortable flat somewhere on the south coast with views of the sea. We shall like that."

She stopped at the gate set in the arch through which we had first entered.

"Goodbye my dear. I feel much happier now that I have met you. I know that you will think it silly, but from the moment I first saw you this afternoon I had the feeling that somehow you belonged here. It would be lovely to see it brought back to life as a real home again with children."

Jo touched her hand and turned away.

"Goodbye Mr Bradley. I have every faith in you."

We walked in silence to the parked cars. Jo walked ahead of me with her head down as if she was studying the ground.

"That went easier than I had expected." I ventured. "Rollo will be impressed."

"Damn Rollo!" I was surprised, as much by the agitation of her face as by the vehemence with which she spoke.

"Did you hear what she said to me as we came away."

"What? That bit at the end about bringing the house back to life?"

"Yes, that bit at the end as you put it. Has it not registered with you yet that she thinks that I am going to live here."

"Oh, come on. I think you are reading too much into it."

"Do you? Well I don't. You saw how she opened up to me. There was a real rapport there. Now I feel that we have deceived her."

"Don't be silly. We have not done anything of the sort. She probably saw as I did that you liked the place. That does not mean that you are planning to make it your home. Any conclusions she may have reached are of her own imagining."

"You know, you're beginning to sound like a lawyer."

"I'm only stating fact. Rollo has asked me to restore the house to its original state. That is all she has been promised."

"And then the house will be sold."

"Probably."

"To whom?"

"I have no idea. I did not discuss that with Rollo."

"Well didn't you think to ask him?"

"No. It didn't occur to me at the time."

"It did not occur to you, because you are too much in awe of him. You always have been. Anyway, it is probably something to do with that ghastly crowd he associates with."

She paused and looked hard at me.

"Don't get involved. Tell him that you don't want the job."

"But I am involved and I do want the job. We have shaken hands on the deal."

"Don't be such a bloody gentleman."

She climbed angrily into her car. My face must have registered some of the shock I felt for she wound the window down and her final words had lost the edge of anger.

"Oh Brad! Don't you realize that he is just using you, the way he uses everyone."

"Jo. What is the matter..." I began to say.

The sentence went unfinished. She had already started to swing the car in a wide crunching arc.

I watched her drive away. I was shaken by her outburst. Strange knots were forming in my stomach. I turned towards my own car and then thought better of it. I needed a walk to calm myself down before I could face the city traffic.

9

It was early the following week that I returned to Eastonbury. Miss Tyzack, as promised, gave me free access to the whole complex of buildings which made up the house. In all I devoted several days to my survey, spending my mornings at the house taking measurements, making diagrams and making notes, and my afternoons in writing up a detailed report. As I had suspected on my first visit, apart from the leaking roof at the south-west corner, the underlying structure was sound. Much of the damage was superficial and skilful re-plastering and redecorating would create a transformation. The only real headache was the main staircase.

Each morning Miss Tyzack invited me to have coffee with her and Nanny Adams in her apartment. Other than the difference in age, they were remarkably alike and chattered together like a pair of sisters. For them it must have made a welcome break from the monotony of their normal existence. Each morning they would ask which rooms had I been working in and my reply would unleash a flood of detail and reminiscences, often wildly contradictory. They would still be talking animatedly as I took my leave to slip back to the empty rooms of the main house.

On my last morning Miss Tyzack accompanied me into the walled garden. At the outer gate, she stopped.

"When you next have opportunity, would you tell Mrs Blake that we have settled on a flat in one of the old houses on the cliffs above Lyme Regis. It has lovely views and there is a wonderful communal garden. I think we shall be very happy there. I thought that she would be interested to know."

Then she solemnly took my hand.

"Goodbye Mr Bradley, Nanny and I will miss your visits."

Jo had been correct in one respect I thought as I walked away. There had been a rapport between them. It was another reminder of how much she had changed in the years I had been in London. I had seen the immediate physical difference on the night of the party. Here at Eastonbury I had seen glimpses of a warmth and compassion that I had not seen before and which for some strange reason gave me real pleasure.

There had also been the strange range of emotions that she had displayed at the end of our first visit here. Time and again during the week while working here I had been reminded of them. She had blown hot and cold that afternoon in a way that made no sense to me. Repeatedly my mind pictured the look on her face immediately before she had driven off. What had it shown, pity, anger, concern; and why was she warning me of having dealings with her own husband. That she was deeply unhappy about something was apparent. It was equally apparent that in turn this seemed centred on her marriage to Rollo. That was an area I did not wish to get involved in. I had been too close to both of them. Thankfully I had my work to bury myself in.

One thing I had already decided on. I would stay away from The Cascades as much as possible. Philippa had already offered me the pattern to follow by sending me copies of the contract and bank account documents already signed by Rollo, for me to sign and return. I planned to post my report to him and await his response.

In the event, it was mid-August before he called me. As ever he was brief and to the point. The purchase of the estate was proceeding and contracts had been exchanged. Completion had been fixed for the end of the month.

When eventually the go-ahead came from Rollo it was as if the heavens were in support of our venture. The intermittent rain which had characterized the second half of the summer had given way to a prolonged Indian summer. The sun shone from cloudless skies with a pleasant dry warmth and I set to work each morning with a song in my heart.

It did not occur to me at the time that I was being highly rewarded for what was relatively straightforward work. It was only later that I came to realize that my real value had been in overcoming Miss Tyzack's reluctance to sell to anyone who did not value the house for what it was. For the moment, I was happy to throw myself into my new role.

For the plasterwork restoration, I had booked the services of a specialist team I had used in the past. For the rest of the work I would be reliant on the work of local tradesmen. Rollo's only reservation was that the main reception rooms were to be papered in period style. For the rest, I was to use my own judgement.

The fallibility of that judgement was to be tested almost immediately. For the initial clearance work I had scanned the list of businesses listed under the demolition section of the yellow pages. I settled on a small block advert under the name of William Bedford & Son. Among the services listed demolition and clearance work caught my eye.

The morning after I had called them, two men turned up in a battered pick-up truck. The older of the two was a short barrel-chested man in his late forties. The younger man was taller and more wiry with close-cropped hair and biceps that bulged from a dirty singlet. I found them peering in through one of the windows. They turned at my greeting. Neither had shaved that morning.

"Bill Bedford." The older man extended a strong almost square hand. "Right then. What have you got for us?"

Like many men of similar build there was an assurance in the way he held himself keeping all movement to a minimum. Only his eyes seemed to move. It was unsettling to face him. The eyes never rested. Dark and piercing, there was something reptilian about the way they flicked from side to side while he was speaking. The son seemed possessed of the same restlessness, but in a way that was the exact opposite of his father. With him the eyes were staring and empty of expression, but any deadness in his features was compensated by almost constant movement of the rest of his body. He seemed unable to remain still for even a second. Even as I spoke to them, he was ranging along the front of the house and looking in at each window. Touch seemed important to him. His hands needed to explore every feature and surface. In turn, his fingers ran over each pane of glass, each section of window frame and even the stone blocks of the wall.

I unlocked the main door and took them inside. Bedford's eyes examined the shabby elegance of the entrance hall. His son immediately detached himself from us and began to make his own hands-on examination.

"Nice place once." The elder remarked. "Though it looks like somebody's had a go at your staircase."

The eyes continued to flick around. "Don't nobody live here?"

There was something about the glint in his eye and the merest suggestion of interest across his face that made me uneasy.

"Oh yes. It would not be wise to leave a place like this unattended. This part is being renovated, but the rest is occupied. While the work is in progress I am living in the old coach house so that I can keep an eye on any comings and goings."

The lie sprang readily to my lips. At the same time, I made a mental note to put my words into practice.

The son had disappeared while we were speaking. My unease had developed into downright suspicion, but there seemed no alternative but to play out the charade of obtaining an estimate from them. I led Bedford into the main reception rooms and began to outline what work was needed. I was carrying my clipboard with a ready prepared specification of the work.

"It is a bit confusing," I said, "but it is all here on this sheet. I have listed all the work room by room."

To my surprise he brushed aside the paper and there was a distinct change in his attitude.

"I fink you've made a mistake." He said. "We don't do that sort of fing. Besides, it's too big. I mean there's only me and the lad."

"But your advert said you did demolition and clearance work."

"Well we do in a manner of speaking. You see we re-cycle fings. You know we clear any fittings or old materials that can be used again. Now if you wanted doors taken out or somefink like that, that would be different. Only them have already gone."

He sniffed as if to emphasise his disapproval and his eyes made a final sweep.

"No. There ain't anyfing here that would interest us. It 'ould only be rubble. There's no profit in rubble. Now where's the lad got to?"

"Ronnie! Ronnie! Come on we're going."

He walked back to the entrance hall calling his son's name. Presently the lad appeared from the direction of the rear of the house. He walked with a loose almost careless gait. One hand trailed along the wall as he walked. There was a strangely satisfied look on his face.

"Come on we're going. Ain't anyfing for us here."

"Naw." The lad replied, speaking for the first time and shaking his head in a mime of disappointment.

They stopped in the middle of the forecourt and

conversed briefly while the elder lit a cigarette. They seemed to be looking at the coach house. I made a point of watching until their pick-up truck had driven out of sight. Then I made a thorough inspection of the ground floor. In one of the smaller rooms in the old wing I found what I had suspected. A window had been eased and its catches left undone. It was obvious that preparations had been made for a later return and that I would have to stay on watch.

Steve was lunching in a local pub when I ran him to ground. For once there was no jollity when I told him of my need for a makeshift bed at Eastonbury. He had immediately cut short his break in order to lend me a hand. I was touched by the obvious concern on his face when we had finished heaving my mattress into the car.

"Are you expecting trouble?"

"I don't think so. I just want to make sure. Show that there is someone there."

"Make sure you leave it at that and don't even think of anything heroic" he said. "that sort of thing is not our scene."

It was only when I arrived back at the estate and reversed up to the coach house steps that I realised that I had given no thought to the other rudiments of everyday living. That would obviously have to be addressed, but for the moment I was content to have a bed, even if it meant having to grope my way into my sleeping-bag in the dark.

Rollo made an unexpected visit as I was still weighing up how best to move the mattress up the stone stairway. I walked across to the archway to see who the arrival might be and was in time to see him climbing out of a powerful tourer. There was none of the usual grace about his movements. Even from across the forecourt his face seemed angry. The car obviously had another occupant for he made a final comment before slamming the driver's door shut. His words carried over to me.

"Just keep your nose out of my affairs. They are none of your business."

I had been on the point of hailing him, but thought it best not to show that I had heard anything. Instead I waited a few moments before revealing myself. Jo was standing by the passenger door. Her face seemed flushed, but she smiled as I made my way across to them. Rollo put on his usual show of bonhomie. There was no hint of the ill-humour I had witnessed. It disturbed me for he had revealed a side to his nature that I had not seen before. It also led me to wondering how much of his behaviour was simply a front. I did not have much time for such thoughts before he was running things.

"I thought that I would drop by and see how you were progressing," he said. "As you see Jo decided that she had to come too. Anyway, what have you got to show us?"

"Apart from some tidying up, not a lot." I replied. I am still sorting out the sub-contractors."

I took a deep breath and told him about my morning's visitors and my suspicions of them. A flash of anger crossed his face briefly.

"Who were they?" He demanded.

"A father and son named Bedford." I replied.

"Oh Christ! That is all we needed. You invited Billy Bedford here. I do not believe it." He said shaking his head with incredulity. "You really do take the biscuit sometimes Brad."

It was my turn to flush. Thankfully Jo had turned away.

"Don't forget I'm new to this area." I replied. "Who is he anyway?"

"Billy runs a yard that sells anything that can be sold on to people tarting up old buildings. That side of his business is legit. The problem is, he seems to sell more than he buys in, if you know what I mean. Both he and his son have served time. He has probably taken a fancy to the fireplaces and light fittings. There is good money to be made from that sort of thing."

I told him of my plans to sleep in the coach house for the time being.

"Good idea. And leave your car out here where it can be seen. In the meantime, I'd better have a word with Oliver."

"Meadowes?" Jo spoke for the first time. "What does it have to do with him?"

"He runs the biggest building outfit in the area. Lots of guys work for him. A word from him should do the trick."

"You mean he'll lean on them." I added.

"He won't need to. A word will be enough."

He paused to give me a knowing look.

"For God's sake Brad, in future check people out or ask me; and get things moving here. I want this sorted out by New Year."

I remembered that I still had to unload my car.

"Can you give me a hand with my mattress?"

My request was brushed aside with a frown.

"No, I haven't time. I have more important things to do. You will have to do it yourself."

He turned to Jo.

"Are you coming with me? Or do you want Brad to drive you home?"

She turned away from him without answering.

"Silly question. You do not like my friends."

With that he walked to his car. He was whistling as he climbed back into it and drove away. It was only after he had gone that I realized that he had not really said why Oliver Meadowes would wish to involve himself in our affairs.

For a while Jo stood staring out over the parkland. I could only guess what was going through her mind. She turned with a tired smile.

"Not a good day." She said. "Now let's get your things moved."

I protested, but she was as determined to help as Rollo had been indifferent, and together we struggled up the stairway with the bulky mattress. She looked concerned when we deposited it in the empty room.

"Oh Brad." She said. "Are you going to be alright here? It's so bare."

"No problem." I replied. "I've roughed it before, and tomorrow I'll arrange for the services to be reconnected to Miss Tyzack's flat."

"Good." She said. "Now promise me you will be careful."

"There's not going to be any trouble." I assured her. "People like the Bedfords prefer to operate when no one is about."

"I hope you're right." She said. "Now would you please take me home."

She sat without speaking throughout the short journey. I glanced at her a couple of times, but she was wrapped in her own thoughts. She finally broke the silence when I pulled into the driveway of the Cascades.

"I'm sorry that Rollo was so rude to you."

"He was rude to you too." I replied.

"Yes, but I'm his wife. It's allowed in a marriage."

"In front of others?"

She shrugged for answer.

"He's changed." I continued. "It is difficult to pinpoint, but he seems colder and harder in some ways.

She looked at me for a moment before she answered.

"He has grown to love money."

"But he's always had money."

"It is not love of money for its own sake. It seems to be the thrill of making it in new and exciting ways that gives him a buzz. He has some scheme lined up for that house and he will not tell me what it is. I'm certain of it and I am equally certain that it involves that bunch he associates with."

"Do you think he is involved in anything underhand?" I was half surprised to hear myself ask the question.

"I don't know Brad. I honestly know more about the

surface of the moon than I know about Rollo's business dealings."

She spoke with a conviction that I could well believe after what I had overheard earlier.

"All that I do know is that he doe not seem to have any scruples and enjoys living on the edge."

She unfastened her seat belt and paused with the car door open.

"Would you like to come in and have tea?"

I declined the invitation. In other circumstances, I might have taken up her offer, but it did not seem a good idea. Besides, I reckoned I still had about an hour or so to get myself a flashlight and other odds and ends before shops closed for the evening.

I took Rollo's admonition to heart after that false start. From then onwards I made a point of not only making thorough checks of any business I approached, but of also vetting their premises. The people I eventually sub-contracted all proved sound and in the joiner Robin Johnston I found a craftsman of the old school who showed a real interest in the task of recreating the missing interior doors. We spent a whole morning taking measurements and discussing woods and styles. He declined any prepayment.

"We have shaken hands," he said. "That is good enough for me."

By the beginning of the third week the place was beginning to come alive. The general builder I had hired quickly sent in a team to remove all the remaining partitions and trolley ramps that had been left. The men worked hard wheeling their debris away into skips as fast as they created it. It was a relief when the roofing contractor arrived and I was able to turn attention to the damaged bedrooms.

All the time, in between directing operations, I was continuing with my own specialist work. I had picked on the coach house on the spur of the moment when dealing with the Bedfords. It proved to be a good choice. It was deceptively spacious. Fading pin-ups torn from magazines and a hollow circle of dart holes suggested that it too had seen wartime use. It was surprisingly clean and two or three days hard work saw two of the rooms repainted and ready for use. The smaller room beneath the bell tower I used as my bedroom. The larger room that overlooked the end of the drive and the greater part of the forecourt I fitted out as my base.

I had already produced large detailed plans for each floor of the house on which each room was given a number. These were set out on a table at the end of the room. To these I now added a separate plan for each room with detailed notes of the work that was needed on each wall. As each drawing and sheet was completed I mounted it on the wall along with all the other pieces for that room and tied them in to the room plan with strips of red tape pinned at each end. Gradually the walls filled up giving the room the appearance of a busy site office.

Finally, I began the painstaking work of making drawings of wall sections of each room on which I experimented with colour washes in order to decide on the appropriate decor. I was deeply engrossed in this work one morning near the end of the month when I heard my name being called. I recognised the voice and sprang to the window to confirm it as Jo's. I think I took the stone stairs two at a time in my hurry to join her.

A smile lit up her face as I called to her from the archway.

"Where have you hidden yourself? I could see your car and knew you could not be far."

"I have set up shop in the coach house. Come and see."

I allowed her to enter the office ahead of me and stood watching from the doorway. She walked to the centre of the room and slowly turned taking everything in.

"You have been so busy. I had no idea ..." She left the thought unfinished for another thought had struck her.

"Which is the room with the view?"

I knew which room she meant. I had devoted extra care to it as if somehow anticipating this moment. I walked across and drew her to the master-plan laid out on the table.

"Here it is. Room Eight. Now trace round the wall from the door until you reach the Room Eight group."

She did as I indicated and stood studying each sheet. I had made coloured drawings of the outer wall showing the windows with the original fold-away shutters repaired and painted and suggested drapery. I had done the same with the opposite wall with the fireplace restored to its original beauty and its missing ironmongery replaced. She spent a long time looking at each drawing.

"This is all so right." She murmured. Then she turned to me.

"I had not realised that you had all this talent and organizational skill. Why do you keep it hidden? I would have thought that you would want the whole world to know."

"Like Rollo you mean."

"No not like Rollo. This is very different. There is so much knowledge and assurance in your work. You have grown Brad. You were so young before."

She halted aware that she was heading into deep waters and turned back to the wall display.

"Has any of the work been done yet?" She asked.

"None of this. I am preparing for my specialists. They arrive the week after next and I want them up and running from day one."

A look of disappointment crossed her face, so I hurriedly added.

"Most of the clearance and patching up has been done and the roofers are at work at the back of the house at the moment. Come I will show you."

She took obvious enjoyment from using the main entrance for the first time. Again, I let the work speak for itself. She did not say anything until we reached the dining room.

"It seems different, yet I can't see why."

"It is bigger." I said. "Remember this had been used as an operating theatre. That end there had been partitioned off and a screen had been built to seal off the fireplace"

"Aah!" She nodded her head slowly with understanding.

"Over there," I continued, "I have started to scrub away some of the ceiling paint. It is some sort of whitewash. You can see a bit of the old decoration."

We must have spent almost half-an-hour reviewing the changes room by room. As I expected we lingered longest in the sitting room. I could see from the way she looked at the windows and fireplace that she was trying to visualize what I had shown in my drawings. Upstairs she merely peeped into the rain-affected bedrooms where I had had the damaged plaster stripped away leaving the rooms looking gaunt and unfinished.

"You have worked wonders already," she said when we were back in the entrance hall. "I can't wait to see it when it is finished."

"That will be a long time yet. It is the finishing work that takes time if it is done properly."

"And I'm sure you will make a beautiful job of it. So I'll just have to wait."

"I'm afraid so."

She beamed at me then. It was the sort of smile that suggested a secret - or a surprise.

"Anyway. That's not why I came. Have you had lunch?"

"Not yet. I usually go down to the pub in the village and have a sandwich."

"Good. I have a much better idea. I've brought a picnic lunch for us. Why don't we find somewhere nice to eat it."

She had wedged a wicker basket in the passenger well of her sports car. She handed it out to me and took a rug and a cool-bag from the passenger seat. Nothing was said. I think we both assumed that we were heading for the grounds behind the house.

A paved alley led away from the forecourt, separating the kitchen garden from the open parkland. On one side a low wrought iron railing marked the edge of the grazed area. On the other side the long wall of the kitchen garden provided support for a variety of climbing plants. At the end of the alley we passed beneath a stone arch and found ourselves in a flower garden.

It was laid out to an irregular design. Flower borders, in some places twenty feet deep or more, in others no deeper than an arm's length, lay on either side of a broad path of random flagstones that curved sinuously between its planted banks. Drifts of perennial flowers marched with flowering shrubs and delicate trees creating a pattern of varying heights, textures and colours that was constantly changing, but never dull.

The full bloom of summer was over, but there was still enough colour from late flowerings to slow our passage. Temporarily thoughts of food were forgotten as we paused to take in each new delight. Our enjoyment was all the more strong from the realization of our shared knowledge of many of the plants we found. It was all so unexpected after the plainness of the front of the house.

A little way along, after rounding a pronounced curve, we reached a fork in the path. The left-hand branch seemed to double back on itself and I guessed that it led eventually to the terracing at the rear of the house. The roofing contractor's men had erected scaffolding there and would be now taking their lunch break. We took the right-hand fork and passing through a trellis entwined with climbing roses, found ourselves in a rectangular formal rose garden. At the end of this a further stone arch led out into the landscaped parkland.

"Look Brad," Jo exclaimed, as we emerged from the arch and found ourselves mid-way along the ridge on which the house had been built. The path continued along its spine for another hundred yards or so. At its end stood a small domed temple. No attempt had been made to break the symmetry of its circular form with any entrance portico, so that its outer wall was a perfect circle of fluted columns that created exciting patterns of light and shade in the midday sun.

"Its beautiful," Jo breathed. "Let's eat here."

She spread the rug on the grass immediately beyond the temple. To our left lay the landscaped lawns and the bridge we had seen from the sitting room. To our right we were surprised to find views of a further section of the grounds. Below our ridge the stream had been used to create a series of small lakes that shone in the sun like the jewels of a necklace.

"What a marvellous spot," Jo said. "I don't think we could have found a better one."

My lack of response must have alerted her that my thoughts were elsewhere. My attention had been caught by a pair of stone benches set against the base of the temple.

"What's the matter?"

"Nothing at all," I replied, aware that I was grinning from ear to ear.

"What are you grinning for?"

I pointed to the stone benches.

"Look." I said. "I think we have found the missing staircase sections."

"What, those."

"Huh-huh. They are upside down. That is the flat base we can see. It is the way the further one is lying at an angle that was the give-away."

"Oh Brad, I'm so pleased."

I am sure that she could not have felt as pleased as I did just then. What to do about the staircase had been a major headache. I could have kissed her. Somehow, she had turned what had begun as a very ordinary day into something very memorable. I think she too felt my mood for she took my arm.

"Come on. Let's eat."

We sat on the rug and I watched as she unpacked her

picnic.

"I have not done anything special." She said. "Just simple things: ham rolls, cheese, fruit . . . and this!"

She unzipped the cool-bag as she spoke and produced a large bottle.

"Fresh lemonade. I made it specially this morning."

There is something that gives an extra quality to eating and drinking in the open air. That simple picnic was no exception. No dish of ambrosia set before the gods could have improved on it. We ate slowly relishing the taste of the food and drank deep draughts of lemonade. Then, when we had finished, we lay back with sighs of heartfelt satisfaction.

"That was very enjoyable," I said.

"Mm, the simple things in life are always the best."

I did not look at her. The wistful tone of her voice said everything.

We lay silently for a while. Eventually I turned and propped myself up on an elbow to face her.

"Do you believe in fate?"

"What? Predestination and all that? I don't know really.

Why do you ask? Do you?"

"I didn't before, but lately ...It is how I feel now. It was strange coming here that first time to meet Miss Tyzack. I can't explain it. It was as if I was coming home."

"You think it was predestined that you should be here?"

"I don't know. It is all confusing. I just sense that in some way this place is going to be significant in my life. Do you think that is silly?"

She smiled. "No. Not silly. I know that you react to buildings in a way that most people do not. What is so special about this one?"

It was not easy to provide an answer. There was simply some strange indefinable sense about this place. Already I had adjusted to its slower pace of life so that it felt as if I had been here for a very long time. Perhaps I was unsure of the magical quality the day was beginning to adopt. Instead I ducked the question and turned the conversation in a different direction.

"Perhaps it is all part of some great masterplan of Rollo's."

"No!" She said with real conviction. "Whatever plans he may have for this place, I'm sure yours is only a walk-on part. In any case he has no great masterplan. He is strictly a short-term operator."

She had a way of signalling the end of a conversation with some sort of abrupt movement. She did it now by jumping to her feet and brushing her dress with her hands.

"I would like to walk round the lakes. Are you coming?"

She began to walk away leaving me little choice but to follow her.

We followed a path which looped down from the ridge and joined the stream at the point where it began to broaden behind the first of the dams.

I returned to where she had broken off the conversation.

"I have been thinking about what you said about Rollo just now. I've never seen him in that way."

"That's not surprising. You have a different viewpoint. You're his friend. You know, his friendship with you must be the only lasting thing in his life."

"It is not much of a friendship these days." I said ruefully, but she seemed not to hear.

She seemed happy to continue with the subject after all. Perhaps she found it easier to talk whilst walking. Perhaps she had decided that it was time for certain things to be said.

"Think back," she continued. "Has he ever stuck with anything for very long? . . .There you can't. He has this craving for anything new, for doing things that have not been done before, for creating a stir.

"Are you referring to The Cascades?"

"That's a prime example. I can understand a young architect wanting to make a name for himself and a house made of glass with this fantastic atrium and waterfall does just that. But ..."

She paused.

"You don't like it."

"Is it so obvious?"

"Huh-huh!"

"I was thrilled with it at first. That was before I realized that it was not for us. It wasn't meant to be a home: just an ongoing advert for Rollo Blake."

We walked in silence for a few moments before she continued.

"Did you know that it got a spread in one of the Sunday colour supplements?"

"Steve mentioned something about it."

"They sent down some gushing brunette to cover the story. You know the type, long glossy hair and bright red lipstick. Rollo made sure he got a good write-up. He spent a whole afternoon giving her a guided tour, pouring on the charm. She loved it all; the marvellous setting, the fantastic house, the handsome young architect. He must have fucked her on the settee behind the waterfall while I sat out in the garden. I found a pair of lace knickers there that evening."

"But they could so easily have been seen by you or any of the staff."

"Living on the edge. That would have been part of the thrill ... Don't look so shocked, Brad. She is only one of many."

I was shocked, but not by her revelations. I had no real illusions about Rollo. It was her choice of words that had surprised me. They were so out of character with the Jo I had known.

She seemed to sense what I was thinking.

"Or is it me you are shocked with? You're right. That is not the real me. It is just difficult sometimes not to let a little bitterness creep in."

I let her talk without attempting any response.

"When I married Rollo, I thought that he would settle, that we would build a good life together. I think that I was blinded by the glamour. It did not take long for that to wear off. I soon came to realize that everything we did had to be on his terms. I was expected to be the dutiful wife stuck in that glass showcase while he could carry on being Rollo. That is what I find hardest to bear: being expected to carry on smiling and playing the gracious hostess at his parties and entertaining all the awful people he brings home."

"Am I included in that last category?"

A smile fought through the tears that threatened to engulf her. She took my arm.

"No. You are not. You are the exception. It was such a lovely surprise to see you on the night of that last party; a lovely reminder of all that is good and honest."

She did not say anything more after that, but she continued to hold my arm.

We had reached the first of the dams of earth and stone that had been thrown across the stream to hold back its waters. We stood for a while admiring the simple beauty of the landscaper's design with its succession of lakes, each set a little lower than its predecessor following the fall of the ground. Each was beautiful and each differed from the others in shape and the choice and siting of the trees and shrubs that clothed the banks.

"Miss Tyzack mentioned there were lakes." I ventured. "They were created by the ancestor who built the house. He made a new lake to celebrate the birth of each of his children."

Jo's face lit up.

"What a lovely idea, and each is different too, just as children are." She counted each small lake. "Nine. Oh! the poor woman. All those pregnancies."

"You have no children." It was as much a question as a statement.

"No."

"But you would like to have children?"

"Yes."

"And Rollo would not."

"Not in any way. He is extremely hostile to the idea. I think he sees them as a threat to his freedom of movement."

She put on a brave smile and her shoulders gave a tiny shrug of acceptance. Again, she looked close to tears. This time she fought off that threat in a different way. She gave that characteristic shake to her hair and began to question me.

"And what of you Brad?" she asked. "Have you sewn your wild oats. Have you left a trail of fatherless babes throughout Italy and the Home Counties?" She squeezed my arm. "No. Of course not. You would never behave so irresponsibly. But there must have been other girls."

She gave me a long sideways look as she spoke.

"Oh Brad! You silly boy!"

It was my turn to shrug.

"Nothing serious." I said. "I've not had time. I've been too busy."

The words sounded lame and we both knew they were only partially true.

We had reached the furthest lake when we became aware of a steady rhythmic whirring in the air behind us. A pair of swans passed low overhead, their long wings beating the air in unison. We watched as they circled the lake and then swung in to land on the water in a display that momentarily combined the skills of hang-glider and water-skier before they were transformed again into a pair of swans gliding sedately across the lake and still together as if joined by some invisible cord.

The significance of what we had seen was not lost on either of us. I put it into words.

"I think we have a lot in common with them." I remarked.

"The swans? What makes you say that?"

"They are very simple creatures." I replied. "I read once that they mate for life. Isn't that what we both want?"

"Yes. I suppose it is."

"Does Rollo love you?" It was something that I realized I needed to know.

"I don't know." She said. "I thought he did at the beginning."

"But now you are not sure." I added.

"The romance did not last long after we were married."

I walked in silence for a while daring myself to voice what was in my head. It was a thought that had come to mind eight years earlier. It had seared then, sharp and painful like a cancer. I had blanked it from my mind, buried it deep where its baleful pain could not burn. Now unbidden it sprang up again. Now it had to be said whatever the pain it might cause.

"What you said earlier about Rollo needing to live on the edge. Perhaps it was another thrill." I said grimly. "It would have been a fine challenge to take you from under my nose."

"Don't Brad." She whispered. "You are only hurting both of us. It does not matter now. The fact is, whatever his reasons may have been, I married him and my marriage vows were not given lightly."

We walked back in silence. She still held my arm as we walked but neither of us spoke. When we reached the picnic site she began to collect up the remains of our lunch and put everything back in the basket. I folded the rug.

"Thank you for a lovely lunch." I said.

"It has been good. I felt that I owed you that."

"Why? Because you spoke your mind last time you were here?"

"No. Unfinished business. We never did have that picnic on Brandon Hill. But I am sorry for that outburst."

She took the rug from me.

"Now I must go. You stay here. I can find my own way."

She walked back along the path and passed out of sight through the arch. I sat for a long while after she had gone slowly digesting all that she had said. It came to me then, when I reflected on my question about Rollo's feelings for her, that I had asked the wrong question. What I really wanted to know was whether she still loved him.

10

Looking back on that time of Indian summer, there seems a strange unreal air about it. In the days that followed Jo's visit I seemed to go about my work in a daze. At one level, I still functioned as normal, but my mind seemed to have divided into two distinct spheres. One controlled my day-to-day activities, while the other ... the other seemed to have no sense of where I was or what I was doing.

It was not a dreamtime as an Australian aboriginal would know it. I did not leave everything to wander off into some rural outback; in a sense I was already there, and my wanderings were confined to the now familiar rooms and passages of the house and the garden pathways. It was as if part of me had become detached and had entered another realm.

The two realms merged and mingled in a chaotic mix. In this strange half-world one day ran into the next in a way that left me unaware of their passing. In the one I continued with my normal range of work. In the other I engaged in strange reveries that featured the same smiling face, the same blue-grey eyes, the same musical voice. I slept, I ate, I completed my preparations for the final stages of the renovation, but there was no rhythm to my days. I worked at strange times.

On one day I would arise early, on another I would work late into the night. Between periods of work and often within them, my mind slipped unbidden into that other world of silent reverie.

Between periods of work and wakeful dream I walked. I found pleasure in retracing each of the tours of the house we had made together. Indoors I relived each moment, looking anew at each feature that had caught our attention, remembering each word spoken. Outside I retraced our steps on the day of the picnic. I sat in the same place by the temple and I paced out the same route we had followed around the lakes. Everything she had said during that last visit was analysed and dissected over and over again.

It is difficult to describe my state of mind during this period. There were no fixed times. All thoughts and moves were random and involuntary. Thoughts came unconsciously to mind and just as effortlessly slipped away. For long periods, I must have drifted through time in a warm haze in which the central cortex of the brain disengaged itself and in which time and place and all the other parameters of everyday life had dissolved. I was aware of this phenomenon, but could do nothing to prevent its occurrence. No observer of my condition could have done anything to alleviate it; though all would have recognized the symptoms.

Fortunately, there were no outsiders to break into my disordered state. The roofers had completed their work and decamped. I was left entirely alone to enjoy this strange idyll. I thought back to earlier times, remembering the way we had first met and the way she had kissed me after that first date. I had been strongly attracted to Jo from the beginning. Then I had badly wanted her to like me, but perhaps I had been too diffident, too unsure of myself. I could admit it now. Even when things were at their most painful I had not stopped liking her. There had been no one else during the years in London, but this was different. It had crept up on me without me knowing. Slowly, very slowly, I came to realize that I had fallen in love.

The realization came as a shock to the conscious half of my brain. This was the sensible factual half that had taken me away to London and had kept me well away from Bristol after she had linked herself to Rollo. It kicked in immediately countering the musings of the dreamy half with facts and cold logic. I was Paul Bradley, it reminded me. I had little in the way of material wealth and my prospects were at best uncertain. She was a married woman: not simply married, but married to Rollo Blake. He was famous, wealthy, well-established. Eight years earlier she had preferred him to me. How could I stand comparison with that. Doggedly the dreamy half marshalled its arguments. She wanted stability, it argued. She would like to have children. Rollo was unfaithful to her and probably did not love her - perhaps never had. She had changed. Eight years ago, she had been a girl. Now she was a woman and with that change had come a deeper realization of what she really wanted from life.

In an argument like this there could be no real winner. Optimism gave way to pessimism only to yield in turn to optimism in a continuing giddy cycle. Constantly I reminded myself that I did not know when, or even if, I would see her again. Yet, despite all, the dreamy optimist would not be entirely suppressed. Perhaps it was only fancy, but with love comes strength. It was, perhaps a measure of the progress my self-development had made that I could even contemplate a challenge to the long supremacy of Rollo's will, that I could think myself man-enough to make her happy where he had so singularly failed.

It was in this mood of dreamy optimism that many days later I took up my pen and drawing board and made my way out through the flower garden to the temple. This time I went a little beyond it. I wanted to sketch it standing on its ridge before the sun moved too far round to the west. I worked slowly for I wanted to draw it exactly as it had been on the day of our picnic. I had almost finished and was concentrating on getting the intricate carving of the capitals as accurate as possible. When I next looked up I was aware of a figure in a pink dress standing next to the columns. It took several moments for the realization to sink in.

She walked over to me. I returned to my sketching, but it was mere pretence. For the moment, my hand could not be trusted to deliver pen to paper with its usual precision.

"I thought I might find you here."

She had walked behind me to look over my shoulder.

"Romantic or what?"

"Just keeping my hand in." I tried to sound nonchalant.

"I like it," she continued. "I might even trade a slice of quiche and a mixed salad for it."

"That sounds a good deal." I said and handed her the drawing. "It's yours."

She looked at it for a moment and then handed it back.

"You haven't signed it."

I scrawled 'Brad' in the bottom corner.

"Jo!"

There was a curious strangled sound to my voice that I could not explain.

"Ssh!"

She knelt and laid her finger tips against my lips.

"Don't say anything. I am here. Just accept that."

I knew that she was right. I felt like a high wire artiste who had just made a slip and had momentarily glimpsed catastrophe. I could so easily have ruined everything by impetuosity. I said nothing. I looked at her and breathed deeply. Slowly my tightrope walker recovered his equilibrium.

After we had eaten, we lay back and talked. It was strange. We had walked out together as boy and girl for many months once before. We had even slept together on the night of the storm. Now it was as if we were meeting for the first time. I realized how little I really knew her. We talked and talked. We talked of little things and important things. We talked of hopes and fears and all the details of our innermost selves. We talked as we had never talked before, and the talking seemed to be the most natural thing in the world.

She became a frequent visitor after that, sometimes calling twice in the same week, but never, I noticed, on Tuesdays. That day, I assumed, was when she was busy with hostess duties at The Cascades. We made no formal arrangements. She would simply turn up at the end of the morning when she judged I would be ready for a break. Always she arrived bearing something she had prepared herself for us to eat for lunch.

We managed to fit in two further picnics before the fine weather broke. On both of these occasions we chose spots by the side of one of the lakes. Then for a short period we took advantage of dry mild spells between showers to sit on benches in the flower garden. Finally, when November brought more prolonged rain and the onset of colder temperatures, we retreated indoors. I bought a pair of canvas director's chairs and we set these up in the sitting-room. We would sit there sipping mugs of hot soup that Jo brought in a large flask, watching the winds slowly stripping the parkland trees to their winter nakedness.

We had drifted into a strange amorphous relationship. It was an arrangement that for the time being suited us both. She had said nothing since that first picnic about Rollo or the state of their marriage. I was conscious that she needed time to sort out the contradictions of her allegiances. She seemed relaxed when we were together. Already the strained lines were beginning to disappear from her face. She had even begun to tease me. I had learned wisdom from that first false step. Now I was content to live for the day. Each morning my thoughts were of what I might profitably do that day. I tried not to think of whether or not she would come. Her visits were bonuses. They were unscripted, but all the more welcome for that. Those hours by the lakeside or in the flower garden seemed to flit by in an instant. Days when she did not appear seemed to have no end. All the time we were conscious that this state of affairs could not last for ever.

It was in the course of this idyll that I heard the music. I was in the rose garden when it drifted in over the trees. At normal times the estate was remarkably peaceful, with only the occasional cough from an ewe or a snatch of birdcall to break the silence. In such stillness, any sound carries. There was no mistaking Puccini's swelling chords as Rodolfo declared his love for Mimi. It could only mean that Dan Landis and his team were here, several days before I expected them.

I hurried through the garden and along the alley to the forecourt. I arrived in time to see a high-sided van with an assortment of galvanized tubs and plastic buckets lashed to its roof lurch around the corner of the coach house. Behind it a low, four-wheeled trailer clanked its load of builder's planks, ladders and sections of scaffolding towers. La Boheme blared from the cab stereo as they swung on to the gravel with all the bravado of a travelling circus proclaiming its arrival to the world at large. In a way that is what they were, travelling self-contained and hawking their skills from site to site. Unlike a circus they did not need to advertise their coming. They were known all over Europe and their services were booked months in advance.

I hurried across to greet them as they emerged from their vehicle and stretched stiff muscles. I had to shout above the noise of the stereo. I had met Dan while working with Henry Hutchings on a restoration scheme in Central London. He had impressed me then, and he had been the obvious choice to replace the delicate plasterwork. He was a man of middle height with an open handsome face that was rarely without a smile. His hair, already thin when I had first met him, had receded further. The extended forehead served only to emphasize the strength of his features.

He lived in an old house in Kew, where his wife painted delicate watercolours of flowers in a studio at the bottom of the garden while he was away. I had had to call on him one week-end and had been surprised to find that inside the house had been remodelled in modern open-plan style. All walls were painted in a soft white that relied on splashes of colour from vivid abstract canvases to break its uniformity. I had not expected this from a man who spent his working life restoring the plasterwork of period houses. Amused by my obvious surprise, he explained with a grin that he did not believe in taking work home with him. The same rule obviously applied to his wife, for there was no evidence of her work either.

Long Tom Willis provided an obvious contrast. A tall thin figure with lank hair he towered over the other two. His face had a lugubrious air which masked a dry sense of humour. He had never married, preferring as he said to do what he wanted, whenever he wanted, without having to compromise with anyone else. Doing what he wanted seemed to consist of relaxing with a pint of beer whenever opportunity presented itself. He kept a small flat in a regency terrace on the sea front at Brighton - Hove actually he said, repeating the local joke - where he relaxed in periods between contracts.

The trio was made up by Claudio Valonnes, a stocky figure with a shock of dark curly hair. He was a truly cosmopolitan figure, the hybrid offspring of an Italian mother and a French chef. He spoke both languages fluently and had appeared to have inherited the other cultural characteristics of both parts of his ancestry in equal measure. From his father, he had drawn the culinary skills which made him the unanimous choice as cook for the group. His Italian genes by contrast had bequeathed a love of opera which was augmented by the gift of a strong tenor voice. It was he who provided the opera recordings which set them apart from any other group of craftsmen I have encountered. For some reason I had never established, he was invariably referred to as 'The

Boy' by the other two. Alone of the three he appeared to have no fixed place of address. He claimed that it was not worth it when they spent so much time away from home. In the periods when the group were resting between contracts he simply moved in with one of his innumerable girlfriends.

Dan had paid a short visit several weeks earlier to assess the situation. We had arranged then that they could have the use of the flat. I showed them the way in through the walled garden. They inspected the flat with interest. It was obvious they had experienced much worse. A working kitchen and carpeted floors were greeted with enthusiasm and the bathroom with its separate shower cubicle produced a sigh of 'luxury'. Within minutes the door of the van had been thrown open. Folding tables, chairs, camp beds, bedding, kitchen utensils, a portable TV set and several boxes of foodstuffs were quickly ferried inside. That done and when everything had been squared up, they made a pot of tea and a mound of toast and sat down to slowly and deliberately work their way through them both. Only when the final crumb had been consumed and the last dribble squeezed from the pot did they declare themselves ready to view their work.

The laid-back attitude was much like the Spartans combing their hair before the battle at Thermopylae. It was just a bluff that disguised a very thoroughgoing professionalism. Before the sun began to fade into dusk they had made a detailed tour of the house and transferred the contents of the trailer and other work equipment into the entrance hall. I left the other two pouring over my drawings and schedules while Claudio prepared their evening meal. The presence of extra bodies on the premises had given me the first opportunity for weeks for an evening away from the estate and I had telephoned Steve to arrange a night out. They were already at work when I slipped across to the flat for my shower at eight the following morning.

Overnight it had become a different house. Rooms had become furnished with scaffolding towers and mixing tanks.

Piles of planks and ladders lay ready to hand and hoses snaked from any convenient tap to their water butts. There was an easy camaraderie between them which allowed work to progress with a smooth efficiency. Dan was the acknowledged leader of the group and handled all their bookings and financial transactions. On site, no one seemed to be in charge. All were equally skilled and undertook specific sections of the work. This was covered in small sections, broadly the area that could be worked while the plaster remained in a plastic state. Judging when plaster was workable was the real test of their skill. As Dan explained it was an art rather than a science, and something that each practitioner had to master alone. As a result, although to my eye the finished work appeared of a similar standard, the methods each employed to arrive at that point varied widely. Even the preparation of the materials differed in small, though each would claim, significant ways. Just what those differences were remained a closely guarded secret, as each man insisted on preparing his own plaster mixes. Only the erection and dismantling of their work platforms and other general labouring was shared by all.

All the time there was the glorious sound of opera. In the manner of a Radio 3 presenter, Claudio chose the day's programme from the huge collection of tapes that accompanied them on tour. Alone with Dan and Tom one day, I asked if they had ever objected to the imposition of Claudio's music on their ears.

"Maybe, at first." admitted Dan, "but not any more. It seems to suit."

"It is hard to explain." Tom had added. "There is a rise and fall in the intensity of this type of work. Some of it is boring and repetitive, some is finely detailed and creative. Opera is much the same with its emotions. The two seem to complement each other."

So, it had come to stay. Tape after tape flowed from Claudio's portable machine. He knew them all by heart, humming along to the overtures and quietly joining in any of the mixed voice choruses. He was silent for the female arias, listening intently during their performance and murmuring words of appreciation in Italian at their close. His great moments came when any of the great tenor arias was imminent. Then he would turn down the volume of the tape-recorder and take on the role himself. Work would temporarily halt and all the empty rooms and corridors would echo to the sound of his powerful voice. His two companions would stop whatever they were doing to listen to him. "The Boy's in good voice today", might be the verdict. Or occasionally, "I have him heard him sing that better", might be the comment before they returned to their work.

I had wondered briefly after their arrival how their presence might affect the situation with Jo. The question was settled the very next day. She turned up a little earlier than usual, as I was deep in discussion with Dan about the complete re-creation of a ceiling panel. I introduced her to them and she made an instant hit. Claudio was quick to show his appreciation. The tribulations of Tosca had filled our ears for much of the morning. Now, after a brief foray outside, a shower of rain had driven us indoors at the moment that Tosca's hapless lover was about to sing his adieu. It was too rich a moment to resist. With the starkness of the entrance hall making a passable stage-set dungeon, Claudio for a few moments became Cavaradossi, singing of his love for Tosca. It was a controlled performance made all the more beautiful by its simplicity. Jo listened entranced. There was silence as he finished. Jo crossed to him.

"Thank you, Claudio! That was beautiful." She said and kissed his cheek.

Claudio beamed. From above there was more applause. Unknown to us Claudio's colleagues had witnessed the performance from the galleried landing.

On her next visit Jo arrived bearing a chocolate cake she had baked for the trio. She made a point of presenting it to her soloist. By the end of that week she had become a firm favourite with them. They seemed to look forward to her visits almost as much as I did.

"Your lady not coming today then," would be the invariable comment on days when she did not materialize.

It gave pleasure to hear her described as my lady. I had not introduced her with any claim to special standing, but simply as Mrs Blake. My best efforts went unrewarded. They assumed from the very beginning that she was 'my lady'. Much as they gave pleasure, such comments had a double edge. They were a reminder that as yet nothing was settled between us.

At each visit, there was some new finished area to show her. During one hectic week Robin Johnston and one of his carpenters fitted the new doors and repaired the damaged shutters, dovetailing their operations around the plasterers' movements. The following week I had my builder back to rebuild the staircase. They carefully excavated around each of the temple seats and moved them piece by piece back to the house on a hand trolley. Each section was hosed down and then given a good buffing before being re-sited in their true positions. Everyone gathered in the hall to view the finished article. All agreed that the replaced sections looked none the worse for their spell underground.

I particularly remember standing with Jo in the sitting room after it had been fully restored. I had mentioned to Dan that this was her favourite room and the team had worked with particular attention to make sure that it was perfect. She had spent a long time examining their work. When she finally spoke, there was a wistful note to her voice.

"It will all be finished soon." She said.

We both understood the hidden meaning in that simple statement.

Throughout those final stages in late November, as room by room the house took on its true form, I had held back from contacting Rollo. Now I had no alternative. The structural repairs were complete. There remained only the re-decoration and I knew that he wanted to make a personal input in that area. By ill-timing he arrived as Dan and his team were stacking all their gear in the forecourt ready for loading up their van and trailer. He roared into his usual space regardless of the fact that Claudio was stacking scaffolding sections there. He was in a tearing hurry and seemed to hurl himself from the vehicle almost before its wheels had come to rest.

"Watch what you are doing with those things. That's an expensive car," he hurled at the unfortunate Claudio as he strode into the house.

"Where is Brad?" I heard him demand as he entered the hall.

Unusually for the time of day, he was wearing a suit. More unusual still was the frown that occupied his face. It was the first time I had seen him displaying real emotion.

He became a little less agitated when I greeted him.

"I can only spare five minutes." He said. "Just tear yourself away from your workforce and show me round."

I particularly wanted him to see the dining room and led him towards it. I saw Dan and Tom exchange looks.

Rollo gave only a cursory look at the finished work.

"It's very good Brad." He said. "But then I always knew it would be. It is just that it has taken so long."

"It's skilled work." I said. "It cannot be rushed and those fellows in the hall are booked up months ahead. We were lucky to get them."

"I know." He admitted. "It is a pity we could not have got them sooner."

There was obviously something on his mind which he was finding it difficult to say.

"What I said about only having five minutes I meant. I know it isn't what I promised, but we shall have to put things on the back burner for a while. Something has turned up that may delay the deal I had arranged."

He relaxed then having finally come out with it.

"I know you will not mind waiting a bit. I'm on my way now to try to sort something out."

I accompanied him back out to his car. Dan and his team had begun to load their van. A thought occurred to Rollo at the door to his car.

"Have you fixed anything with decorators yet?"

"Only provisionally." I replied. "I have to confirm the contract."

"Hold off for the time being," He said. "I will let you know when to go ahead."

Then with a flurry of gravel he was gone. I could hear the throaty roar of his tourer along the avenue long after it had passed out of sight.

The threesome had stopped to watch his departure.

"I would say that man was in a hurry." Said Dan. "Who was he?"

"That was Rollo Blake the architect." I replied. "He's the man behind all this. It will be his signature on your cheque."

"He's an arrogant bastard whoever he is," Said Claudio, still smarting from the uncivil reprimand he had received.

Tom was still following the roar of the car. As the last sounds faded away he turned to us.

"Did I hear you say his name was Blake?" He asked.

"Yes Tom." I replied, catching the drift of his thoughts. "As in Mrs Blake."

"Aah!" Said Tom. "Well, you give your lady our best when you see her. Tell her she can come and make tea for us any time ... and good luck to you lad."

I helped them with the remainder of their loading. Then it was time for them to go. I shook hands with each of them in turn.

"Thanks for everything."

"It has been a pleasure." said Dan. "We shall honestly miss this place."

With that they climbed into the van. As they swung out between the gatepost lions the first notes of the overture to

Tannhauser drifted from the cab stereo. I smiled ruefully to myself. The circus was on tour again.

The day felt suddenly flat after their departure. I should have felt satisfaction on the completion of my programme, but I felt nothing. The moment I had long anticipated had come, but the ending was not as I had expected. There was no ending. Everything had simply stopped and I was in limbo.

There was still much of the afternoon left. I decided on a walk around the estate. It was a strange reflective walk I took. So many people had flitted in and out of my life; so much had happened. The house too, in a way that I had not anticipated, had already begun to exert a hold on me. The decision to sleep here had been taken as a security measure. Now I realized that I enjoyed waking each morning to the peace and beauty of the place. I tried not to think of the time when I would have to leave.

I had walked for some time engrossed in thought. It was not until I began my circuit of the lakes that I became aware of the stillness. Even allowing for the time of year it was strangely silent. Then I saw the reason. High above the estate a sparrow hawk slowly circled.

11

The gentlest of breezes played through the trees seizing the pale flecks of sawdust as they fell. It whirled them in slow pirouettes before casting them in wide drifts. They formed a thin uneven coat between the tufts of grass. They coated the leaves long since fallen and partially decayed. They clung to the bark of the tree and they found an easy hold on the rough texture of my protective leggings and around the eyelets and laces of my shoes.

The snarl of the chainsaw reverberated through the woods. I applied more pressure and it responded with a tortured scream that changed to a roar of triumph as it cut through the final fibres of the wood. The newly cut log rolled against the others already filling the hollow. I paused in my work and killed the motor. The sawing was proving warmer work than I had imagined and I needed a breather.

The day was developing far better than it had earlier promised. That initial morning of limbo had dawned grey and chill. For the first time since taking up my temporary quarters in the coach house I had awoken stiff and cold. It had not taken long to make a decision when I reviewed my situation over a mug of coffee. There had been no problems with the Bedfords. Oliver Meadowes had no doubt warned them off. Freezing in the coach house seemed pointless when I could be much more comfortable in the flat and almost as close to hand.

The financial review that followed that decision could not offer a solution with the same speed and effectiveness. For the past six months, I had been living on the redundancy settlement Henry and James had paid when I left their employment. Lodging with Steve and staying here at Eastonbury had provided cheap living, but my earlier Italian travels had eaten into this reserve. There was now little left. The Windsor project and two smaller consultancy contracts had been completed, but as yet I had not received payment for them. It would be some time before my name came to be sufficiently known for work to flow in at a rate that would support me. I had accumulated a little capital during my years in London and the sale of the lease on my flat had made a healthy addition to that. There was a difference between capital and income, as Steve had never tired of telling me, and I was determined if possible to avoid digging into my savings. Rollo's visit, short as it had been, now cast everything in a different light. It seemed that there was no cut and dried arrangement. There would be no quick sale of Eastonbury.

Deep down I do not think I had ever trusted the promise of a painless step into self-employment. If nothing else, my father's experience had taught me that much. During the summer and autumn, I had put out a number of feelers and one had borne fruit. I had the offer of a temporary lecturing appointment. There was no promise of anything permanent, but it would stretch to the end of next summer. I had a few more days before I made a decision, but I knew already what my answer would be.

It was the first weekend that I had not been pre-occupied with work on the house. It came as something of a shock to have to think how I had filled my time before Rollo's offer. I had given no thought to my book for over three months. Now there would be time to develop my drawings and to liaise with Tomaso. If I accepted the lecturing job, there would be lectures to prepare. Hopefully too, linking everything, there would be time with Jo. Limbo need not be unproductive, I reasoned.

I began with the basic aspects of living that had occasioned this review. Winter was here and I would need to keep warm. The flat had an old large bore radiator system heated by an oil-fired boiler on the ground floor. The oil tank was still almost one third full. I could not at the moment afford to fill it, but used sparingly to provide a low background warmth I thought it would last through the coldest months. For more immediate warmth I would rely on the open fire. The source of my fuel was not hard to determine. It could be seen in the woods that massed on three sides of the estate. By mid-morning I was on my way home from Bristol. An axe lay across the rear seat and a galvanised wheelbarrow with a broad bulbous wheel rode upside-down atop the roof rack. In the boot was a chainsaw I had hired for the week-end. It took no more than fifteen minutes to wheel my bed and other effects across to the house. Then I was free to spend the rest of my time laying-in my fuel.

A walk into the wood behind the house had revealed a choice of material. Almost immediately I had come across the great lower bough of an oak, itself the size of a lesser tree, which had been torn away from its stem. Further on a birch tree, uprooted but standing propped against a weaker neighbour, had caught my eye. Finally, I had found a virtually full-grown beech lying along the edge of the deep hollow that had betrayed it when some great wind had struck it after rain.

I had been confident enough when hiring the saw, but I was apprehensive when the time came to make use of it. I had decided to tackle the smaller boughs first. With my heart in my mouth I pulled the starter cord to fire the engine into life. My first application of the fearsome blade to timber had been tentative, but it had seemed to slice through it with astonishing ease. With adjustments to my footing and with a stronger grip of the handles I had soon begun to master it. The smaller branches, the birch and then the great oak bough all succumbed in turn to its voracious appetite. Encouraged by early success, I had found enjoyment in the power of the machine and with my confidence sky high I had finally taken on the beech tree. I had already made a deep impression on one side when hot and tired I took a rest.

Refreshed, I refuelled the saw, oiled the teeth in the way that I had been shown at the hire shop and began again. I worked purposefully through the rest of the afternoon. I followed a systematic approach, slowly working my way around the tree, cutting back each branch a piece at a time until only the great girth of the trunk remained. Cut logs lay around in an untidy circle, their clean ends contrasting with the sombre tones of the earth on which they lay. More marked my way home as I trudged back to the house in the fading light. I was hot and dog tired, but I was supremely happy. In my wheel barrow was the saw and fuel can and enough small pieces of sawn wood for my first fire.

Much of the following morning was spent in the same way. This time my work was less urgent and I stopped early so that I had time to undertake the labour of carting the many barrow loads of logs back to the house. I stacked them in the coach house yard beneath my office. The stack filled all of one bay and much of the next. I looked at my handiwork before heading indoors for the night. I reckoned I had enough wood to keep me warm for most of the winter.

That second day's labour had produced one unexpected side-effect. Returning from the woods with a barrow piled high I crossed a shallow hollow. The load bounced up and down with a thump. It is strange how old memories can be stirred. For a moment, I was a child again riding in Dad's wheelbarrow and squealing with pleasure as he bounced over dips in the nursery paths. It was the merest flash of remembrance, but it was enough to remind me that, along with the book and everything else, I had given no thought to him. The feeling of guilt I experienced was sufficiently strong to decide me to go to see him.

I was reluctant to move far on Monday. It had been several days since I had seen Jo and I was sure that she would come. I busied myself splitting some of the larger logs. I used a tree ring as my base and set each larger piece end up on this so that I could swing at it with my axe. I quickly found that there was a surprising amount of skill needed as well as force. Each piece was different in some way and I enjoyed the challenge that each presented.

I needed something to keep my mind occupied. From mid-morning onwards, I was listening for the first sounds of Jo's car along the avenue, expecting at any minute to see her swinging into the forecourt. As the afternoon wore on I realized that she was not going to show up. I returned to the flat carrying an armful of logs for my evening fire. The seasoned wood burnt brightly, but it was a cheerless glow it created that night. I went to bed disappointed and not a little puzzled.

Tuesday had been fixed in my mind as the day for my trip home. I reasoned that this was the one day in the week I could be sure she would not come. I left early. It was a crisp, clear morning. At other times, I might have enjoyed the drive and the sight of the winter countryside, but I was in no mood to enjoy anything. My thoughts were elsewhere. One minute I would be wondering why Jo had not turned up and the next I would begin to concern myself over what reception I would receive from my father. I pulled into the driveway of the nursery without having settled either issue.

My visit proved every bit as difficult as I had thought it might, but in a way that I had not imagined. At first, I thought that things might be taking a turn for the better. The front garden was tidier than I had seen it in the summer. A look around the back soon showed me that this was a false impression. The business area looked even more untidy than before. Every bed was filled with weeds and decaying matter. None of the greenhouses seemed to be in use. He seemed to have given up.

Dad too had changed. I was surprised to see how thin he had become. His face had the same gaunt look about it. The same dark hollows surrounded his eyes, but there was a difference. The eyes had lost their brightness. I remembered the tension of my last visit and how fiercely he had tamped the potting compost around the seedlings. There had been anger then. Now the anger had gone. Now there was only hurt and an apathetic acceptance. He said that he found it difficult to concentrate on anything for very long. He did not sleep well at night. I tried to question him about the business and how was he managing in the house, but in the end, I gave up. The answer was the same to all my queries. He would look away, give a shrug and mumble, "What's the point?" When I was a boy such an answer from me would have produced a sharp reprimand. He had turned into a man I scarcely recognized.

On the way up, I had stopped to buy food. I prepared lunch for the two of us. He ate a little, but then merely toyed with the food. Then without a word he pushed the plate away and sloped over to his chair by the fire. It was the prelude to a difficult afternoon. He did not want to say much, so I had to do much of the talking. I told him about Eastonbury, the sort of work I had been doing and what I hoped to earn there. He perked up a little when I told him about Miss Tyzack's walled vegetable garden, the flower garden walk and the lakes. I thought it best not to say anything about Jo. My parents had not met her, but they knew about our friendship and they knew what had driven me away from Bristol eight years earlier. Now Dad bridled at the first mention of Rollo's name.

"He's no friend of yours." He said. "I never trusted him. He was too clever by half when he was a boy. I'm surprised you want anything to do with him."

It was a relief when it was time to leave. I was about to

drive away when I noticed him coming out to the car. He opened the door as I tried to wind the window down to speak to him.

"Will you be coming home for Christmas?" He asked almost fiercely.

Christmas! I had not given it a thought. Now the very mention of it filled me with dread. I looked at his tired thin face. There could be only one answer.

"Yes Dad." I said. "I'll be home for Christmas."

As an afterthought, I called on Steve on the way home. His face had a relieved look when he saw me.

"I have been trying to get hold of you all afternoon." He said by way of a greeting.

"Good news or bad?"

"Interesting." He replied. "Come on up."

He led the way upstairs.

"I have just started knocking something up for supper, so you will have to come through to the kitchen."

He went directly to the cooker and stirred the contents of a large frying pan. The aroma of onions drifted across. I took a seat at the small table. I suddenly felt very weary.

"Right. That's OK." He said turning to look at me. "Am I cooking for one or for two?"

"Make it two." I said.

"You have not asked what it is."

I sighed with a slow shake of my head.

"I'm too tired to care. I've had an awful day ... I went back home to see Dad."

"Ooh!" Steve made a knowing sound. He took a bundle of long spaghetti from a tall glass jar and fed it into a pan of water boiling on a ring. Then he turned to face me.

"Well here's something else to make it a memorable day. That friend of Rollo's you told me about, the builder."

"Oliver Meadowes?"

"That's him. Meadowes. Thought you ought to know he has been arrested."

"What!"

The shock of his statement drove away all tiredness.

"The story did the rounds this morning."

"Are you sure?"

"Oh, it's kosher right enough. There is talk of nothing else. I thought it might be significant for your operation."

"You may be right."

I nodded thoughtfully. I was thinking of Rollo on the morning that the Landis team had been loading up to leave. There had been something on his mind then and there had been no mistaking his hurry when he had driven away.

Steve turned back to his cooking. He opened a large can of tomatoes and emptied them into the pan. He dropped the can into his waste bin and reached for a jar of dried herbs. His movements seemed well-practised.

"What's he been charged with?"

"VAT fraud." He called over his shoulder.

"Oh!" I felt strangely relieved.

"You sound relieved."

"Well I am in a way." I replied. "I thought at first that it might be something directly involving Rollo."

"I wouldn't sound the all clear yet. The enquiry is continuing and more arrests are expected."

"When did this happen? The arrest I mean?"

"Early last week."

He placed an opened bottle of chianti on the table with two wine glasses.

"Pour the drinks while I finish off." He said. "It should be almost ready."

"Do you know what triggered the arrest?"

"Silly sort of thing really. He'd done a cash deal with a small outfit. You know the routine. Discount price. Cash payment. Nothing declared."

He began to strain the spaghetti as he spoke.

"It seems that someone forgot or got greedy. At any rate input relief was claimed on the deal and this alerted Customs & Excise. They must have had their suspicions for some time. There was no preliminary chat. They raided his house and the company offices. Smashed in the office door with sledge hammers before the staff turned up for work and grabbed every scrap of paper they could find. There is talk of a diary that lists names."

He had lost me at one point.

"What is input relief?"

Steve was more like his old self as he came across to the table bearing two plates of bolognaise. He grinned as he set them down.

"I was forgetting that you artistic types can't handle the technical stuff."

I was in no mood to tussle with him.

"So?"

"So." He said. "Let's take an example. XYZ makes widgets. It charges VAT on each one that it sells. That is called output tax. But XYZ itself has paid VAT on the parts and materials it needed and on things like telephone bills. That is its input tax. What it actually pays each quarter to Customs and Excise is the difference between the two. In some cases, if inputs are greater than outputs then a VAT rebate is received and nothing paid."

He looked at me pityingly.

"That wasn't too difficult for you, was it?"

"No. It's very straightforward when the jargon is explained. So how is the fraud carried out?"

"That is the puzzle. VAT is a huge complex system, but everything should balance out. Builders are in an interesting position. New work doesn't carry VAT, but repair work and renovation does. My guess, for what it's worth, is that one sector has been played off against the other. A big outfit like Meadowes' would provide plenty of scope and it would have had to be systematic and long-standing. One way or another friend Oliver appears to have been a very naughty boy."

"Prison sentence?"

"Almost certain." Steve said.

He twirled spaghetti carefully with his fork against his spoon.

"I would say that he will be out of circulation for some time."

I thought of the bluff hearty character I had lunched with at Rollo's house.

"He will have opportunity to catch up on his reading."

"Eh?" It was Steve's turn to look puzzled.

"Forget it. Just a private thought."

I did not stay for long after the meal was over, although Steve was ready to open another bottle and make an evening of it. He came down to the front door with me.

"How are things at Eastonbury? Are you OK for money?"

"I'm afloat for the moment." I assured him. "And I've been offered a couple of terms of lecturing for the New Year. I'm still thinking about that."

"I would take it if I were you." He said.

He gave me a long searching look. Somehow, I got the feeling that he knew a lot more than he had told me.

I drove home in sombre mood. It had been a long day and there had been little of Steve's customary good humour to buoy my spirits. Quite the reverse. He had left me with so much to think about. He had talked of trade gossip as his source, but he seemed to have information that was very detailed in places. He had seemed quite certain that Oliver Meadowes was facing a prison sentence and had been quick to squash any hopes I entertained that Rollo was not involved in some way. That approach would certainly explain Rollo's recent behaviour. If Meadowes had been in the frame as the eventual buyer of the Eastonbury estate, that possibility now seemed dead. I felt relieved that none of my own capital was tied up in our arrangement. Even so it would be some time before I saw any of the profit Rollo had suggested I might expect.

It was a long time before I fell asleep and when it came my sleep was fitful. I awoke several times, my mind still full of the day's affairs. Eventually, some time after three, I drifted off into a deeper slumber. Then it was time for dream to take over from conscious thought. There was an almost nightmarish quality to my dreaming. I seemed to be sharing a prison cell with Meadowes and Rollo. We sat facing each other unspeaking. The only sound came from the voices of people I had known. They appeared briefly at the open door of the cell pausing long enough to throw their comments at me.

Claudio led the procession.

"Rollo Blake is an arrogant bastard." He said.

Immediately he was followed by Steve.

"Rollo is a self-centred bastard." He intoned. "Everyone else has always known that. It is just that you were blind to it."

Jo followed close behind him. She had been weeping.

"Why could you not see that he was using you?" She said. "The way he uses everyone."

Finally, it was the turn of my father. He appeared at the cell door looking much as I had seen him that afternoon. There was a disembodied tone to his voice as he spoke the words he had used when I was still at school.

"Make sure he doesn't lead you into anything."

The sentence was repeated over and over like a litany. It was still sounding in my head as the cell door clanged shut. I awoke with a shudder. I felt more wretched than when I had gone to bed. I looked at my watch. It was already gone eight. Outside, the day seemed to have taken on my mood. Rain fell steadily from a leaden sky.

I lit a fire, so that it would establish itself while I

showered. After breakfast, I wrote an acceptance of the lecturing post and drove down to the village to post it. Then I settled down at the table I had brought across from the office and began to work on the annotations for my Italian drawings. Twice I thought I heard a car outside, only to be disappointed. I began to find Jo's absence disturbing. I was about to take a break when I heard the unmistakeable sound of a car drawing up outside. I hurried down to the entrance hall. Before I reached it, I was surprised to hear the sonorous clanging of the doorbell.

Two men were standing under the portico. Both wore suits and had mackintoshes draped over their shoulders.

"Paul Bradley?" The elder of the two asked.

"Yes." I replied uncertainly.

"We are police officers." The elder continued, holding out his warrant card as he spoke. "I am Detective Inspector Richards and this is Detective Constable Grainger. We would like to ask you a few questions. May we come in?"

"Yes, of course." I replied. The memory of my night's dream rose in my mind.

I opened the door wide and they filed in. Both looked around them with interest.

"It's being restored at the moment." I said.

"Does anyone else live here, Sir?" Grainger, the younger man, asked.

"No. I am only here to keep an eye on the place. We were worried about break-ins."

"Very wise, Sir."

"I have a fire upstairs. It will be warmer than here."

I led them upstairs. Neither man said anything.

"I am sorry that I cannot offer you anywhere to sit." I said. As you see it is all very spartan. I can offer coffee. I was about to make some when you arrived."

"That would be very welcome," said Richards. "We both have milk, but no sugar."

I went through to the kitchen. The coffee making gave me

time to get over the shock of their arrival. When I returned to the sitting room I saw that they had moved. Grainger was warming himself in front of the fire. Richards was leaning over the table studying my drawing board. I handed them each a mug of coffee and went to collect my own.

"Are you an architect, Sir?" Richards asked when I returned.

"Sort of." I replied. "That is a drawing for a book I am working on. It's a house in Verona. That's my field. I specialize in architectural history and period restorations."

"Ah! I see. And is that what you are doing here?"

"Yes. I have been handling the restoration."

"And how long have you been here?"

He straightened up and looked at me with a steady unwavering gaze.

"Since late August."

"And before that?"

I lodged briefly with a friend in Bristol. I was just back from a three-month spell in Italy. Doing research for my book."

I looked at each of them in turn.

"What is all this?"

"Nothing for you to be concerned about, Sir." Richards replied. "Just routine enquiries. We are tying up a few loose ends."

"How long have you known Roland Blake?"

Grainger took up the questioning from his position by the fire.

"Quite a few years. We were at school together."

"You also studied architecture at the same college."

I was surprised by how much they already knew.

"That just happened that way." I said. "We are interested in totally different fields."

"And you stayed in touch?"

"No. I was working in London until April this year."

"From when?"

"From the time that I left college."

"Which was?"

I gave him the date, although I was sure that they already had it. He jotted the information down in his notepad.

"So how long were you in London?" He continued.

"Eight years."

"Eight years." He echoed my words. "You say you had no contact with him for eight years and then you suddenly become his partner. Wouldn't you agree, Sir, that is unusual?"

"Not really." I stammered. "If you knew Rollo, you would not find it at all unusual."

"We are getting to know your friend quite well." The older man cut in from across the room. "I would agree. He is certainly not your Mr Average."

"Anyway," I added. "I am not his partner. I am contracted to complete the restoration here for a share of the profit when the house is sold. That is all."

"But your name is on a joint bank account." Richards continued.

"Well yes." I replied, vainly trying to remember what I had signed. "And there was a formal profit sharing agreement."

Richards gave me a knowing look.

"I would say that made you a partner, Sir. Wouldn't you?"

"And is this the only venture you have engaged in with Mr Blake?" Grainger returned to the fray.

"Yes."

"So why after a gap of eight years did you suddenly go into partnership with him?"

It was such a long story, I thought. How could I possibly begin to explain how it had all come about. Instead I just gave them the bare facts.

"When he bought this house, it was a condition of the sale agreement that he would restore it to its former state. He needed someone with my professional background."

"So why did you accept the offer?"

"I needed work and it seemed a good way of establishing my own consultancy practice. You see I had just left my old employer."

"And who was that, Sir?"

I gave him the name and address of Hutchings & Hardy. Grainger made a careful note of everything. The two interrogators exchanged a look and Richards took over again.

"When was the last time you saw Mr Blake, Sir?"

"He was here on Friday," I replied. "The last of the plastering had been done. I called him. I thought that he would want to see it."

"Did he discuss anything with you?"

"No. It was a very brief visit. He did not really look at anything. He told me not to undertake any further work until he contacted me. Then he left. He seemed in a tearing hurry."

"Yes, I'm sure he was." Richards added sardonically. "Did he say where he was going?"

"No. I got the impression that he had someone to see in Bristol."

"Do you have any idea of his present whereabouts?"

"He is probably at his house. It is home and office."

"That would the modern glass building?"

"Yes. That's right. Inspector, why are you asking me all this? What has Rollo done?"

By way of an answer Grainger handed me a card.

"If you do learn of Mr Blake's whereabouts, you can contact us here." He said.

The interview was obviously at an end. I led them back to the main entrance.

"Thank you, Sir." Richards said at the door. "You have been most helpful. Oh, and good luck with the book."

Grainger nodded to me as he followed him out. His face bore a look of distaste at the prospect of stepping out once again into the rain.

I went back upstairs feeling drained. I sat reflecting for a few minutes. Then I rang Steve.

"You're lucky." He said. I was just on my way out to grab an early lunch. I am out of town this afternoon."

I was in no mood for small talk.

"I've just been interrogated by two policemen. They are looking for Rollo. What the hell is going on?"

He did not say anything.

"Last night I got the impression that you knew a lot more than you were telling me. Was I right?"

Again, there was a pause. I could almost hear him thinking.

"Yes. You were. Pam my secretary is married to a detective. I am told things which are related to finance, but it is on the strict understanding that I stay shtum. I said more than I should have."

"Right. Well can you tell me what is going on?"

"I don't know the whole picture, but it's big. It is not a simple tax fraud. That seems to be a sidelight. When Meadowes' house was raided, a diary was found. It has opened up a whole can of worms. The police have taken over."

"What sort of worms?"

He paused before he replied.

"Corruption."

"Corruption!" I echoed. "What does that mean?"

"Bribery. Rigged contracts. False accounting. It's anybody's guess. There are a lot of big projects involved. A lot of it is local, but there is other national stuff, you know, schools, hospitals, MOD construction. That sort of thing. The diary listed payments and named names."

"And Rollo's name was there?"

I did not need to ask. His strange choice of cronies was beginning to make sense.

"There's a whole raft of people named: councillors, planners, civil servants. The police are turning the city inside out. There have been vague rumours about Meadowes for years, but this is different. The shit has really hit the fan this time."

My mind reeled.

"I've taken your advice and accepted the lecturing job," was all I could think to say.

"Good. Your stately home project looks a dead duck."

"I think you're right." I said. "And thanks Steve."

"Keep what I have said to yourself and stop worrying. Other than the knock-on effect on your work, you are not involved."

I put the telephone down in a state of shock. Not even the visit of the two detectives had brought me to fully accept that Rollo could be involved in any kind of illegal activity. Risk-taking I could believe, but not criminal conspiracy. I remembered what Jo had said about him needing to live on the edge. The line between what is legal and what is illegal is often finely drawn. It seemed that in the hunt for excitement he had found the temptation to cross that line irresistible.

How much had Jo known I wondered. That night of the party at the Cascades she had talked of it being part of Rollo's public relations efforts. Had she known that Rollo's idea of engaging support from local and national politicians and officials went much deeper. Had she any inkling that a number of her guests and many others not present were being suborned to award important contracts to him and his associate Meadowes. What had she known of Rollo's cronies. She had warned me in no uncertain terms about getting involved with them. To what extent had that been motivated by disillusionment with or even outright distrust of her husband I wondered. Had she any real evidence of their unsavouriness, or had it simply been woman's intuition.

The more I thought about it the more important it became that I found answers to the hundred and one questions running through my head. Only two people could supply those answers and they could both be found in the same place.

I drove out to The Cascades in a mood of grim deliberation. Along the way that mood underwent change. A slow-burning anger began to develop that was ready to burst out by the time I pulled into Rollo's driveway. It looked strangely quiet. At first, I thought that the house was closed, but then I noticed that the front door stood open. I was in no mood for formalities. I strode straight in and made directly for Rollo's offices.

The smooth operation I had seen on my last visit had gone. The reception desk where Philippa had held court was unoccupied. The contents of the desk drawers had been emptied on to its surface. Behind it a number of black rubbish sacks lay against a wall. I glanced briefly at their contents. They seemed to be full of drawings.

As I finished checking the last of the sacks Philippa came in, struggling with the weight of another. This was a different Philippa. She was wearing a kitchen smock and her hair had been pinned up. She looked hot and stressed. As if to emphasize her lack of chic a lock of hair had escaped its clip and hung down the side of her face.

"Oh. It's you," was all she said.

"Where's Rollo? I need to see him." I demanded.

"He's not here."

"Where is he?"

She gave me a look of total disdain.

"I have no idea. I'm just clearing up here."

I strode past her to the offices. Both the main drawing office and Rollo's own office were empty. Philippa followed me into the main office.

"Satisfied!" She gave me a steely smile.

My anger was fast changing to bewilderment.

"Where is everyone?" I asked.

"Judge for yourself."

She walked past me to the drawer units that lined the wall of the office and began to fill another sack with unwanted drawings. I breathed slowly and tried to quell the anger that was beginning to develop again.

"I need to see the file on Eastonbury."

My request was greeted with a deep theatrical laugh.

"Well you've come to the wrong place. You will have to ask the police. They've taken everything except this stuff."

I cursed my own stupidity. I should have guessed that the police would have called here long before they got around to checking on me. I had been too wound up to think straight.

"Is Jo here then?"

"No. She is not here either. Now if you don't mind, I have work to do."

She continued filling her sack. I stood for a moment. My mind was racing. What was happening here. The evidence suggested that Rollo's whole business operation was being wound up. I had come on a fool's errand.

I turned without a word and strode out. As I passed back through the reception area, something on Philippa's desk caught my eye. There was no mistaking the shape of air tickets. There were two of them. Both bore the Air France logo. I had time only to flip open the top one before the click of Philippa's heels warned me of her return. It was made out to Roland Blake from Paris to Rio de Janeiro. I hastily replaced them. I did not need to see any more. Everything was perfectly clear now. Rollo was jumping ship and he was taking Jo with him.

<h1 style="text-align:center">12</h1>

Clifton looked forlorn in its wetness. Rain fell steadily from the endless greyness that all day had driven in from the south-west. It formed pools in every depression of the streets and pavements. It dripped from trees and street furniture to join the water running off the camber of the road. Strong flowing rivulets formed that overwhelmed the rainwater drains and ran on down towards the old village and the zig-zag of terraces that would lead it down to the river. Cloud shut out what was left of the daylight. Around the green most of the houses had lights burning.

Few pedestrians ventured out into this watery world. The only movement came from the cars hissing along the street in streams of spray. None stopped, so there was no shortage of parking spaces in the approach to the bridge. As if by instinct I had driven to this place after leaving Philippa's office. It had been my haven during those first unhappy months of student life. Now without thinking I had turned to it again.

The emotions I felt were raw. They burnt in my gut like a cheap whisky swallowed too quickly. The burning seemed to inflame my whole being. I felt violently angry without being altogether sure what or whom I felt angry about. My mind cast about for someone or something on which to unload this burden of anger.

The most obvious target was Rollo. The word betrayal was uppermost in my thinking. I piled all the weight of my feelings behind this charge. He was self-centred, I thought with bitterness. His first instinct when facing trouble would always be to cut and run for cover. He had assets in South America, a house in Chile and dual nationality. He was hardly likely to hang around here to face certain arrest and a probable prison sentence when he could be safe and comfortable in the continent of his birth. What would it matter there, that his reputation here lay in tatters.

Strangely, the more I reflected on it, the harder I found it to feel betrayed. I had walked into the deal with him over Eastonbury with my eyes wide open. These other affairs of his were not part of that arrangement. They were quite separate. It was my bad luck that my own dealings with him were being wrecked by the turbulence erupting in this other part of his life. For the rest Rollo was merely being Rollo. I had long ago accepted that that was the way it would always be.

My feelings towards Jo were more ambivalent. I had been confused from the moment I saw her again on the night of the party. Old emotions had been stirred then and I had felt the first barbs of jealousy towards Rollo on that account. In part, my own confusion had perhaps been created by the ambivalence of her actions. She had promised nothing, yet at the same time the way she had behaved towards me had suggested something else. I remembered the first of our picnics and that first walk around the lakes. I had been excited by her closeness. Had that made me too ready to believe that she was developing some feeling for me. Was I guilty of seeing only what I had wanted to see. Should I have listened more to what she had been saying. She had spelled it out for me. I had not been ready to listen. We liked and wanted the same things, that much was true. She had seen that that would never be enough. We were very different sorts of people. My swan could never be more than friends with her wild goose.

The more I reflected, the more things fell into place. I was friends with each of them, but in entirely different ways. Over the past few months I had seen each individually on a number of occasions. It occurred to me now that I had seen little of them together. I had forgotten how strong had been their rapport at their first meeting on the afternoon Rollo had driven us to Blagdon. They were well suited to each other. They both looked for colour and excitement in their lives. They both needed to follow the sun.

All the things we had talked about during the autumn came back to me. I had taken her comments at face value, using them to gauge any weakening of their relationship. I realized now that I had been looking at things in the wrong way. Her only real complaint against Rollo was that she was not getting much of the fun and that she disapproved of some of his associates. Away from them and The Cascades there was the opportunity to begin again. It had been idle presumption to think that she would ever leave him. She needed the excitement he created. For that she would accept his infidelities. Now that she had chosen to stand by him and join him in exile, my guess was that she would enjoy the experience.

My musings had led me to a single inevitable conclusion. The only act of betrayal had been my own. I had betrayed myself. In the process, I had scorched my fingers and had my pride dented. Other than that, I had suffered no lasting damage. They were hurts I would soon get over. Why then was I so angry. I remembered DC Grainger questioning my renewed association with Rollo. Why had I resumed my friendship with him after a clean break of eight years. I remembered the reaction when I had received his letter. That had been the point when the jealousy had begun to emerge. It was then the answer came to me. It was not a renewal of friendship. Nor did I love Jo in any real sense. The two were entwined in a different way. It was the desire to compete that had motivated me.

In our earlier years Rollo had been the dominant partner in our friendship. He had been more mature in a worldly sense. My own maturation had developed at a much slower pace. Now we were more evenly matched. Time had made me more fully aware of my own strengths and abilities. I was ready to compete with him now on more equal terms.

His letter and the offer had been the opportunity that I had been seeking. It was quite clear to me now. Deep down, I think, the way he had moved in on Jo still rankled. I had been ready to make her the battleground. That, I realized now, would have been a contest which I never could have won. There would be other opportunities to prove myself I reasoned. Hopefully they would be on issues where the odds would not be so hopelessly stacked against me. Perhaps it was as well then that I did not know that fate already had arrangements for that trial of strength well in hand.

My anger subsided. For the first time since I had parked the car I became aware of the rain. Deep in thought I had followed the old familiar path that skirts the edge of the gorge. It came as an uncomfortable surprise to discover that I was at the far end of Durdham Down and that I was soaked through to the skin. My hair was plastered down over my forehead. Trickles of rainwater ran down my face and round my ears. Some of it found its way beneath my collar. My trousers clung to my legs and more trickles of water percolated down through my socks to soak on the inside shoes which were fast being penetrated from without. I felt cold and miserable. Clifton and the bridge had suddenly lost their appeal. I wanted to be home again in front of a blazing log fire.

It had felt better then for a while, warm and dry after a hot shower. The improvement in my spirits was to be short-lived.

The following morning the reality of my situation began to sink in. I experienced the emptiness of a bereavement. The frustration I had felt earlier in the week had been but a foretaste of what was to come. Then, I think, I had still expected Rollo to pull something from his hat. Any delay, I had thought, would be temporary.

That belief had persisted through all the upheavals of the past two days. In the face of all the evidence to the contrary, I had clung to the notion that Rollo was not involved in any significant way with the police investigations. I had believed that, somehow, he would conjure some quick solution to everything and emerge unscathed. The discovery of his flight had finally destroyed that illusion. The magician had run out of rabbits and was quitting the stage. The air tickets were for flights from Paris. He was probably out of the country already.

Whichever way I looked now, there seemed no way forward. I was left as little more than a caretaker at Eastonbury. For the moment, the police held all documentation relating to it. When that would be returned I had no idea. Looking further ahead, the time when I would be relieved of my role here seemed ever more distant and uncertain. I was left suspended in time. I had felt this at the weekend. I was wrong then. That had been only a warm-up. This was the real limbo.

Those drab days of December are a period I now try to forget. I drifted through them in as uncertain a state as I have ever known. A deep ennui enfolded me that took me to the edge of depression. I trailed around the estate half-heartedly doing little and appreciating nothing. When hunger drove me out of the house, I shopped in the village without enthusiasm. Back at home again I cooked and ate what I had bought without interest. I saw the headlines of the newspapers. They all centred on the burgeoning corruption scandal. It was old news to me and I was not tempted to read further.

For much of the time I simply sat before the fire. The

flickering flames and the subtle changes of their colour had a mesmerising effect. I spent whole days doing little else but watch them. There was a primeval satisfaction in the warmth of the incandescent centre. I found an endless fascination in observing the stages by which each tree stump was slowly transformed into the glowing embers of heat energy. I timed how long it took for each log to pass through this ritual transformation. I watched fire and flame but what I saw was time and energy. Each new piece I added was a period of time bought. I can see quite clearly now that that is what I was doing - buying time, using time to make adjustments in my mind.

I lived like this for almost two weeks. Slowly the dead weight of my thoughts lifted. I was ready to function again when the telephone call drove the last vestiges of lethargy from my head.

The bank was situated in the old commercial heart of the city. I left the car at Steve's and walked along the edge of the Floating Harbour into the centre. I had experienced few dealings with banks. What little I knew suggested that a call from a branch was not usually good news. This I assured myself was different. This after all was Rollo's bank. I walked to the appointment intrigued to find out what this had to do with me and why my meeting was scheduled with no less a person than the manager.

I was shown into a large office on the upper floor. The room was panelled in oak and furnished with a traditional desk and chairs in the same timber. A balding man of spare build offered his hand and introduced himself as John Gregory. There was something forced about his smile as he went through the routines of greeting. Behind the assurance, I sensed a man ill-at-ease about something.

I took the seat he offered me and awaited events. Gregory returned to his own side of the desk. He sat for some moments toying with the papers of a file which lay open upon it. He seemed to be searching for the right form of words. Eventually he found it.

"Thank you for responding so promptly Mr Bradley," he said. "I have been reviewing the account which your partner Mr Blake opened in August."

There it was again, that word partner. He was taking exactly the same line as the two policemen.

"Excuse me, Mr Gregory," I interjected. "You used the word partner. When I agreed to work for Mr Blake, nothing was said about us being partners. I was simply to carry out work for him on the property at Eastonbury. In return, I was to be remunerated by a share of the profits when it was re-sold."

Gregory looked at me with a frown.

"This is a matter of semantics," he replied. "You were engaged with Mr Blake on a joint undertaking and were party to a joint account with him at this branch. As far as the bank is concerned, the key issue is the date on which your involvement commenced."

He stopped to examine the file once more.

"Yes. Here it is," he continued. You signed forms to act as co-signatory on August 23rd.

He looked searchingly at me across the desk. I felt my face reddening. Silently I cursed myself for not bothering to get advice on what I was doing. I had been naive and charged in like a complete beginner.

Gregory had not finished. His voice carried to me as if from another world.

"One week later, on August 30th, the loan agreement was negotiated by Mr Blake. Now that Mr Blake would appear to be, as it were, no longer with us..."

"What loan?" My voice sounded strange to me. I felt my inside quivering.

Momentarily a look of puzzled unease crossed Gregory's

face. It was there for only an instant before his professional demeanour took over.

"Mr Blake arranged a loan for the purchase of Eastonbury Court. Did you not know?"

He said that he was providing the finance. He did not say anything about borrowing money. I would never have agreed to that."

A sickly smile played at the corners of Gregory's mouth. Whether it was scorn or an attempt at sympathy I had no way of knowing.

"It makes no difference in law whether you agreed or not," he continued. "A loan was arranged by Mr Blake on this account. As his partner, you are bound by his actions."

"You mean I am responsible for the repayment of this loan, even though I knew nothing of it?"

"Yes. That is the legal position."

"How much?"

My voice trailed away. I had attempted to keep my voice from betraying any sign of nerves, but I was only partially successful. I cleared my throat and began again.

"How much was borrowed?"

Gregory consulted a page of figures in the file. It seemed an eternity before he replied.

"The package arranged was a drawdown facility with an overall credit limit of five hundred thousand pounds. Half of that was drawn immediately, presumably to purchase the property. The remainder was available when required to cover the planned renovation costs."

He glanced across to check that I was taking it all in.

"Fifty-one thousand five hundred pounds has since been drawn to cover a number of cheque payments. Then at the end of November a final sum of two hundred thousand pounds was drawn. There is also interest accruing to date of seven thousand and ninety-five pounds. That makes a grand total of five hundred and eight thousand and ninety-five pounds."

My mind repeated the total. Five hundred and eight thousand and ninety-five pounds. It sounded very ordinary said in that way. It was when I looked at it in a different way that it began to hit me. Slowly the realization sank in that I was in debt for over half-a-million. My throat had suddenly gone very dry. Beneath my belt my bowels contracted in a most unpleasant way and I broke out in a cold sweat that left my shirt clinging to me. There was a roaring in my ears. For one desperate moment, I thought that I would faint or else succumb to blind panic. I reached out for the edge of Gregory's desk to steady myself. The touch of something hard and familiar reassured me that the floor had not opened up to swallow me. Slowly my nerves settled. I was about to blurt out that I did possess more than a fraction of the sum owing when I realized that Gregory was still speaking. Strangely he looked more nervous than ever.

"This type of loan is always made on a purely short-term basis. In this particular case, fifty thousand pounds plus interest was scheduled to be repaid at three-monthly intervals until the line of credit was cleared. The first of those payments fell due on December 5th. Under the unusual circumstances I am prepared to overlook this breach of the contract."

He paused for a moment. His hands fidgeted with the papers in front of him and he licked his lips nervously.

"However, as I made clear earlier the bank now expects you to honour the terms of the agreement. In addition to the first instalment, you will also be required to clear the small amount by which the credit limit has been exceeded. That will mean an immediate payment of fifty-eight thousand and ninety-five pounds."

My mind was still reeling from shock. I said the first thing that came into my head.

"I can't write you a cheque right now," I stammered. "I will need to transfer money."

Even as I spoke I thought how feeble it sounded. I need not have worried. Gregory seemed to be tuned in to a different wavelength. As I spoke he visibly relaxed. He permitted himself the first real smile of the afternoon as he wrote something to add to the file.

"Of course, Mr Bradley," he purred. "Shall we say by the end of the month?"

It was mid-afternoon when I left the bank. The streets were still busy with Christmas shoppers. I felt strangely detached from the life thronging around me. All I could think was that in under two weeks I had to find fifty-eight thousand pounds when my total wealth amounted to little more than three-quarters of that. Then every three months for the next two and a-half years I would have to find the same amount. It was impossible.

The thought of the debt seemed to crush me. I felt alone and very frightened. I could understand why people in such extremes have been known to fling themselves from high buildings. It would have been simple enough to throw myself into the Floating Harbour. Fortunately, the shock worked itself out in other ways. Against all reason I suddenly felt wildly elated. I wanted to sing and shout and dance in the street. It was all too ridiculous to be true. The world was going mad and I wanted to join in the crazy revelry. This manic reaction coursed through me as I walked back to Steve's. It was only as I neared this bastion of everyday reality that it deserted me. Suddenly I had the desperate need to share this burden, I had so suddenly acquired, with someone.

Steve was working in his office alone. He took one look at me and sat me down.

"What's the matter old son," he said. You look as if the sky is about to fall in on you."

"It already has," I said simply. I have just been informed that I am bankrupt."

"What! How come?"

There was real concern in his voice and on his face. I told him of the interview with the bank manager. Concern gave way to concentration as I gave my account. He stopped me when I had quoted the key figures.

"Hold it old son. Run through those numbers again."

I reeled off again the amounts Gregory had quoted. Steve jotted them down.

"The bastard!" he exclaimed to himself. "He transferred two hundred thousand shortly before he disappeared."

He swung back to me.

"Think," he said. "Can you remember if this chap Gregory mentioned who that transfer was made to?"

"Southern Cone Trading."

"Are you sure?"

I nodded. It was not difficult. The name had burned itself in my memory.

Steve was shaking his head.

"I've never heard of them. I'll have to check them out."

"There's no need. You will not find them."

"You know who they are?"

"I don't know who for certain, but I can guess. I can also guess where. The cone is the way of referring to the lower half of South America. It's a term Rollo used to use when he was talking about the holdings he inherited there."

I could see Steve's mind rapidly adding two and two to make a sum far larger.

"So you think this company is one that Rollo has set up in South America and that he's paid the money to himself?"

I nodded.

Steve digested the idea.

"That would not surprise me. He has always lived by a different set of rules to everyone else."

He had turned back to study the figures, his face a mask of concentration. His fingers drummed on the desk.

"Well," I ventured eventually. "What now?"

He gave me one of his old grins.

"Well, what springs initially to mind, is an old saying about a creek and a shortage of paddles."

My mind had returned to a different issue.

"What puzzled me," I said. "was that Gregory the bank manager seemed very nervous."

"I'm not surprised. In his position, I would have been nervous."

He noticed my look of surprise.

"It's an unusual sort of arrangement. This type of loan is only normally advanced to established businesses with proven track records. I would not have thought that Rollo would have enough clout to swing a deal like this. Someone was obviously putting in a good word for him. Now suddenly our blue-eyed boy is on the run ... It's official by the way. There's a warrant out for his arrest."

He slipped in that item of news by way of an aside.

"Now, where was I?"

"Rollo on the run."

"Right. Back at bank head office when the quarterly returns come in Big Chief Banker wants to know who was dim enough to lend him half-a-million without any collateral."

Light began to dawn.

"So that's why Gregory wanted the loan to carry on."

"Too right. The last thing he wants is for you to go belly up."

"But I am going to go belly up."

"Not necessarily, just so long as you can meet that first payment. That will give us time to sort something out."

Imperceptibly he had switched from friend to professional adviser. He now looked directly at me.

"How much can you raise?" He asked.

I ran my mind over my various assets.

"Very roughly, about forty-seven thousand."

"Right! That leaves you eleven thousand short."

He reached into a drawer in his desk and drew out a cheque book. Then he wrote out a cheque and handed it to me.

I looked down at the figures he had written.

"This is for twelve thousand. I can't take this."

"All right," he said holding out his hand for it's return. "You can go back to your nervous bank manager and tell him that you are broke."

"But, what if I can't repay you."

"That's a chance I'll have to take."

He gave me another of his old grins.

"Besides, you have such an honest face. Just don't make a habit of this sort of thing."

There was something about his last comment that made me realize that the loan he had just made had probably cleaned him out. It meant a lot to me that he had made such a gesture of trust and friendship. Somehow it marked the turning point in this whole sorry mess. From that moment, the clouds of despair began to thin and the first gleams of hope began to appear. Things were bad, but they no longer seemed completely hopeless.

Steve took a clean sheet of paper and headed it.

"Now that is settled, let's start planning the next phase," he said.

I stopped him in his tracks. My mind was working again and something had come to me.

"There's something I need to know," I said. "Who owns Eastonbury? I mean it would seem that I shall be paying for it."

"Good question," he replied. "I think the answer will be that you do. Assuming it was purchased by you and Rollo as partners, it should become yours now that he has more or less walked out on the partnership. I will need to get a second opinion on that."

He paused to make a note on a stick-it pad and stuck it to his telephone.

"Right. Let us assume then that you are the sole owner. The problem is one of liquidity. Everything is in fixed assets -

bricks and mortar to the unenlightened - and you need liquid assets to pay off the bank."

He drummed his fingers again as he thought.

"There are two ways out," he continued. "You either find a new partner, who will put up cash, or else you sell the assets ... No. That's no go. Eastonbury is not worth half-a-million."

I had not really been paying much attention until this point. My mind was still back dealing with the ownership question. The thought that I was the owner of the estate had lit a slow fuse that was spluttering into life. There was a strange feeling of excitement as my subconscious ran with Steve's final point. I was thinking of schemes I had worked on with Henry Hutchings. He had explained then that sometimes the parts add up to more than the whole. It seemed that this might be just such a case.

"It could be," I said. "Converted into luxury flats, it might fetch more than that."

Sleep came surprisingly easy that night. I had gone to bed with plans and ideas flooding through my head, but the strains and tensions of the day had taken their toll. I soon drifted off into a sound slumber and did not awake until eight-thirty. I felt refreshed. More importantly some vital piece had been removed from the log-jam of my mind. The river of consciousness flowed in full spate. The period of limbo had come to an end.

Eastonbury had filled my waking hours for so long that I was familiar with all its parts. Already I had in my mind a rough idea of what could be done. Now the precise length of the piece of wall between two windows or the exact position of a doorway became factors of prime importance. I needed details and lots of them.

Armed with my surveyor's tape and a sketch pad I spent three whole days measuring and recording. As I worked I built imaginary walls and paced out the movements of everyday living in imaginary rooms. I made plans and sketches as I went. The irony of what I was doing was not lost on me. Having spent the last few months remedying the damage caused by unthinking wartime restructuring, I was now about to embark on a new programme of structural change. The only difference rested in the aims of the work. In my own case, my sole hope of salvation lay in effecting a remodelling that would pass the most searching test of all - that of the market.

I had reflected at one point on my original commission from Rollo. It was not clear to me what he had had in mind. The more work I did now, and the more I thought of how to extract maximum value from the estate, the more puzzled I became. The greatest value I could envisage would accrue from breaking up the house into carefully presented units. Rollo had intended to maintain the house as a single unit and anticipated clearing a sizeable profit when it was sold. Something did not add up. I put it at the back of my mind with a mental note to follow it up at some point. For the moment, I had more than enough to occupy me.

I was quite adamant that there was to be no quick fix aimed solely at maximising profits. I had seen too many examples of shoddy flat conversions during my years in London. I was determined to respect the integrity of the original design. I was aided in this by the way in which Eastonbury had been developed. A more homogenous design might have proved more difficult to handle.

Eventually I settled on a scheme that would create six apartments. Four of these would be approached by means of the main entrance hall and would incorporate the fine formal rooms in their pristine state. The only construction work needed would be on either side of these in the older original house and in the kitchen wing where additional bathrooms and kitchens would have to be created. In addition, there would be a seventh flat, much like a mews conversion, occupying the upper floor of the coach house. I intended to reserve that until the end and only sell it as a last resort. I had become so used to working in my office there that I had hopes of keeping it as my permanent base. I surveyed the final plan that I had drawn up. It was not perhaps what Miss Tyzack had hoped for, but times had changed. I think she would have realized that and would have not been unhappy with what I had in mind.

That week my emotions fluctuated wildly. There had been the high point when Steve rang to say that he had checked on the ownership question. I need not do anything it appeared. As the remaining active partner the house was in effect mine. He had been advised however that I should get a court to formally dissolve the partnership in my favour. That had bucked me for a time, but that was soon to be countered by the effects of paying off the first tranche of the loan. What at first sight was a very positive move had had a surprisingly negative effect. It had made me realize how thin my resources were and how large the scale of what I was undertaking. It left me feeling very exposed.

Between these emotional ups and downs I continued to work feverishly. I completed outline drawings of my scheme and felt encouraged enough to call the Bristol branch of the estate agency which had handled the London schemes I had worked on. Someone turned up from the office the next day, a fellow of about my own age, but light years ahead of me in self-assurance. He looked over the house and walked the estate before finally studying my drawings. To my relief he seemed to like them.

"Bear in mind," he said, "that the market for this type of property is small and very discerning. However, within that market, I think these apartments will be an excellent proposition. I would not envisage any difficulty in finding buyers, providing that the conversion is of top quality and is carried out as sympathetically as you have indicated."

Before leaving, he made some quick calculations of floor areas and reeled off the approximate price each of the apartments might realize. I made a careful note of everything.

Later that evening I totalled up the figures he had given me. I added in the various grants the work would attract and subtracted an approximate figure for all building work, fittings and finishing. I then made a final deduction to cover estate agency commissions and all legal fees. The eventual was lower than I had hoped for. If I included the sale of the coach house it worked out only a little below the figure I needed to break even. It was close enough. My earnings would cover the rest.

I sat back more relieved than elated. For the rest of the evening I relaxed listening to a Mahler symphony. Before going to bed something prompted me to cast a final look over my calculations. The figure for the building and finishing work seemed to stand out. It hit me then that this was not a simple balance sheet transaction. These figures represented hard cash that would have to be paid out in advance of any sale. Even if I completed the conversion one unit at a time, selling each completion before commencing with the next, there was no way that I could see of financing the up-front costs. I had no money and, with several hundred thousand pounds of debt hanging over me already, there was no possibility of borrowing what was needed. My mood evaporated immediately. It seemed that there was to be no escape after all.

It was in that same mood of despondency that on the following day I drove home to spend Christmas with my father.

13

Christmas can be a cruel time. The season of goodwill to all has always had a darker underside. For the lucky few it can be a wonderfully exhilarating time. For the lonely or bereaved its emphasis on loved ones and family life ruthlessly exposes any absence of such factors. Driving home, I remembered the emptiness I had felt at this time of year during the awkward teenage years. This Christmas I feared would see a return to that emptiness.

I had always spent the break with my parents and with the years of maturity had come a simple pleasure in the family ties. Mom had always loved Christmas and took great pains to make it special. I could never understand why puddings had to be made so far in advance, but autumn was the time for the long ritual of preparation and they always tasted good. In mid-December, she would decorate the Christmas tree. Delicate baubles dating back to her own childhood which spent most of the year cosseted in a box in the loft would be disinterred and fixed in place. She would painstakingly trail wisps of cotton wool along each branch so that to my childish eyes the simple tree became a magical fairy land. In the final week she made mince pies, deep filled with mincemeat to which she added extra flakes of apple and a measure of brandy. Proudest of all would be the rich cake swaddled in marzipan and icing that would stand at the centre of the table at tea time.

This year it would all be so very different. I had arranged to provide our provisions. An assortment of foodstuffs filled the rear of the car. None was of my own making. I could not avoid drawing the uncomfortable parallel with the past. It promised to be a strange homecoming.

Dad at least had made an effort. He had bought a small tree and had attempted to decorate it in the usual way. He had also filled a large bowl with apples and oranges and another smaller one with nuts. I was relieved to see that there was an improvement in his appearance. He still looked gaunt and tired, but in part the dejection that had worried me on my last visit had lifted and he seemed to take more interest in things.

There was something that I wanted to be out of the way before Christmas Day. I waited until after we had cleared away the evening meal before I broached what was on my mind.

"Dad," I began. "There is something I want to tell you."

"Oh yes."

"You have seen in the news about this corruption business and ... and Rollo's involvement in it."

"Yes," he said guardedly.

I saw the thought run across his face. His expression was almost fierce as he posed the question.

"You're not involved in that, are you?"

"No Dad. I'm not." I looked him directly in the face as I answered him. "But it has had an effect on what he and I were doing together."

I had given him an outline of the work I was doing at Eastonbury on my last visit, but I went over it all again, ending with my interview at the bank and the financial problems that I now faced.

"I thought it would be safe and straightforward," I ended lamely. "I was wrong and you were right. He has finally landed me in trouble."

I waited for his reaction with trepidation. I half-expected him to explode in angry recrimination or at least to vent his wrath on Rollo. To my surprise he did neither. Instead he came across to me and looked at me. There was the glint of a tear at the corner of his eye.

"I've been hearing about all this on the TV news," he said. "And I knew it would mean trouble when I heard that Roland was involved and was wanted by the police."

He placed his hands on my shoulders.

"I wanted to ask you, but I thought, no, if he is in trouble he will come to me and he'll tell me himself like a man. And you have."

I reached up and clasped his wrists. We stood like that for a while. We did not need to say any more.

It was not the Christmas I had feared. Things could never be as they once had been. There was still much sadness, but we were not miserable. Countering one area of loss was another of gain. The barriers that had grown between the two of us in recent years had dissolved. We were father and son once again.

He sprang his surprise on the morning of Boxing Day. As is so often the case in the period around the end of the year, the morning was crisp and bright. We had finished breakfasting when he went to the window.

"It looks as if it is going to be a fine day," he said. "Why don't we go out for a ride?"

"If that is what you would like," I replied. "Where would you like to go?"

He turned to me from the window with a smile on his face.

"I would like to see this stately home of yours," he said.

· · ·

There is something about Eastonbury that seems to exert a magic on whoever visits it, and so it proved again. It was late morning when we turned into the avenue between the first pair of lions. Sunlight lit the bare branches of the trees and the valley looked at its best. He had said little on the way down. Now he began to look around with real interest.

His first move on getting from the car was to walk to the fence at the edge of the parkland and look across to the nearby woods. Only then did he turn to look at the house.

"Do you own all this?" He asked. There was a note of wonder in his voice.

"That's a good question," I replied. "Nominally I think I do. The problem is, I still have to find a way of paying for it."

Abruptly he became very businesslike.

"Well," he asked. "Is this all I get to see, or are you going to show me inside."

I unlocked the main door and left him looking round the entrance hall while I walked across to the coach house for an armful of wood. I had expected him to wander off, but he was still there when I returned. He was content to follow me up to the flat and watch while I lit a fire. I waited until the wood had caught and put the guard in place.

"Right," I said. "I'll show you round the house while that is burning up. We can have a cup of coffee when we get back."

We made a tour of the house. As we went I told him of the state it was in when we had taken over and pointed out all the work that had been done. I attempted to get him to visualize how the place would look divided up into flats. He tried to show interest in what I was saying, but I could see that buildings were not really his scene. The one thing that caught his eye was the view across the park to the bridge that Jo had so taken to. I knew that his real interest would be in the gardens.

How four bare brick walls built in the shape of a rectangle

could create such interest is something I could not fathom. When I led him into the walled garden, he stopped and stood quite still. He scanned around slowly, first to the right and then to the left. Then he breathed a deep sigh. There was an animation to his face that I had not seen since returning from Italy.

"This would have fed the whole house in the old days," he finally said. "Every big house had one. There would have been all manner of vegetables and salads in the middle there, all grown in rotation according to the season. And in those borders against the wall there would have been fruit, smaller plants at the front and trees trained against the wall. The soil would have been good too. They would have all the manure from the horses."

He sighed a sigh of deep satisfaction.

"That was real gardening."

Miss Tyzack had only worked the section of the kitchen garden adjacent to the house. The remainder was much overgrown. Although he had not seen it before Dad seemed to know that there was once a path following the rectangle of the walls and separated from them by a broad border. The only visible section was the path I had used from the gate to the kitchen door. I was puzzled when he spoke of the path forming a circuit. It was there sure enough. Its old flagstones well-hidden by the grass and weeds that had taken over.

Dad happily traced its course. I followed mystified in his wake. Every few yards something would catch his eye and he would stop to make comment. At one point, he drew my attention to the rusted stumps of nails in the brickwork of the wall.

"Those were for pinning the branches of espalier fruit trees," he explained.

Further round the remains of a low wall protruded from the undergrowth.

"That would have been the greenhouse," he said.

He continued in this manner until we had completed our circuit. His enthusiasm had revealed a side to him that I had not seen before. Superficially our interests had little in common, I thought, but under the skin we were not so very different.

The flower garden produced the same glow of enthusiasm. He knew every plant by both formal and everyday name and maintained a flow of commentary throughout. I do not think it was specifically aimed at me. I might not have been there. In reality, he was talking to himself, re-awakening the enthusiasm that as a youth had first taken him into horticulture.

Surprisingly the walk around the lakes did not elicit the same level of response. He expressed admiration for the design and identified the various trees and shrubs, but his reaction was much more muted than before. I commented on the difference in his appreciation.

"Don't forget," he replied, "I began my career working in the parks department back home. This is a bit like that. The overall design is fixed. All you have to do is keep it neat and tidy."

He turned to look back up to the house.

"I'm a plantsman," he said. "Now back up there is what interests me. Vegetable gardens and herbaceous borders are alive. You are working at them all the time and they keep on evolving."

We walked in silence after that. I was left with so much on which to reflect. How was it possible, I thought, that I could have grown up in his house without really knowing him.

We completed the tour with an inspection of the coach house. He cast an appreciative eye over my stack of logs and for once noticed details of the building.

"It is interesting how this has been built on top of the old stonework," he remarked. "What period is it?"

"The upper storey is eighteenth century," I replied.

"I thought it was old," he said. "I noticed the bell turret when we drove in."

He spent much longer over the contents of the site office than I would have expected. All the preparatory work I had done for the restoration was still there and he spent time studying the various drawings. Finally, I showed him the new work outlining the division of the house into flats. He could appreciate it more now that he had seen everything.

He made no comment until he completed his perusal.

"You intend to go through with it then?" He looked directly at me as he put the question.

"I have no alternative." I began. Then I became aware of the searching look and realized that he was asking something different. "Yes," I said. "Goodness knows how, but I am going to see this through."

We left for home shortly afterwards. The afternoon was well advanced and the sun was setting in a golden blaze that threw long shadows across our road. We drove in silence. I had attempted to make conversation at first, but that had soon lapsed. He seemed to want to sit with his own thoughts.

As we neared home I turned my head to him.

"Does the name Francis Fielding mean anything to you?"

He looked at me, puzzled by the question.

"You have not heard his name mentioned in connection with the corruption scandal?"

"No." He shook his head. "Who is he?"

"He's a lawyer I met at Rollo's. I thought he might have been involved."

I don't know why Fielding had suddenly come to mind. Perhaps it was the result of a few days of relaxation after all the stress of the past weeks. Whatever the reason it was very puzzling. I was not sure of the exact nature of his involvement in the unfolding scandal. I had only the evidence of a single meeting to go on. The impression I had gained then was that he was the acknowledged leader of the group who had lunched with me that day. I dismissed the thought, but immediately started another. It occurred to me that, if Fielding was not assisting the police, he would be available for me to meet him. There were a number of questions to which I needed answers and it seemed that he was the one man who might be in a position to supply them.

14

The minute hand of the electric clock that faced me from the wall behind the reception desk jerked forward another step. It had caught my eye when I had taken a seat and made a general sweep of the room. I had returned to it after finding nothing of interest in the pages of Country Life. For the past twenty-seven minutes, it had been my sole distraction.

It must at one time have been the latest word in modernity. Now, like the rest of the office it showed the passage of time in another way. Age had added a further dimension to its functionality. It had given it the charm of idiosyncrasy. Whereas the hands of most electric clocks move by imperceptible degrees; this one recorded time in a manner that was entirely its own. For periods of between twenty and ninety seconds the minute hand would show no discernable progress. Then in a single twitch it would catch up on lost time. With the aid of my wristwatch I timed the intervals between movements. I attempted to trace some pattern to its operation, but found nothing that admitted of regularity. No two intervals I timed were of the same length. Frustrated in this, I fell back on attempting to second-guess the machine. I tried to anticipate when the next movement of the minute hand would occur. With a mechanism so devoid of reason and so singular in its operation I did not expect to succeed, but then I was not conducting scientific research. I was bored to the back teeth and the clock was a simple pastime.

Henry Hutchings had always impressed on me that an appointment was a mutual arrangement. It fixed a time that was convenient to all parties, and that time should be honoured as strictly as possible. Exactness in business is not always possible and a certain degree of latitude is permissible. With Henry, the line had always been drawn at ten minutes. Anything beyond that in his book showed either incompetence or deliberate rudeness. Francis Fielding had not seemed to me to be an incompetent person. Nor, despite the evidence of an erratic clock in his reception office, had he seemed in any way disorganized. Everything about him suggested a man who took great care over small details. It made it all the more puzzling why he had failed to meet the time of our appointment by so wide a margin.

The minute hand jerked again. I had now been waiting for twenty-eight minutes. I decided that I would wait no longer than thirty.

The thought returned that I was still not entirely clear what I was doing here or what I was going to say. It only served to increase my discomfort. Perhaps it was a mistake to have come here. Might it not be better, I thought, if I simply slipped away. I squirmed uneasily in my seat. The clock showed twenty-nine minutes. I would definitely make a move at thirty.

A muted buzzer sounded at the receptionist's desk. She looked across at me and smiled.

"Mr Fielding will see you now Mr Bradley," she said. "His room is at the end of the corridor upstairs."

My doubts made a momentary return as I mounted the stairs and walked along the short passage that ran to the rear of the building. A door faced me at the end. I tapped and entered.

Fielding was sitting at a large modern desk set at right angles to the window. He rose as I entered. His appearance was exactly as it had been on the day of Rollo's luncheon. I wondered if he would remember me.

"Ah! Mr Bradley," he said, giving me the same flaccid handshake as before. "I thought that it might be you when I saw the name on my appointments list."

I knew then that he had remembered and that my long wait had been deliberate. Thirty minutes was too neat to be anything else. But why, I wondered.

"Do sit down," he continued. "Good. Now what can I do for you?"

There seemed no point in any preamble. I came directly to the point.

"I want to find Rollo." I said.

A thin smile ghosted across his face.

"You are not alone there," he replied. "There have been others looking for him."

"I had a visit from the police too," I said. "This is a personal matter."

Fielding spread his hands in a gesture of helplessness.

"Sadly, I have to give you the same answer as I gave the others. Your friend Mr Blake is a client of mine. I am bound by the principle of client confidentiality."

"I am not asking for anything about his affairs. I would simply like to know how I might contact him. He was your friend and he was my friend too. I am asking you on a purely personal level."

He sat back and looked directly at me.

"That is a fine point you have drawn," he said. "However, I am not sure that the Law Society would appreciate the distinction."

"So, you won't help me."

"As I have explained my hands are tied. First and

foremost, Mr Blake was my client. I cannot help you."

There was something about his sanctimonious smoothness that caused disgust and anger to rise in me in equal measure.

"Are you claiming that he was not your friend?"

"I am simply saying that I am a professional man and have to behave in a professional manner. Had I been less professional I might not be sitting here now."

"You were happy enough to eat at his table," I exclaimed.

My accusation left him unperturbed.

"My relationship with Mr Blake was a purely professional one. Dining with a client is not incompatible with that position."

He had taken up his fountain pen and rolled it between immaculately groomed fingers. He sat like this, thinking for a moment, before he continued.

"Bear in mind," he said, "apart from ourselves, there were three other people at that table. Two of those people are on remand awaiting trial for conspiracy and corruption, and the third is on the run: whereas I am sitting here in my own office talking to you. Now why is that do you think?"

"Because you took care to protect your own skin," I declared hotly.

"You would make a poor juror in a criminal court," he replied. "You would be prepared to convict on any shred of circumstantial evidence. Fortunately, I am not on trial. The police have questioned me of course. They suspected me of involvement with the others, as you do, but like you that is all that they have, their suspicions."

Again, he allowed another thin smile to play around his mouth.

"I know it outrages your schoolboy notions of rightness and fairness, but there is not a scintilla of evidence that could be cited against me in a court of law."

The anger that had flamed briefly in me had subsided. I found that I could admire his guile with a detached equanimity.

"You do not deny that you made money from their activities." I said coolly.

"What is there to deny?" He replied lightly. "I supplied professional legal and financial services to three clients. I charged them fees for those services. The fees were declared in my accounts and I have paid tax on them. Is that illegal?"

"That was cleverly done," I said.

Fielding nodded in pleased acceptance of the compliment. This single evidence of pleasure was the sole human trait I had noted in his make-up.

He was toying with the fountain pen again. I sensed that he was debating whether or not he should say anything further. Like many clever men forced to work in the shadows, he suffered the frustration of never being able to show the real extent of his cleverness. My ready acknowledgement of his manoeuvring had given him a rare opportunity to indulge his vanity.

"I had a bad start in life," he said. "I won't bore you with the details. What it taught me was the importance of having power. I have made it the central canon of my adult life that I would never again put myself at the mercy of anyone, and the easiest way to effect that is to turn that situation about, to have other people at my mercy. Believe me, it is much more satisfactory to exercise power than to suffer from it."

He paused for several seconds during which his gaze did not waver.

"To achieve such a position of power," he continued, "it is necessary to remove all trace of emotion from one's life. Emotions are our Achilles heel. They create weakness and all weakness creates opportunities for others to exploit. Once I had understood this it was easy enough to reverse the whole principle. I make it my business to look for weaknesses in others and turn them to my own advantage. That is easy enough; the skill lies in directing their thinking so that they actually believe it is their own clever doing."

He placed the pen back on the desktop.

"The builder Meadowes and that strange fellow from the planning department had a very obvious weakness. They loved money. It was very easy to lead them on. Your friend Rollo on the other hand was a much more complex character. It occurred to me that there was something missing in his life. He seemed to need excitement to fill that void. It was rather like a drug. As time went on he needed stronger and stronger doses to achieve the desired effect. It made him very reckless. Such a pity. He was a very gifted man."

I noted his use of the past tense without comment. It was as if Rollo had ceased to exist once he had passed outside Fielding's control.

"Sadly, all that is now at an end. They made a lot of money and I in my own way prospered more modestly, but then the price of taking the greatest cut is that one also takes responsibility. That is why Meadowes is in prison and I am here."

I had heard Fielding out in silence, appalled as much by the monstrous ego he had displayed as by the cold and calculating way in which he had manipulated others. His final expression of sorrow for the end of his lucrative scheme with not a word of compassion regarding the fate of his dupes was too much.

"Have you no regret for what you have led these men into," I cried out.

Up to this point he had seemed relaxed, as if enjoying his recital. My words produced an immediate change. His face reverted to the stiff coldness I had first noted. There was no expression in the eyes that stared across the desk at me.

"Regret." He almost spat the word out in distaste. "What others choose to do is their own affair and they must accept the consequences of their actions. My only regret is that the petty greed of that fool Meadowes has ruined a new scheme that I was developing that was very dear to my heart."

"Eastonbury." I knew intuitively without really understanding why.

"Exactly so. It was so simple. All I had to do was to suggest that a modern-day version of the Hellfire Club would be a sure-fire money-spinner. It suited their personalities so beautifully. Meadowes was positively drooling at the thought of all the money he could make and your friend Blake I think was equally attracted by the risqué nature of the operation."

"You were going to turn Eastonbury into some kind of vice den," I said disbelievingly.

"I would not have put it so crudely," he responded coolly. "I would have described an opulent Country House Hotel where guests could indulge in any form of pleasure known to man. The best foods and wines, a casino - that was why the house was being restored. There were to be various pleasure domes and other accommodation in the grounds overlooking the lakes. It would be the sort of place where the bored or the dissolute could go for an exciting weekend, and all very discreet. The Eastonbury estate is ideally suited don't you think. So very secluded."

I listened in growing disbelief.

"Imagine," he continued with an almost messianic ardour, "just imagine, all the human weakness and folly that would be paraded in such an establishment. Think of all the delicious opportunities that would be revealed."

For a moment, he was lost in thought. Then abruptly he returned to the original thread of his discourse.

"All of that has been brought to nothing because Oliver Meadowes could not resist cheating on his VAT payments and you ask if I feel any regret for him. I find the very idea nauseating."

The man was mad. I could think of no other explanation. He inhabited a world of which I wanted no part.

"Thank you. Mr Fielding," I said rising to my feet. "You have answered the two questions that brought me here."

"Sit down Mr Bradley," he said icily. "I have not done with you yet. You pretend to yourself that you have answers to questions that have been running through your head. Allow me to disabuse you. You have information, but you have no answers. You have not yet even begun to realize why you are here."

There was a cold edge to his voice that made my blood turn cold.

"You are here because you are in financial difficulties. Is that not so?"

I made no response.

"You have completed your work and wish to receive payment. Unfortunately, you are unable to trace your former partner. In the meantime, you have discovered that you are legally responsible for any commitments he undertook, including bank loans."

"You seem well informed on my affairs," I said.

"Naturally. You were brought in at my suggestion to overcome the Tyzack woman's scruples. I took the trouble of checking you out. I also took the added precaution of suggesting that you sign partnership contracts and bank documents to make sure I had some leverage over you. A wise precaution as it has turned out."

The arrogance of the man was breathtaking. I could feel an impotent rage rising in me. I had thought him reptilian in his coldness. I realized now that I had chosen the wrong species for my comparison. He was more like a spider spinning webs to trap the unwary. He played the spider now watching me from across the desk with the fingertips of each hand placed exactly against each other, judging whether or not he had me securely enmeshed.

"The question is," he mused, "what am I to do with you? You are of no further use to me. You appear to have no vices and are far too upright and moralistic to suit my purposes."

"I'll take that as a compliment."

"Do," he said. "Your only weakness was your inexperience of business matters and I think that has been remedied by the sharp lessons you have received of late."

He reflected further.

"No, I think the best course of action will be for me to buy you out. Let me see. The estate was sold for two hundred and fifty thousand and you have spent countless thousands improving it. Against that, this is a distress sale so you would not expect to receive full price."

He looked at me directly.

"I will offer you two hundred and twenty thousand," he said.

It took a moment or two for his offer to sink in. I almost laughed at his wild underestimate of my debt position. He obviously had no idea of the precise nature of Rollo's arrangements with the bank, nor of his final plundering of the account. I remembered Steve's assessment. The size and irregular nature of the loan were points in my favour. I still had another two months before the next instalment was due. On any of these counts there could be only one answer to the offer.

There was another issue too. I had made a promise to Miss Tyzack and would do all I could to honour it. It was not just a point of honour either. Over the last few months I had grown to love the house and its grounds. If there was one person on earth I was now determined should not come into possession of the Eastonbury estate, that person was Francis Fielding.

My anger made me surprisingly calm. I even found the assurance to give him a broad smile.

"I think not," was all I said.

Fielding remained unperturbed.

"I will give you until the end of the week to decide," he said.

"The answer will still be no if you give me a year."

"Bravely said," he replied, "but no matter. I can buy at a similar price from the bank when they foreclose on the loan. Think about it."

"Fielding," I said, "I could tell you to go to hell, but I think you are there already."

15

David Ramsay leant back in his chair. The thick cardboard folder of a student portfolio rested on his knee, its back propped against the edge of his desk. He sat quite motionless studying a design. His face, normally relaxed and cheerful, displayed a mix of intense concentration and something that bordered on rapture.

He seemed unaware of my presence as I entered the office and crossed to my own desk. I had shared an office with him since the start of the term. He was a pleasant enough young man, but this was his first post and he was still very keen and, to my taste, a little too eager to please.

I ignored him for the moment and leafed through the assignments I had collected at my morning seminar. At first glance a number of them looked promising. I placed them in my briefcase. There would be no opportunity until much later to begin assessing them. Behind me Ramsay sighed deeply. I heard the sounds of the portfolio being re-assembled.

I swivelled my desk chair to face him.

"You seemed far gone when I came in," I said. "Something interesting."

"I've been digging in the archives for old final year presentations. Some of this work is staggering."

The reply came easily enough, but all the same I thought that he looked a little uneasy.

"Anyone in particular?"

He made a point of looking at the name on the portfolio's label.

"Rollo Blake." He read.

I had not needed to ask. Even glanced at upside down as I had entered, there was no mistaking the style of the designs.

"Why the sudden interest in old students? You have not by any chance been talking to Andrew Walters have you?" I asked.

Walters had been on the teaching staff in my student days and had now risen to the rank of Senior Lecturer. I found him an irritating man. I did not question his ability, but he was not the sort of man one could trust. He made it his business to find out everything that was going on and was only too ready to gossip about what he knew. I avoided him as much as possible.

Interestingly Ramsay reddened at the mention of his name.

"No," he said. "I read in a newspaper article about the big scandal that Rollo Blake had been a student here. It intrigued me. I thought I would look up some of his work. Wasn't he here at the same time as you?"

There had obviously been talk in the Common Room.

"You should not encourage Andrew," I said. "He likes to gossip. And yes, we were here at the same time. We were also at school together."

"What happened?" Ramsay asked. "I mean what made him behave the way he has?"

He looked at me as if I had the answers to everything. I could only guess at what titbits Walters had fed him.

"I have no idea," I said. "I have had very little to do with him since we left here."

He accepted my reply without question. His mind had

already moved back to the designs in the portfolio lying on his desk.

"I find it strange," he continued. "These designs are absolutely brilliant. Why would he want to throw everything away?"

"I'm as baffled as you as to what motivated him," I replied, "but I would not say that he has thrown everything away. His skills and talent are still there."

"That's what I mean," said Ramsay decisively. "Don't you see. He will never be able to practice architecture so long as he is on the run."

He re-opened the portfolio case and spread a number of the designs across the desk.

"Just look at these designs," he continued. They are all different, but each is unmistakably by the same person. He might just have well have signed them."

I began to see his point.

"You mean his work will always be recognised."

"Absolutely. The minute he produces a design, even if he uses an assumed name, he will be telling the world where he is. As an architect, he's finished."

It was a sobering thought. Even in such run of the mill structures as the schools and hospitals which he had designed for his syndicate, the flair, which had featured so strongly in his earlier work, was still there. Would he be able to live without exercising it, I wondered.

Ramsay had delivered his verdict. His curiosity about Rollo sated, he re-assembled the portfolio.

"Coming to lunch?" he asked.

"No." I replied. "I'm meeting someone."

It was good to get outside again. The lecturing job was not shaping up as I had imagined. God knows I needed the income, puny as it seemed when ranged against the overburden of my debts. Yet deep down I knew that, come the end of my contract at the end of the academic year, I would not want to extend it.

Perhaps it had been a mistake to come back to teach at the college where I had studied. It is hard to make the transition from Junior to Senior Common Room. In my own case, the result was that I felt that I did not belong in either. Worse, the whole college set-up I found claustrophobic. I had lectured before and been desk-bound for much of the time when working with Henry. Neither had worried me. Now at times I felt a sympathy for Oliver Meadowes. It was as if I myself were serving a form of prison sentence with my movements restricted and all my time accounted for.

The truth was I had become used to the space and peace of Eastonbury. For months, I had been answerable only to myself. Each day now I looked forward to battling my way out of the city through the evening traffic. Each evening the feeling, when I turned into the avenue past the lion sentinels, was one of real homecoming. I had enjoyed a taste of freedom and there could be no turning back.

For how much longer I could enjoy Eastonbury, I did not know. I had left Fielding's office in a mood of cold anger, determined that he would not prevail in his scheming. That had been almost a month earlier in the dog days between Christmas and the New Year. Those feelings had not changed, but as each day brought me closer to the date of the next repayment instalment to the bank, the more hopeless everything seemed. I was in a bind. Short of a miracle, I could think of nothing that would save me. I pulled my scarf across my throat against the raw wind that was blowing up the river and headed for the pub where we had arranged to meet.

Steve was already there and was half-way through his first beer.

"What are you having?" he said by way of greeting. "I'm going for a steak sandwich and a beer."

"Fine. I'll have the same."

He drained his glass. Then he walked to the bar, placed our order and returned with our drinks. He sat down and raised his glass. There was a curious pleased expression on his face.

"Cheers!" he said burying his lips in the froth that had already overflowed the edge of the glass.

"Well?"

"Well." he replied archly.

I was in no mood for light-heartedness.

"Steve, what the hell is going on? You ring up asking me to meet you here. You say there is something important to tell me, but won't say what. Now I'm here you just sit and grin at me like a Cheshire Cat."

"Alright," he said. "I've had my fun. I'll come clean. I have a sleeping partner lined up for you."

The shock of what he had said left me unable to speak for a moment.

"This isn't a joke, is it?" I finally managed to mumble.

"No. Straight up."

"Who is it?"

"I can't disclose his name. He wants to meet you first. He's a client of mine. A retired businessman. He's coming to see me this afternoon. I thought that you would like to meet him."

"Of course, but I am lecturing for the first two hours after lunch. I can be with you at about four o'clock."

"That will be fine," Steve said grinning.

I grinned back at him and belatedly raised my own glass.

"Cheers," I said.

I must have cut a poor figure in the lecture room that afternoon. My thoughts were on Steve's client and the implications of what his introduction might lead to. Fortunately, I had produced copious illustrations and the group found plenty to interest them. It seemed to take an age to reach the time when I could decently end the session. The late afternoon traffic was already building up and there were the usual hold-ups for roadworks. Everything seemed to conspire to delay me and it was five minutes past four when I parked in Steve's yard.

Steve was in the outer office going over some papers with his secretary when I walked in.

"Brad," he said, beaming at me in a way that reminded me of his lunchtime behaviour. "Come on through. We are all ready for you."

He waited while I hung my car coat on the office coat stand and then ushered me into his office. A figure was seated with his back to the door. There was something about the jacket and the balding crown that I recognised immediately.

Steve was wearing his best silly grin.

"I don't think I need to introduce you two do I."

"Is this your idea of a joke," I said to him icily. Then I turned to confront his visitor.

"Dad! What are you doing here?"

Steve took his seat. For once he looked ill-at-ease. Perhaps he had expected me to respond to the humour of the situation, if so I had failed miserably to come up to expectations. In other circumstances, it might have been different, but I had been through too much of late and, with so much riding on this meeting, had been keyed up all afternoon. I sat down, furious with the pair of them.

"Your father asked me to..." Steve began.

"It's alright Stephen," Dad cut in. "I'd best explain."

He looked at me in the straightforward way I remembered of old.

"This charade was my idea, so don't take it out on Stephen. I know how stubborn you can be and I didn't think you would come if you knew it was me."

"Well you were right there," I replied. "I know you mean well, but you don't have the sort of money I need."

"Perhaps you should hear your father out," Steve said simply.

"Alright. Now I am here, I might just as well."

It was not put very graciously. After the raising of my hopes during the afternoon and the struggle to get here on time my spirits had taken a heavy knock. I felt very tired.

Dad cleared his throat.

"You see Paul it's like this. Stephen has been telling me for some years now that I needed to invest more in the business to match what the big nurseries and garden centres were doing. The trouble was there was never enough money and there did not seem much point as you were not interested in taking it over. That was before your mother became ill."

He stopped to blow his nose into a large handkerchief.

"I'd had a number of offers to buy me out, but they were all from builders. Nobody was interested in the business as a going concern, but the land was going up in value all the time. Things really went downhill while I was nursing your mother. I could see that the business was finished. I couldn't see what to do until you came home at Christmas."

His words came to me as if in a dream. It seemed unreal that I could be holding a business meeting with my own father. Physically he was much improved on the state I had seen him in during the autumn, but he still looked old and tired. He was the one who appeared to need a helping hand, yet if I understood the drift of his thinking, it was he who was hoping to come to my aid.

I shook my head.

"Dad, no," I said. "You don't know the full picture."

"Hear me out," he continued. "I've been in contact with one of the builders that was sniffing around. The upshot is they have upped their offer and I have accepted."

"You've sold the nursery," I said incredulously.

"Yes. They have paid me an advance of ten per cent, and I get the rest on completion which has been set for two weeks today."

Steve had sat patiently as Dad had filled me in on his doings. Now he chipped in.

"Don't worry Brad. Your father has consulted me all along

the way. The business was failing and he has been offered a very good price for the land."

"I'm not concerned about the price," I cried turning back to Dad. "What are you going to do? It was not just a business. It was your home."

"That was part of the problem," he said flatly. "It has been tearing me apart living there without your mother. I could not stay there. Then it struck me that you and me could work together. Anyway, it's done now."

There it was again. After all these years he still had not let go his dream of a family business.

"No Dad," I said. "I can't take your money."

"It's what your mother would have wanted."

"Not like this," I said. "She would have wanted you to look after yourself."

His face was a mask of disappointment. I cast around in my head for the right words to soften what I had to say to him.

"Don't think I'm ungrateful. It's a wonderful offer and I'm proud of you for making it. But I can't let you pour your money down my drain. It's too risky. There is a fair chance I could still go bankrupt even with the use of your money. Where would we be then. No money. No home. Nothing."

I turned to Steve for support.

"Explain to him Steve."

"It's what I have already warned him of," Steve said.

"He's right, Mr Bradley. You have to stay outside this."

"I know what you are saying," Dad said, emotion all too obviously welling up in him. "I can't stand by and watch my own flesh and blood go under like this."

"You don't have to," Steve said. "There is a way round this if you will both stop arguing from extremes."

He spoke quietly. The look on his face told me that he had switched into professional mode. We both waited to hear what he had in mind.

"What you need Brad is working capital," he began. "At

the moment, everything you have is tied up in fixed assets, that is the house and the land. To make matters worse those assets have been purchased with borrowed money. In technical terms, you are very highly geared. The safe gearing ratio banks normally work to is fifty per cent. That is, they will advance one pound of their money for every two pounds of yours. Your gearing ratio when Rollo left you high and dry was closer to one thousand per cent. You need money and fast."

He paused for a moment to allow what he had said to sink in. Then he faced Dad.

"If you were to undertake the simple partnership that you have in mind, the assets you would bring to the business would reduce the theoretical gearing rate to something between two to three hundred per cent. That would be still very dangerously high, and it would still leave you dependant on selling apartments in Brad's conversion scheme. If the housing market faltered in the meantime, you would be in real trouble."

"I don't understand all this money talk, Dad said. "but you're the accountant. If you say what I've suggested is unsafe, then I had best take your advice."

There was a note in his voice and a look on his face that suggested that he was none too sure all the same. He still hankered after his family business. If anything, now that I was his only close relative, it made that desire all the stronger.

I thought back to what Fielding had said about emotions being our Achilles heel. In that respect, his assessment had been all too accurate. I was thankful that in Steve I had an ally whose judgement Dad trusted.

"What are you suggesting?" I asked him.

"You need to sell an apartment to break the logjam. Right?"

I nodded agreement.

"You also need to find another Fifty thousand or so by early March."

I nodded again.

"What I propose is that you sell your father a lease on one of your apartments for ... shall we say One Hundred Thousand. That should be enough to keep you in business and gives you a fighting chance of pulling yourself out of this mess."

"And if I don't..."

"And if you don't, your father is not legally involved with you. He would still have a roof over his head and the rest of his capital intact."

He looked at each of us in turn.

"Well what do you think?"

Dad pondered for a moment.

"I could still give Paul more money if he needed it, could I?"

"You could lend him more." Steve corrected him. "Remember it is important that you keep your finances separate from his."

Dad nodded.

"Alright. If you think that is the best way."

"Brad?"

I did not need to think. It was beautiful. Dad needed a home and at Eastonbury I could keep an eye on him. At the same time, I had the chance to pull through. I was about to agree when the thought of Fielding and his grand design crossed my mind.

"I'm broadly in agreement," I said at last, "But with one extra proviso. I think Dad's lease should also cover the grounds. That way, if I go under, we would still control the site."

Steve gave me an old-fashioned look.

"Good thinking. We appear to have a businessman in the making."

Dad was not listening. His thoughts were elsewhere.

"You say grounds," he said. "Does that include the kitchen garden?"

"Who else would want it," I grinned at him.

We stayed on discussing the finer point of the arrangement until after six. Steve made detailed notes as we went through everything.

"I'll get on to Elizabeth tomorrow to get the lease drawn up," he said as we broke up to go in search of dinner.

We settled on Steve's local, as Dad was catching a train home at 7.45pm. The walk to the pub gave me time to reflect. The more I looked at it the more sense it made. Dad too was warming to the idea. By the time we had settled at our table he was already airing plans for what he could do with his new property.

"I shall do mail order," he said. "Something out of the ordinary that the mainstream nurseries don't offer."

"Anything particular in mind?" I asked him.

"Perhaps something exotic or maybe I'll develop my own hybrids. I don't know yet. I shall have to think about it a bit more."

Steve nodded appreciatively.

"Sounds good. You will have a good address for anything like that."

Afterwards I drove Dad to Temple Meads. We had cut things fine and his train was already standing at the platform. We stopped at the nearest carriage.

"We shall be working together in a way, shan't we?" he asked.

I nodded agreement.

"Yes. We shall. There are lots of things I can involve you in."

"That'll be good."

The guards whistle sounded.

"You've got the cheque safe?"

I patted my wallet.

"Yes. It's safe. You had better get aboard."

I ushered him on to the train and shut the carriage door behind him. He barely had time to lower the window before the first gentle lurch of motion. There was a new light in his eyes as he looked out at me.

I walked a few yards along with him as the train eased forward.

"Get that flat ready for me as soon as you can, and don't worry. We can beat this."

He waved from the window as the train pulled away.

"Don't go buying any gardening equipment yet," I called after him.

I don't know whether he heard me. He gave a final wave and passed out of sight.

The world seemed a more comfortable place as I drove home to Eastonbury. It was as if a great weight had been lifted from my shoulders. I felt a lightness and a confidence that had been missing for many months. One of Claudio's arias came into my head and I hummed it for much of the short drive. Perhaps it was just a trick of the shadows thrown by my headlights, but as I turned into the avenue, I could have sworn that there were smiles on the faces of the lions.

I parked in the forecourt and stood looking at the house. It was a fine night. Wisps of cloud drifted across the moon veiling its light to a pale silvery luminescence. Against this the house stood massed in silhouette. Looking at its shadowy bulk I had the feeling that a corner had been turned. In my mind, I could already picture the glow of lights behind drawn curtains. I felt a promise that before long all would be brought to life again. It would not be the comfortable leisured lifestyle that Miss Tyzack had known as a child. Nor would it be the sordid glitz of an underworld that sought to profit from human weakness. It would simply be peopled again. They would come in the haphazard mix of ages and genders, occupations and interests that forms the normal mould of human society. With luck, they would meld into a small community that would accept each other's differences and peccadillos and if confronted with weakness would offer aid and toleration rather than seek to exploit it.

When I finally unlocked the main door and went inside, I found a letter bearing the logo of Rollo's bank. I carried it upstairs and laid it aside while I busied myself lighting my evening fire. Driving home I had resolved to ignore the assignments in my briefcase and to put aside any thoughts of lecture preparation. Instead I had promised myself an evening of relaxation - a log fire, a good book, perhaps a glass of wine. I felt that I owed myself that much.

16

Time had passed by the north-west corner of Eastonbury's kitchen garden. The mark of its passing was everywhere around. It could be seen in the unchecked profusion of grass and weeds. It showed starkly in the broken glass and rotted timbers of a greenhouse that had simply collapsed from age. It could be measured in the crumbling cement of the decaying brickwork and the rusted studs of the nails which had once supported climbing plants. Closer inspection would reveal its evidence in the pockets of rich soil scattered among the debris of human artefacts, for these were the joint product of years of vegetable decomposition and the earthworms which made it their home.

This was the good soil which Dad's experienced eye had noted in the course of that one short visit in late December, but which had remained unnoticed during my much longer sojourn.

"Don't lose any of the soil," he had written. "It's good stuff."

He had then gone on to explain, with the aid of a simple diagram, how to construct a sieve that would separate soil from debris. His comments marked the end of an episode that, for all its comic overtones, had left me fuming that the first day of the college's Easter break would be spent on garden clearance.

There was a second diagram showing me exactly where he wanted to position the new greenhouse he had ordered. He wanted me to clear the site ready for it. He had posted the letter with a second-class stamp. By the time it reached me, the greenhouse had already been delivered. I had found the sections stacked against the garden wall in the forecourt when I returned home from college.

I had telephoned him that evening. He had been almost obtuse in his inability to comprehend the pressures I was under. I had had to bite back the words which had first come to mind. It could so easily have escalated into one of those quarrels where harsh words are spoken and quickly regretted. Instead I had pictured his sad face at the other end of the line and remembered the obvious pleasure he had felt at the prospect of creating his own walled kitchen garden.

"There is nowhere to put it," I had finally said.

"It's a lean-to," had been his response, as if this somehow provided sufficient explanation. "I thought that it could stand where the old one stood on the north wall."

"That part is overgrown. Nothing has been cleared," I had countered.

It had been a dialogue with the deaf. Nothing I had said had had the slightest effect. He had simply returned to the game plan he had already worked out.

"I thought that if you could get the site ready for me, I could erect it myself when I move down next week."

I remember having yelled into the phone at this point.

"Dad! Do you have any idea how much work I have on my plate at the moment?"

There had been a pause before he had answered.

"It'll have to be done. The season will be gone."

He had not needed to elaborate. We each had our own timetable. Mine was dictated by the constraints of financial contracts, his was controlled by an older and more demanding taskmaster. I had given way finally. Already the tight timetable I had set myself had begun to slip.

My first consideration had been to make the flat ready for Dad. We had decided that much at our dinner with Steve.

"I wouldn't want a room with those great windows," was how he had dismissed the suggestion of a flat in the main house. He was a plain man and there was an element of show in the height of the ceilings and the corresponding proportions of the doors and windows that he disdained.

This disdain did not extend to walled kitchen gardens. To him they were working arrangements. He saw no social pretensions in the height or cost of the walls. They served the practical purpose of protecting the plants and creating an ideal micro-climate. The obvious solution had been for him to have the existing flat, suitably modified, and to have the door from the garden as his means of access.

It was an ideal solution from my point of view. Not only did it place Dad within his own realm, but he would be able to move in before the date arranged for the sale of the nursery. Most of the work I needed to carry out in readiness for him was on the ground floor, where I planned to convert the former pantry and store rooms into a kitchen and dining-room. When that was done the existing kitchen would make a small office for him.

There was a financial advantage to this scheme which I had not realized at the time. Architecturally the kitchen wing was different to the rest of the house. It had been designed as a work area with staff accommodation. The remaining apartments would all be of a different quality with period features. If converted in the right way they could all be marketed as luxury apartments and priced accordingly. All of this had been explained to me by Jonathon Gardiner when he visited me a second time.

My experience of estate agents was limited. What I had seen of them in London had left me wary of a profession which produced a seemingly inexhaustible supply of young men and women who were all of a type: personable, articulate and possessed of an unbounded fount of optimism and enthusiasm. Twenty years earlier Jonathon would have matched this description, but the era of high inflation had produced rich pickings for men of his calling. Under the onslaught of good living the youthful Jonathon had given way to a figure who would not have looked out of place in the pages of Charles Dickens. The three-piece business suit he wore struggled to contain the girth of his waistline, even with the lower two buttons of the waistcoat left undone, and the ruddy colouring of his cheeks continued down to his shirt through thick folds of flesh.

Whatever the years might have done to his person, they had not dimmed his enthusiasm. He spoke rapidly with much waving of his arms to emphasize the points he was making. At frequent intervals, he would pause in mid-flow to smooth down his hair, grown long across his head to disguise his advancing baldness, and which, like all thinning hair, seemed ever wayward.

He had spent most of an afternoon making notes on the projected apartments and measuring room sizes. Afterwards we had sat over a pot of tea discussing marketing strategy.

"The work has to be done properly," he had stressed, punching the air for added emphasis. "Everything has to shout quality at the client. There can be no skimping on detail. Bathroom taps and door handles are what everyone notices, but everything else has to be of top quality too."

He tapped the clipboard with the sheaf of notes he had made.

"The same goes for this. A run-of-the-mill sales leaflet will not do. I'm thinking of a small brochure – perhaps cream or off-white parchment inside a card cover. The cover printing will cost a bit more, but it will be worth the expense. We can insert colour photos later. I shall need to take the outdoor shots when there is good sunshine, so I will wait until one of the apartments is complete and furnished."

"Furnished!"

"Oh, don't worry about that," he said carelessly. "I'll get one of the big stores to supply everything. They are quite happy to do that. It's good advertising for them. I'll also get them to provide a table for the entrance hall. It is a bit bare at the moment, but with a few touches it will make an ideal sales office. It has to look right. First impressions are all important."

Lecture over, he had drained his cup and jumped to his feet.

"Right then. Must crack on. I'll get everything set up ready at my end while you push on here. How soon will you be ready do you reckon?"

"If planning approval is given this month, then I could have the first unit ready sometime in June and the rest of the main house by the end of summer."

"Good," he said briskly. "I shall be ready and waiting. Just give me a bell when you are nearing completion and I will set things in motion."

He had it all planned out. In the event it all worked out quite differently, but that still lay in the future as I commenced the task of clearing the site for Dad's greenhouse.

The skip I had hired was positioned ready in the gateway to the garden. I had constructed a ramp of builders' planks so that I could wheelbarrow loads of rubbish directly into it. I had also constructed a rectangular sieve to Dad's specification, which would be supported at a near-vertical angle by two stout posts. When I began the actual work of clearance I found progress disconcertingly slow. It was only after I had stripped an area for the sieve and could begin to throw shovelfuls at it, as I cleared, that I began to see a pattern and find a rhythm to my efforts.

The work was heavier than I had anticipated and progress was made in fits and starts with frequent breaks to draw breath. As mid-day approached the bottom of the skip had disappeared beneath a deep layer of rubbish. I was hot and running with sweat. My hands and clothes were filthy. I loaded a final shovelful of debris from the foot of the sieve into the barrow and determined, that once this had been transferred the skip, I would take an early break for lunch. It was as I mounted the makeshift ramp with the barrow that I heard the voice.

"Excuse me," the voice said. "Could you tell me where I can find the owner?"

I retraced my steps to ground level, set the barrow down and walked round the skip into the forecourt. At the side of the gate stood a slightly built lady. Behind her was the small saloon car in which she had arrived unnoticed. Flecks of grey in her hair suggested that she was in her early fifties. She was dressed in a lightweight hip-length coat with a silk scarf loosely knotted at the throat. The clothes were of a type that any moderately well-off lady of middle age might have bought, but there was something about her bearing and the warmth of her smile that seemed to make them different.

"I am the owner," I said.

"Oh!" She responded with an unrestrained giggle that made me instantly warm to her. "I was expecting someone rather different. Mr Gardiner referred to you as the developer."

"Well I am in a way. I wear several hats. Today I'm labourer and general handyman. I'm clearing a site for a greenhouse," I added lamely.

"I was hoping that I might see the apartments. I know I have come without making an appointment, but I have to go back to London this afternoon."

Again, she made that half-apologetic smile. Silently I cursed Jonathon. He had gone on at such lengths about the importance of presentation and first impressions. He had also agreed that either he or one of his staff would drive prospective clients to the house and escort them round. Instead someone had turned up out of the blue. The brochures had not been printed and the work of conversion was still under way. The original kitchen had been gutted and there were gaping holes in walls where new doors were to be inserted. There was mess everywhere. That was just the house. I could not bear to think about my personal state of unpreparedness. There could not have been a worse time to show anyone round.

I looked down at the shoes and trousers noting the marks of the morning's work. It was as if she read my thoughts.

"You're fine," she said. "I can hardly complain if I come unannounced when you are hard at work, and I would like to see inside the house. It is such a lovely building. I'm already getting a tingle."

I did not enquire as to what the tingle signified. She had that easy manner that carried one effortlessly along. Instead I was already making rapid plans as to how I would deal with this unexpected problem.

"At least let me wash my hands." I said. "Perhaps you would like to look at the plans while I clean up."

I led her across to the coach house and left her browsing over my drawings in the site office, while I dashed back to the flat to wash and slip into some clean clothes.

She looked at me reproachfully when I returned to the coach house.

"It really wasn't necessary to change," she said and then switched subject abruptly. "This is your work. Isn't it?"

I nodded.

"I thought so. It's very good. I particularly like the way in which you have made sketches of possible decors. Could you do something similar for me?"

"The drawings on the walls are old plans. I was restoring the house for a business syndicate. That has fallen through, so I'm now converting the house into apartments."

"Much nicer," she said. "It would be a shame to waste such a lovely house on some dreary old business."

Fielding's plans for the estate would have been far from

dreary I mused, but that was ground on to which I did not wish to stray. Instead, I attempted to be businesslike.

"Are you ready to see the house?" I asked.

We walked across the forecourt.

"In another month or so the troughs at the centre will have their summer plantings. It looks very colourful then. Now, I'm afraid nothing is ready," I continued lamely. "I had not planned to begin marketing for another six weeks. Everything is in a very rough state."

"Mr Gardiner explained all of that," she said. "But your scheme seemed to be so exactly what I was looking for. He thought that you would not mind giving me a preview."

She said very little after I ushered her in through the front door into the hall.

"The hall will be maintained in its original state and will be the entrance for all the apartments in the central part of the house. The grandest rooms were in this part of the house and I'm attempting to keep those largely untouched."

We had stopped in the sitting-room with the view across to the bridge. "This is the design you were admiring in the site office."

"I had rather guessed it was." She had a way of holding her head to one side and studying me as I spoke. She did it now, looking directly into my face. "This room is a favourite of yours."

"Mm." I nodded.

As we spoke we had approached the stone fireplace, the largest and most ornate in the house. I was expecting some form of appreciative comment. Instead, to my surprise I noticed a look of distaste cross her face. It was followed in quick succession by a look of shock which quickly turned to horror. She stopped and put her hands to her head. She stood like this for some moments.

"Oh dear!" She gasped.

"Is anything wrong." I was temporarily nonplussed. Perhaps she was ill or felt faint.

"No. It was nothing. I'm fine."

She gave a reassuring smile and moved away. She seemed to have regained some of her poise and made a point of examining Robin Johnston's new doors before moving on into the next room. Once there she made a point of firmly closing the door behind us. When she turned back to face me, her face had lost its earlier animation. She appeared grave.

"Are you sure that you are alright? Let me get you a cup of tea."

"No, thank you. I'm fine. Really."

She stood for a moment as if uncertain how to proceed.

"I think, perhaps I should explain," she finally said. "I spoke earlier of getting a tingle. It is a term I use to describe what I believe is a form of psychic experience. I have these from time to time. When I do they are usually significant. This house has been positively shouting to me since I first arrived. Such good, strong vibrations. And you too. You seemed very much a part of it."

I looked at her in astonishment.

"Very occasionally I experience stronger sensations. Feelings; sometimes pictures."

"Really! What do you see?"

"Very little. Just odd glimpses. That's what makes it all so fascinating and at times frustrating."

"Perhaps I should cross your palm with silver."

She smiled briefly. "It would not do you any good. I can't summon them to order."

Inexplicably her face took on its former seriousness.

"That is what happened just now. It was quite disturbing. I was getting the good vibrations I spoke of, when something else intervened."

She shuddered as she spoke.

"I can't describe it. It was as if there was the presence of pure evil. It only lasted a moment and then the good feelings returned."

I had listened to her with growing astonishment. Had I

not witnessed the whole episode, I would probably have dismissed it as hokum. It seemed incredible, and yet there was something about her mood that asked to be believed.

"What does it mean?" I asked.

She shook her head slowly.

"I don't know. I think it was a premonition of something very unpleasant, possibly even dangerous. It was very strong."

"Dangerous!" I echoed. "In what way?"

Again, she shook her head.

"I can't say. I get this insight. Nothing more. It can be very frustrating."

"But you said the good feeling returned?"

"Yes. If anything, it was stronger than before."

She stopped. Her thoughts were back in the next-door room. There was a look of puzzlement on her face.

"Was there something else?"

"Its so very odd. Normally, when I get one of these insights, I seem quite detached. It's as if I were an onlooker. Just now it was different. I seemed to be involved in what was happening."

"What was happening?"

"I don't know. It only lasted a moment."

"Would there be a repeat if you stepped back into the other room?"

"I don't know. That is, I don't think so. It's not something I can control. It just seems to happen. In any case I don't think I want to experience that again."

I studied my visitor. She seemed composed and behaving quite normally. Yet it was obvious that, for a moment, she had been deeply shocked. I hesitated, unsure of what came next.

"Do you wish to see the rest of the house, or has all this put you off?"

"Oh yes. I don't know what brought me here today, but it was for a purpose. If anything, I am more interested than ever."

Her answer surprised me. It must have shown on my face, for it was now her turn to study me.

"You must not be concerned by what I've said. If what I experienced just now was a glimpse of the future, then it will happen. We cannot change it."

"It's strange," I replied. "I have felt something ever since I first became acquainted with this house. It's hard to define. At first, I thought it involved someone else. A girl I knew. Now I am not sure."

It was my companion's turn to be interested.

"Really! Tell me what you know of the house." She said.

The atmosphere had undergone a subtle change. No longer was it a simple developer and client relationship. I drew her from room to room of the main house and then in stages to the old flat, the kitchen garden and on to the gardens. We talked as friends. I told her of my involvement with Rollo and of the meetings with Miss Tyzack. I told her of the sorry state of the house when I had first seen it and the transformation that Dan and his team had wrought. I told her, without going into too much detail how Rollo, had left me in the lurch when the original scheme had fallen through and I found myself telling her of my hopes for the development I was undertaking.

We had emerged near the summer house where Jo and I had enjoyed our picnics. The lakes shone in the midday sunshine.

"Oh! This is wonderful. Carl will love this." She glanced at me.

"My husband. He has been ill for some time. He has to use a wheelchair more and more. I think this will give him his freedom again." She looked at her watch. "Heavens is that the time. I really must dash. I have to meet someone at Heathrow in a little over three hours time. It has been utterly enthralling and I will come again with Carl."

A thought had crossed my mind.

"I forgot to ask your name."

"I know. Isn't it silly when we have been talking like old friends. It's Renzburg. Celia Renzburg."

"And I'm Paul Bradley." We shook hands laughing at the sudden incongruity of social customs.

It was as we approached the forecourt that the name came to me.

"Carl Renzburg, I said. "The Renzburg Quartet. I saw them play once in London."

A look of infinite sadness crossed her face.

"Yes. Those were happier times. He doesn't play now. Life can be very cruel at times. It can be particularly hard for a musician." She forced a smile back again." Thank you again, Paul. And I really will be in touch."

"I Know."

I don't know why I said it, but some things one instinctively knows.

The lunch break I took after she had gone was a contemplative affair. It was easy enough to remember exactly what had happened and what she had said. Making any sort of sense of it was what created the difficulty. Thinking is virtually impossible in a dimension of which we have no knowledge or experience. Tired of grappling with the incomprehensible, I had soon brushed it out of my mind and returned to the more pressing problems of the present. Celia's final words that she would return with her husband kept returning as a reminder that I still had much to do.

After lunch, I returned to the work of clearing that her visit had interrupted. Somehow the work seemed easier. I worked with determination. By dusk I had cleared the whole of the strip below the north wall and for good measure had dug up the concrete bases of the old greenhouses. Dad would be pleasantly surprised and my own conscience would now allow me to concentrate on my original work schedule.

The remainder of the college holiday passed in a whirl of

work. The builders I had hired moved in. Walls were knocked out and new ones built. The old staircase to the flat was torn out and a new stairway created. The piles of materials diminished and the packs of kitchen units and appliances were transformed into a gleaming new kitchen. Bit by bit Dad's new living quarters took shape. On the other side of the wall that now blocked the old passage from the kitchen to the main house, it was possible to trace the layouts of the first apartments. I sank gratefully into bed each night exhausted from the days labours, but happy with the progress being made.

Dad moved in during the following week. I stood with him in the forecourt as he saw off the removal men who had transferred his effects.

"No regrets?"

"None!" The reply was emphatic. "That place was always a struggle. Well, perhaps just one. Your mother would have liked all this."

He looked around at the house and grounds and sniffed deeply before turning into the house. That evening we sat after a late dinner, tired from the day's exertions.

"Tomorrow we can perhaps make a start on sorting out your things," I ventured.

"Oh no," he replied without looking up from the catalogue of garden sundries he was reading. "That can wait. I've more important things to do."

The following morning, he was already hard at work assembling his greenhouse when I came down to breakfast in the new kitchen. I could see him from the kitchen window. His move had gone more smoothly than I had dared to hope. Over the past few weeks he seemed to have shed years from his age and found new purpose and direction. This house seemed to have the same strong influence on anyone who came near it.

It would have been so easy then to have begun the task of unpacking and arranging his things. For a moment I was tempted, but I sensed that this would have been fatal for our future harmony. So, I washed up my breakfast dishes and left him to his work while I went in search of mine.

I was itching to get started again. There were a thousand and one details to sort out before plumbers, electricians and all the other specialists could begin the fitting out of the first apartment. I was conscious that time was pressing. On Monday, the new college term with its all-important summer exams would commence. Somehow the development process would have to be fitted in around the demands of my lecturing role.

The morning's work took on a new urgency when I answered a telephone call. It was Jonathon Gardiner. He sounded very cheerful.

"Ah, Paul! I've been trying to get hold of you for the past two days."

"I've been away," was all I had time to say before he cut in.

"No matter. You're there now. It's all a bit sudden, but it's great news all the same. We just need to sort out a few details."

"Whoa Jonathon. What is great news?"

"The Renzburgs," he replied. "By the way did you know they are musicians. Apparently, he ran a chamber ensemble. Not my taste. I'm a jazz man. But they are just the sort of people you want for a scheme like yours. Sets the right tone. The daughter's a cello soloist."

"Jonathon, what are you trying to tell me?"

"Didn't you get my letter?" His voice sounded peevish.

I remembered with guilt the pile of unopened mail that was building up.

"I may have. I haven't had time to go through my mail."

"You mean you don't know yet?"

"Know what?"

"The Renzburgs are definite buyers. Their deposit money is already banked."

It took some moments for the news to sink in. Then panic gripped me.

"Which unit do they want? There is nothing ready. When do they want it ready?"

"Wrong pronoun." He chuckled as if enjoying some joke.

"What?"

"I said 'wrong pronoun'. It should be when do they want *THEM* ready."

"I don't understand."

"Them as in plural. More than one."

"Two!" I said incredulously.

"No. Three." He was openly laughing now. "The Renzburgs want three of your apartments. Two on the ground floor and one upstairs. One of them is for the daughter. The other will be for music practice and visiting friends. They'll need some minor changes to your plans, but I don't think that will be a problem... Hello! Are you still there?"

"Yes. I'm still here," I said quietly.

"It's a flyer," he continued. "I've never known a start like it." He paused, conscious that I was not responding as he expected.

"I'll call back later," he said. "You seem a bit overwhelmed."

I put the receiver down and sat back in my chair. Overwhelmed. There was not a word that expressed how I felt. How could he know. How could anyone know. Even allowing for the cost of the current work, the sale of three units together with Dad's money would bring us close to break even. There was no doubt in my mind that Celia Renzburg would complete. Once that was done... I hesitated, not daring to complete the thought. Even the hint of it had been enough to send a shiver of excitement through me. For months, I had lived with the almost inhuman burden of Rollo's debts. Every day since the shock of that first meeting with Gregory my thoughts had been concentrated on how to prevent that burden from crushing me. Jonathon's news had given the promise of escape.

I had allowed myself the merest glimpse of a time when I could start to live again. That short glimpse had been enough. Involuntarily I began to shake. I was aware of this wonderful feeling of relief. It seemed to rise from my feet and course gently through my body in warm streams that finally emerged as tears that trickled unabated down my face.

17

I had spent the morning in the coach house working on the final stage of my plans for the house. The conversion of the central section with its classical proportions had been relatively straightforward. The warren of small rooms that made up the old original wing presented an altogether more difficult proposition. This had been no grand design. It had grown haphazardly over the centuries with rooms and outbuildings added at will to meet the needs of the moment. Making sense of this jumble of rooms and passages was like attempting a jigsaw puzzle without the aid of a picture. I had spent several frustrating hours sketching alternative floor plans on graph paper. There seemed to be no simple solution. The building I had would not allow the size and purpose of all the rooms that modern living demands.

I was on the verge of tearing up my efforts when the answer came to me. I could make my own additions. So long as they were done in a sympathetic style and, on a scale that did not compromise Eastonbury's unique charm, I could not see any major problem in obtaining planning approval. The new work could be tailored to exact needs that would allow me to maximize the full potential of the old house. The more I thought about it, the more certain I became, that I was on the right track at last. It seemed such an obvious step at the time. It was only much later that it came to me that, in that simple way, I had made the momentous step from being architectural historian to architect; from being conservator to creator.

At the time that thought did not occur to me. My attention had been caught by the angle of the sunshine falling across my desk, telling me that it was early afternoon and reminding me that I had not eaten since eight that morning.

I was still on a high as I went down the stone steps of the coach house and into the forecourt. An unfamiliar convertible was parked near the main door. Its hood was down as if enjoying the early summer sunshine.

Celia and Carl were just emerging from the house. They walked slowly, Carl resting his hand on the wheelchair he would use when he became tired. I waited for them to approach.

"Hello Paul," Celia cried. "Isn't it a glorious day?"

"Perfect!" I replied with feeling. "And how are you today Carl?"

"The sunshine is good," he said. His voice still showed traces of German intonation. "Tomorrow I will be reaching the lake, I think."

"We go the long way around," said Celia. "That way we avoid the steep path by the temple."

"Not for long I hope."

"No. If Carl continues to get stronger, I think we might manage that too by the autumn."

"I hope so. Enjoy your walk. I'm off to get lunch."

"Oh! You will not have time for that," said Celia artfully. "There is someone waiting in the hall. Here to look at one of the apartments I imagine."

She read my face. "Did you not know?"

"No. I didn't. Thank you for alerting me."

I made my way across to the main house feeling puzzled. Since Celia's unexpected visit my arrangements with Jonathon had worked well. During weekdays, he drove out to

Eastonbury with any prospective buyers. At weekends, he let me know of any appointments and I showed them round. I had not heard from him and was not expecting anyone.

I pushed open the door and walked into the hall. A familiar figure stood beside the oak table that served as reception desk. She was reading one of Jonathon's brochures. She made no sign that she was aware of my presence as I walked across to her.

"So." I said. "You've come back."

"Yes." She said simply. "I wanted to see you. I hope I'm welcome."

"You're always welcome. You should know that."

I spoke calmly, but behind the words my thoughts were in turmoil. Since the day I had learned of Rollo's flight I had tried not to think of her. After the first few days I had adapted to life without her. It was as if she had suddenly ceased to exist and there had been so much happening to occupy my mind. Seeing her again came as a shock. She was as beautiful as ever. The sight of her had produced a violent punch beneath my rib cage which sent my heart leaping up into my throat. Whatever the calmness of my outward appearance, inwardly all was confusion.

"Thank you. I would have understood if you had not wanted anything to do with me."

She had continued to look at the brochure. Now she laid it aside and turned to look at me. We stood facing each other, unsure of what to say.

"Well." She finally said. "Look at all this. Big changes."

I shrugged. "A matter of survival."

"I would like you to tell me about it. There is also much I need to tell you, but not here. I think we need to be somewhere else."

"I was about to have lunch. Have you eaten?"

"No. I came straight here," she replied.

"Right. Let's go and eat somewhere. Inside or out?"

"I'm surprised that you need to ask."

"I take it that is a vote for outdoors."

"Yes. You decide where. We can pick something up along the way."

We walked out to her parked car. I held out my hand.

"I'll drive."

She handed me the keys without protest and took the passenger seat. A silk scarf had been left strewn across the seat. She tied this carefully to protect her hair as I headed off up the driveway.

I drove fast. I had not given any thought to the matter, but I knew exactly where to go. We rode in silence. I concentrated on my driving; she looked out at the passing vistas.

Clifton on a Saturday is a quiet place after the crowding activity of the working week. This was as we found it now, as we drove in over the Ashton Gate bridge. I found somewhere to park and we hunted down ready-filled rolls and some fruit. Then we walked down the Hotwells Road until we reached the lower slopes of Brandon Hill.

"The first time you brought a picnic to Eastonbury you spoke of unfinished business. We did not wind the clock back properly then."

"Don't Brad." She protested. "You can't pretend that the last nine years never happened."

"I'm not trying to. What happened has happened. We can't change that. What we can do is draw a line under it. This is where the thread broke. This is where we decide whether or not we want to tie it back together again."

She made no further protest and we picked our way up the sloping parkland. We settled near the top, a little below the Cabot Tower. We ate quietly, taking in the view of the floating harbour below. I think we were both conscious of what was to come and neither of us was sure how to broach what was foremost in our minds.

It was Jo who finally broke the silence.

"You've changed. You seem stronger, more assured."

"You mean I've finally grown up."

"No! That's not what I meant. You have always been grown-up. It's just that before, you were diffident. Now you seem to know what you want. There is an element of steel that was not there before."

I smiled ruefully.

"If there is, it is not so surprising. I've been put through the furnace. Underneath you'll find me still the same."

"It is nothing to be ashamed of. I think it's good."

She hesitated for a moment.

"I'm not only judging by what you do and have done. I'm also aware of what you didn't do. You didn't run away or crumple when Rollo walked out. You stood your ground and sorted out the mess. I admire you for that."

She reddened as she finished speaking, aware perhaps that she was revealing her feelings for the first time.

"Did you know that he had dropped me in it?"

"I don't know much about it, but I knew that he was planning to. That was what sparked off the final row with him."

That last phrase resonated in my head.

"You just used the words final row."

"There were lots of rows. That was the last one before I left him."

Again, I felt that sudden shock under my rib cage.

"You've left him." I said dazedly. "When?"

"It was months ago," she replied. "While he was still here in England."

"I thought you had gone with him. I saw the plane tickets.

"Plane tickets!"

"Yes. Air France. Paris to Rio de Janeiro. There were two of them."

"Where did you see those?"

"They were on Philippa's desk at The Cascades. I only had time to see who the top one was made out to. That was in Rollo's name. I assumed..."

"Well, we can guess who the other one was for."

I was still trying to make sense of everything. I looked at her bewildered.

"If you didn't go to Rio with him, where have you been all these weeks?"

"I was in North America, not South. I've been staying with my sister in California."

I shook my head in confusion. "I think you had best go back to the beginning."

"There's not a lot to tell," she said. "It was an awful time. I could sense that something was wrong, he had become very withdrawn and pre-occupied. There was obviously something important on his mind. Then the news broke about Oliver Meadowes' arrest and the corruption scandal, and the police came to the house looking for him."

"They questioned me too."

"Rollo wasn't at home at the time. He was chasing round like a scalded cat. He was probably planning to go off without saying anything, but I questioned him when he came home. At first, he tried to make out that it was nothing to do with him. He said it was just some VAT fraud that Oliver Meadowes had got involved in."

As she spoke she played with the fingers of her left hand. I noticed that she no longer wore her wedding ring.

"I laughed at him," she continued. "I asked him why he was behaving the way he was if it had nothing to do with him. Other things were said too. It got quite nasty."

"And did he admit anything?"

"Yes. He finally came clean. Told me all about their shady practices, all the bribery and manoeuvring. 'Oiling the wheels', he called it. He said it was common practice and that the sole reason that they were being investigated was because Meadowes had kept details of everything. I was horrified, not so much by what he had done – I'd become used to his standards – but by his refusal to see any wrong in it. The only mistake in his eyes was to have been found out. It was then he told me he was going to skip the country. A friend had a boat and would take him across the channel."

She stopped for a moment and lifted her eyes to me.

"I remember thinking at that moment that you would not have behaved in that way. Then it hit me that he might in some way have involved you. When I asked him how this would affect what you were doing at Eastonbury, he shrugged as if it was of no importance. He said the scheme was dead in the water. It meant leaving you in a hole, but he intended to look after his own interests and you would have to do the same."

She shook her head sadly, as if re-living the episode.

"I felt so very angry. Words could not have expressed the total loathing I felt for him at that moment. So, I simply handed him my wedding ring and told him I was leaving."

She obviously had not come to the end of her story. I said nothing.

"He didn't bat an eyelid. He made no effort to talk me out of leaving. He just said that was fine by him. He would be travelling light and I would be in the way. I can see now what he meant. He was already planning to take that whore from his office with him... It's strange isn't it. I used to dream of a life of adventure and travel to exotic places, and yet, when all this started to unravel, I didn't want any part of it. It all seemed as hollow and worthless as the life we'd been living here."

"Was that when you left?"

"Yes. I just threw all my clothes into my car and drove to my parents. Then I went on to San Diego to stay with Jen. She had asked me before. It was exactly what I needed. Plenty of sunshine and the time and space to sort things out in my head. Everything had turned upside down so suddenly. It would not have helped if you had been around. Can you understand that. You men are such simple creatures. We girls need time to adjust."

"I don't think we are so very different. Men simply get on with something practical."

"Like converting a minor stately home into flats."

"Something like that. It helps of course if you have one to hand."

Her eyes were suddenly full of sympathy.

"Has it been rough for you?"

"At times, but let's not talk about that."

"I'm sorry. I didn't know what else to do."

I took her hand gently in mine.

"It's alright. I knew something was wrong when you didn't show up at Eastonbury. I went over to The Cascades. There was only Philippa there clearing Rollo's papers and being as unhelpful as she could manage. That was when I saw the airline tickets. I knew then that he was running away. Deep down it is what I expected him to do. I thought that you were being the dutiful wife and going with him.

Jo shook her head sadly

"What a mess! I have been such a fool. I was taken in by him. I let him use me and, in the process, I hurt you."

"We were both used by him. I've been under his shadow half my life. He always seemed to have all the things I didn't have: looks, money, flair."

"And charm. He certainly had plenty of that, but that never was the attraction for me. I thought he was interesting and exciting. I expected him to open up a whole new world to me. I wanted to be part of it all, to share everything. I came to realize that there was nothing much to share. It was all a façade. There was nothing behind it."

Jo stood up.

"I need to walk. Let's find somewhere to get a coffee."

We walked round the shoulder of the hill past the functional university buildings and through the prim elegance of Berkeley Square. We found a coffee bar and sat looking across at the bulk of the university tower.

I stirred my coffee with a slow rhythm, my thoughts elsewhere.

"What I have never understood..."

"Why Rollo wanted me."

"No. Not wanted. I could understand any man wanting you. What has puzzled me is why he married you. I don't think he loved you."

"I don't think he really knew himself. From things he said, I got the impression that he was very lonely. He adored his father and loathed his mother."

"That I can understand. She could be a bit overpowering at times."

"His father was South American. Blake was a name his mother adopted when they came to England. I don't think he ever came to terms with his father's death and coming here to live. I think in the early years you were the nearest thing he had to family. You were the only person that he was fond of."

"He had a strange way of showing it."

She gave me a quizzical look.

"Didn't it ever cross your mind that he might be jealous of you?"

"Jealous! Of me!"

"Mm. Like sibling rivalry in a way. He seemed older, more assured than you when I first met him. That is probably how he saw it; a bit like an older brother."

"He was always very competitive."

"That's my point. Older siblings always expect to be first at everything. I think Rollo enjoyed competing with you, but he always wanted to maintain his edge over you. He once said how talented and competent you were, but that you had not yet realized it. I think that what he was trying to say was, that when you did realize it, it would not be so easy for him to lead."

"Are you saying that winning you over to him was just sibling rivalry?"

"It was one factor. I think too that deep down he wanted

to be happy as he had been as a child. The problem was he was afraid of being hurt again."

A rueful expression crossed her face and she shook her head.

"Poor Rollo! I don't think he had it in him to love anyone properly."

There was a strange finality about her words and the use of the pluperfect tense.

"Are you trying to tell me something Jo?" I looked at her intently. You're speaking of him as if he were dead."

"Rollo is dead, Brad. That is what I came here to tell you."

It took some seconds for her words to sink in. Even then, it did not register fully. Instead the memory of Rollo bronzed and carefree driving us to Blagdon in his sports car came to mind. It was inconceivable that someone like Rollo, who had always lived life to the full, could be dead. In shock, I could only echo the dread word.

"Dead!"

"It was some weeks ago. He left Brazilia in a private plane bound for Bolivia. It came down in the jungle. The authorities have found the wreckage. There was no sign of any survivors. He has now been officially declared dead."

"And this is the sole reason you came?"

"Amongst other things. I wanted to see you; to explain how things stood." She paused and took a deep breath before continuing. "I also needed to consult my own solicitors and my parents."

As she spoke she had occupied herself re-arranging the contents of her bag. She snapped its clasp shut and looked at me.

"It had been my intention to divorce him as soon as I was able. I still intend to continue with that plan."

The stark simplicity of her words shocked me as much as the news which had preceded them. Nor was it solely the words themselves. It was also the cold determination with which they were delivered. It was a Jo I had not seen before.

"Why do you need a divorce? You're a free woman now that Rollo is dead."

She looked at me pityingly.

"You're too nice Brad. Even now you cannot accept how duplicitous he could be."

I had been too busy fighting the nagging feeling of foreboding that had begun to overtake an afternoon that seemingly had begun so well. The implications of what she had said finally took hold.

"Are you saying that you don't think he's dead?"

"I'm not sure. I need to be certain. All I know is that the Brazilian authorities have closed the file on the plane crash. Officially there were no survivors."

"And you think that he may have survived?"

"He may not even have been on that plane. It might have been set up. I have doubts. Call it female intuition. Wanted man disappears in one of the most inaccessible corners of the globe. Roland Blake, who was not really Roland Blake, is declared dead and leaves virtually no trace that he ever existed. It all seems too convenient. In the meantime, I'm left hanging in limbo."

"Let it go. It's not worth it. You will only damage yourself."

She turned on me fiercely.

"No way! I gave that man nine years of my life. I accepted his infidelities. I was denied the children I wanted. I worked like a slave entertaining his business associates. Do you honestly expect me to walk away while he swans off with that creature from his office?"

She opened her bag again and took out a pack of cigarettes and a delicate lighter. She produced a flame with the lick of a manicured nail, holding the cigarette in a strangely impersonal way. Then she sat back and inhaled deeply. When she continued, she no longer seemed to speak to me. It was as if she were speaking to herself.

"I need to draw a line under all of this. I need to know

whether he is alive or dead and what has happened to all his money and property. Then I can start a new life."

A gulf had opened between us. I had sensed its existence earlier. Now it was all too obvious. She faced me from the other side of that rift and even though we continued speaking the gap between us slowly widened. Moment by moment the girl I had known seemed to recede into the distance.

We left the coffee bar shortly afterwards and walked back to the car.

"Are you going back to America?"

"Yes. Jen is expecting a baby. I've promised to help run her business for a while. I can get a residency permit that way."

"And after that?"

"Who knows. Once you have left England, you realize what a small place it is."

She smiled at me ruefully, almost apologetically it seemed.

"And you?"

"I have to finish off at Eastonbury – the old wing. I was working on that this morning."

It was strange saying 'this morning'. It seemed half a lifetime away.

"I have just about broken even so far. It will be nearly all profit from now on."

"Will you stay there?"

"Probably. Dad lives in Miss Tyzack's old flat and I want to turn the coach house into a proper base. You know. Somewhere to come back to."

We had reached her car. I handed her keys back to her.

"Are you alright for money?"

"Yes. Thank you Brad. That was sweet of you."

She paused as she unlocked the car door.

"That was what first started the doubts," she said. "The money. It was odd. He had made out a will, but the only asset it listed was a single bank account. Nothing else. Just this one account with two hundred thousand pounds in it. Neat don't you think?"

"Very." I replied, my mind instantly noting that two hundred thousand pounds was exactly the amount he had withdrawn from the partnership account on the day before he had fled.

"You seemed miles away then."

I smiled at her. "Just thinking." I said.

She got into the car. I remained standing beside her.

"Don't you want a lift back to Eastonbury?"

"No. I think I will stay on in town. I've not seen Steve for a while."

She started the engine and looked out at me.

"It's best this way Brad." She said. "I'm enormously fond of you, but broken threads don't retie easily."

I nodded agreement.

"I know. Stay well and be happy."

"You too." She said.

She slipped the car into gear and eased forward.

"I'll write when I have any news." She called.

A hand waved briefly from the window and then she was gone.

After she had gone I stayed on in Clifton for a while. I felt empty in the strange sort of way one does after important events. I found myself drawn back to the suspension bridge. This time it was not as a source of solace; it was more a form of habit. This is where I came when I needed to think. Now it was to review past events. I needed a mental unwinding.

It was early evening when I headed down to the harbourside to find Steve. I found him in his local and we decided to make a night of it.

I gave him a brief recital of what had happened.

"How do you feel now that Jo has gone."

"A bit strange, but I'm alright. Deep down I think I've known all along how it would end."

"Good." He said. "Lovely girl, but I never thought she was

quite right for you. Thought that even before she married the Runner."

"You didn't say."

"None of my business."

We sat for a while nursing our drinks in companionable silence.

"Do you think he's still alive?" I eventually ventured.

"The devil is said to look after his own." He grinned with a flash of the old Steve. "I think Jo may well be right. It all looks too neatly packaged. First of all, there's what we know about – the money in the account. All nice and tidy as if it was a non-negotiable divorce settlement. No leads. No loose ends. But then, there is what we don't know anything about. There is the house in Chile and all the other assets he was left when his father died. Then there is the company he transferred the loan into that you

asked me to check out. I have not been able to find any trace of that. If he had disposed of any of these, I would expect there to be more cash."

"You think it might be under another name."

"I'd bet money on that. It has all the signs of a carefully planned disappearing act. Of course, it doesn't prove that he is still alive. He might have arranged all this and then been very unlucky, but I can't buy that. I would say it's odds on he's still alive. Is that what you think?"

I nodded in agreement.

"I thought Jo was being a bit wild at first, but then when I began to think about it more.... "

"You don't think he could have been unlucky?"

"Luck is a word I would never associate with Rollo. Things did not happen to him: he made them happen."

Steve studied his glass

"Sadly, we shall probably never know."

David Ramsay's words came back to me.

"There is a possibility, although it's a slim one. Every architect has his own style, his own way of doing things. To anyone knowledgeable it is something instantly recognizable. Rollo has a very distinctive style. It is almost like a signature."

"You would know if he ever designed anything again."

"Oh yes. I know his work better than anyone."

"Unless of course he disguises his style."

"Difficult. It would mean an entire change of personality."

Steve was enjoying this examination of the hypothetical.

"So how likely is it that you would come across it. I mean if he is alive, he's likely to stay in South America."

"There would be coverage in journals. That sort of thing. It is a possibility, and if it happens it will be pure chance. I don't intend to go looking for him."

"No thoughts of getting even?"

"How could I get even: walk off with his money, put him through hell for months? That's not my style. In any case, when you weigh everything up, I don't think that I have come out too badly."

"You are unbelievable. Do you know that? If I had been treated by him in the way he has treated you, I would want his hide nailed to a tree."

"That's because you are a miserable bean counter with no soul." I answered with a grin. "I think that I will leave getting even to Jo. She was talking of hiring a private detective to find out what he has been up to."

"Was she now," said Steve.

He raised his glass.

"That's something I will drink to."

Too much of the past year had been spent alone and working feverishly to balance the demands of my lecturing job with unfolding events at Eastonbury. Although I would never have admitted to it, had it been suggested, I badly needed a break from work and some decent company. That weekend with Steve provided both. The easy companionship of the days when we shared the Clifton flat returned. It was exactly the tonic I needed. I do not know whether Steve had sensed my needs and had acted intuitively or if we had simply fallen back into old habits. Whatever the reason, it had worked. I returned to the lecture room after the week-end feeling a new man. For the next few days even the banality of teaching could not undermine the simple joy in living that I felt.

It was a little puzzling at first. As the week progressed it slowly dawned on me that other forces might have been at work. It was perhaps not so much what Steve had done, but what I had contributed myself that produced such feelings. Jo's unexpected visit had marked a turning point. I felt a certain emptiness, but no deep sadness at her going. In some strange way, the news she had brought and our final parting had acted as a powerful catharsis. The well-being I felt was the effect of release from emotions long bottled up.

Lying in bed at night reflecting, I could now see what others must have noticed. I had become too obsessed with getting back at Rollo. It had taken over my thinking far too strongly, overruling my normal caution and drawing me into all the many difficulties of the past year. Belatedly I had been shown that I did not need to compete on those terms. I could move forward; lead my own life; make my own plans. It seemed that a whole new world awaited me.

Those sentiments proved premature. The skin of the old life had not been entirely sloughed off. Even as I enjoyed the first days of my new freedom, wheels were in motion that would bring into effect Rollo's last surprising play. I received a letter from a Bristol solicitor advising me that he had been retained to execute a deed of gift made in my favour. It asked me to make an appointment to see him and to bring with me evidence of my identity and domicile.

I made my way to the appointment puzzled by what it could mean. In a final ironic twist, I found the solicitor's office was situated next door to the bank where I had had the fateful interview with Gregory. This new interview proved to be much shorter and far less traumatic than the earlier one. No details were provided. We spoke briefly and I handed over the documents that had been requested. Within ten minutes I found myself back in the street knowing little more than when I entered.

It was some weeks later, after checks had been carried out, that I was asked to make a second appointment. It was then that I learned the nature and origin of my gift. I think the lawyer was enjoying the drama of the occasion, for he gave no clue as to the nature of the gift. He declared that he was satisfied that I was indeed whom I claimed to be and could therefore legally receive the gift. Then with a theatrical flourish he drew a folder from a drawer in his desk and handed it to me. Inside the folder were the title deeds and keys to The Cascades.

The letter authorizing the gift was short and formal. It had been drawn up by a lawyer in Rio de Janeiro. The original was in Portuguese and a translation had been provided. It gave no reason or explanation for the gift. It was dated 17th March and had presumably been written some days before the plane Rollo had hired came down in the jungle en route to Bolivia.

III

18

It had been a strange path which had brought me here, I reflected, as I lay on the leather couch watching drifts of cloud pass over the atrium. Strangest of all had been the way in which this house had been gifted to me. That continued to be greatly intriguing. I had spent long hours questioning Rollo's motives. At the end of that exercise I felt none the wiser. In the end, I remembered Jo's comments about his inner hollowness. Perhaps there was no hidden agenda. Perhaps any attempt at second guessing was futile. The gift of the property was an accomplished fact. It seemed best to take it at face value.

There remained the question of whether Rollo was alive or dead and whether or not the gift and its timing threw any further light on this. I ran over and over all the evidence, probing for any hint of significance. My initial reaction was that here was further proof that his disappearance had been stage-managed. Why else, I reasoned, would he have made the gift as a discrete issue only days before the plane crash, unless it was to keep it separate from the remainder of his estate. Later, after playing devil's advocate against myself, I could see that, equally strongly, it could be taken as proof that the gift had been made at a time when he could have had no anticipation of his impending death.

All such thoughts were pushed into the background when I drove across to take possession of my new property. The initial shock had given way to uncertainty. The uncertainty had deepened once inside the front door. As I moved from room to room one single thought grew in my head. What was to be done with such a property.

I had sat down on the atrium couch to think through that simple question. The splashing of the flowing water and the general atmosphere of the house had then taken over and turned my thoughts in other directions. Whether because of its height or the way it offered its space, this house seemed always to have had an uncanny power to show people in their true guise. That power had worked again now. My review of past events had provided the answer I sought. Looking back, the self I had seen was a shy, self-effacing younger man, who throughout his friendship with Rollo had allowed himself to be dominated. At the end, I was not sure whether he was genuinely trying to help me or simply using me. The Cascades was impressive – Rollo himself had claimed it was by far his best work. That in itself made the point. So long as I owned it, this house would remain a potent symbol of that old dominance. If the burgeoning shoots of my self-assurance were to be allowed to grow untrammelled, this house could form no part of my life. I decided that I would sell it and send most of the proceeds of the sale to Jo.

I had lost all track of time lying there with my thoughts. When I finally let myself out and locked the door behind me the sun had already slipped away to the west and there was a cold edge to the developing greyness.

During the following days, the intense feeling of well-being I had experienced after Jo's visit gradually faded. In its place, a sense of calm purposefulness developed. I worked steadily.

The overall shape for the additions I planned for the old wing took shape and I could concentrate on the detail that would tie them in with the original. There was even time to think ahead to making a prolonged visit to Italy and the completion of the book. I felt at peace and life was good.

The serenity of my affairs might have warned a more experienced head that this would not last. A more cautious mind might have reminded that loose ends from my former problems remained to be tidied away. Almost certainly such a mind would have counselled a degree of wariness: a man with Fielding's love of control would not find it easy to accept interference with long-cherished plans. None of these thoughts occurred to me. Deep in the folds of Eastonbury's valley it was difficult to escape the opiate of its peace.

I had worked late. The end of the college term was approaching with the usual flurry of work. It was well after midnight when I slipped into bed. Sleep did not come at once. I lay for a time, thinking back to my last visit to Italy, sensing in memory all its sights and smells. Suddenly I tensed. I thought that I had heard a sound. It had been very brief and had not been repeated. It sounded like the crunch of gravel, the sort of noise a vehicle might make turning slowly on a gravel surface.

I lay still, listening for further confirmation. There was nothing. Slowly I relaxed and again settled myself for sleep. Then I stiffened again. There was no question now. Across the still night air had carried the unmistakeable chink of metal tools.

Hurriedly I slipped into the clothes I had earlier shrugged off and went in search of a torch. There was no moon and it was quite dark when I quietly let myself out of the flat into the walled garden. The gate into the forecourt seemed to groan more loudly than usual as a I opened it. I peered round it cautiously, uncertain of what lay on the other side. It was too dark to see anything clearly. I switched on my torch and swung its beam round in a broad arc. The forecourt was empty. Behind it the bulk of the house formed a featureless dark mass against the overcast sky. I focussed the beam on the main entrance. It was secure and undisturbed.

Doubt returned. Had it been my imagination at work. Everything seemed fine. I stood for a moment uncertain of what to do next. A voice inside my head urged me to go back to bed. Then the voice of reason cut in. An odd sound did not signify anything it said, but I had distinguished two sounds. Both of them were man-made. Two meant coincidence. I took a deep breath. In my book coincidence is always significant.

A picture formed in my head of a vehicle slowly swinging in from the end of the drive. I had done it dozens of times myself. Instinctively I had already begun to cross to the coach house yard. I flashed my torch as I passed under the arch. My car stood where I had left it. Next to it was the pick-up truck Dad had recently bought. In the other covered bay was Celia Renzburg's car. They were merely noted in passing as the beam of my torch swept round the yard, for I had already sensed there was something else. The torch beam came to rest on a dark coloured van, its rear doors swung wide open. It had been backed up to the door that lead into the old wing.

I moved carefully around the van. Behind it the door into the house stood open. I switched off my torch and edged carefully into the house. Immediately inside I banged my shins painfully against something solid that partially blocked the passageway. I could hear grunting and shuffling noises approaching. There was a dull thud as something heavy was set down. I pressed myself against the wall, but they remained in the first of the rooms. I could hear them breathing heavily as they recovered from their exertions.

"Is that it then?" A voice asked in a hoarse whisper.

"Naw. There's anuvver, a real beauty. Get your crowbar Ronnie."

I froze. The second voice was unmistakeably that of Billy Bedford.

"You'll break the fuckin springs on the van if we take any more."

"Why are you worryin about fuckin springs when there's five fuckin grand in there waitin to be picked up." Bedford growled. "Now get in there."

I heard them moving off. Ronnie whined something about getting on with the other job, but it was indistinct and they quickly passed out of earshot. I waited a few moments until I judged it was safe to show a light and then flashed my torch along the passageway. Ahead of me sections of two of the house's stone fireplaces had been set down ready for loading. Ronnie Bedford and the other voice must have been working here for some time before the arrival of the van had alerted me.

I swung my torch back along the passageway to the outside door. My blood froze when I saw what I had banged against in the dark. Stacked by the door were four five-gallon petrol cans. These could only be part of the other job Ronnie had wanted to get on with. The Bedford's intentions were quite clear. They planned to set fire to the house before they left.

As I took in their preparations, I made out sounds which I guessed were of a door being forced. It could only be the door to the Renzburg apartment on the ground floor. As quickly as I could, I manoeuvred past the stone blocks and rushed through the vacant rooms into the entrance hall. The door to the Renzburg apartment was wide open. A faint glow shone from the sitting room. The three were grouped around the fireplace. Bedford held a torch while Ronnie and the third man attempted to lever the stone blocks free from the wall with a heavy crowbar. Without thinking I threw myself at them.

I remember yelling at them as forcefully as I knew how. I think I was trying to seize the crowbar, but the force of my intervention sent Ronnie sprawling against the unknown figure. The crowbar spun from his grasp and fell with a clatter on the hearth.

Bedford recovered from the surprise very quickly.

"He's on his own." His coarse voice rasped. "Nail the bastard."

I turned to him as he spoke, just as he took a wild swing at me with the heavy torch. It missed my head, but gave me a painful blow on the shoulder. Behind me the other two had scrambled to their feet. I heard strange grunts and snorts and then a roar that was almost primeval in its ferocity. Two long muscular arms wrapped themselves round my body, pinioning my arms to my side. I sensed then that I was fighting for my life.

The work I had been doing over the past year had toughened me up considerably. I think I would have been a match for most normal men, but there was nothing at all normal about the grip I was in. There was an apelike strength to those arms. I tried everything in my power to free myself. I bucked and twisted, heaved and dropped my weight suddenly, but all to no avail. Every move I made was countered by a tightening of that awful hold. I felt that my breath was being squeezed out of me.

As I was held the other man lunged at me. I defended myself in the only way left to me and kicked as hard as I could in the direction of his crotch. My foot made hard contact and he doubled up in the foetal position with a screamed sob of pain. Between gasps I heard him mouthing expletives and threatening all forms of dire consequences.

For the moment, he was out of it and what he might do to me in the future was of no concern. I already had more than I could handle in the form of Ronnie. I felt him slacken his grip slightly and heard him draw in a deep gasping breath as if winding himself up for some new extra effort. All of a sudden, he let go his hold and took my left arm in both hands. Then with another of his animal roars he swung me violently round and hurled me with all his might against the wall.

I could see what he was attempting, but I was powerless to stop myself. The arc of the swing had turned me towards the fireplace. I hit the corner of the chimney breast with a sickening thud and sank to the floor, conscious of a terrible pain down the right-hand side of my ribs. As I fought off waves of nausea I was aware of Ronnie grabbing the crowbar and taking a vicious swing at my head. I tried to roll away, but my actions were weak and he caught me a glancing blow to the side of my head.

I felt a violent slab of pain. Bright flashes alternated with swirling blackness as I passed in and out of consciousness. Suddenly the room was bathed in light. For a moment, I was aware of Ronnie kneeling over me, his face contorted as I had never seen human face before, his eyes glaring red, his arm raised for one final blow. Then a slight figure threw herself between us. Her arms cradled my head in protection. As if from mists I heard Celia's cry, terrible in its fear and anguish.

"Stop it! You'll kill him!"

Between wraiths of grey mist, I saw Bedford trying to wrestle Ronnie away. I felt Celia's body shaking with sobs of relief. Then blackness closed in.

Consciousness came by slow degrees. I seemed as a swimmer immersed in opaque grey waters. I swam seemingly without effort or need of oxygen. For an immeasurable period of time I moved effortlessly through this shadowy world. My arms made no strokes, no current tugged at me, yet I was aware that I was slowly rising. The water through which I moved gradually becoming more pellucid. The shadows of this strange world, though indistinct, developed substance. Finally, there was light. A pale suffusion of sunlight played on the surface of the waters far above. By slow degrees it brightened as I rose until finally I broke its gauzy surface to emerge into the unaccustomed brightness of a still and sunlit room.

It took a little time to become even half conscious of my new surroundings. I yawned away the remnants of sleep and took stock. I was lying in a metal-framed bed in the centre of a small room that had hospital stamped all over it. A clipboard lay on the invalid table that spanned the foot of the bed. On a chair alongside the table a familiar figure sat. His face was drawn with tiredness. I gave him a tired grin.

"Hello Dad."

"Hello son."

He jumped to his feet at once and moved closer so that he could take my hand. He stood holding it in both of his without attempting to speak. I think he found this an easier way to express his feelings than words.

"How are you feeling?" He finally asked.

"Not so bad. My head feels a bit sore though."

Instinctively I raised my right arm to touch the place. The movement produced a stab of pain down the right side of my chest. I grunted audibly.

"My chest hurts like hell."

"Three of your ribs are broken and the rib cartilages have been sprung. They will mend. It was your head we were worried about."

"I'm fine Dad. Honestly. He didn't catch me full on."

"It's just as well he only had one go at you. You have Mrs Renzburg to thank for that. She saved your life you know."

"I know. I may have saved hers and Carl's too. The Bedfords were planning to torch the house."

"Cowardly bastards!" He spoke with a depth of real venom and disgust. It was the first time I had ever heard him use strong language. "What exactly have you got yourself mixed up in?"

"I'll tell you everything soon, but not now."

I was saved from further questioning by the arrival of a young nurse.

"Oh! You're awake." She said. "There's a policeman called to see how you are getting on. I told him you were still asleep."

I was about to say that it would be alright for him to come in, but there was no need. Inspector Richards had already appeared in the doorway.

"This will take only a moment." He said. "How are you?"

"Apart from a sore head and some broken ribs, I'm fine."

Dad was looking narrowly at him. "Is this the new policing we hear of," he asked, "or is there some other reason?"

Richards gave a half smile.

"Your son's state of health has a bearing on what charges we shall bring against the Bedford clan."

Dad gave a snort of disgust. I was more interested in what Richards had revealed.

"You have arrested them then."

"Have you not been told? Yes. We had quite a party last night. I would like you to make a statement when you are feeling up to it."

He began to move towards the door, but paused for a moment to make a parting comment to Dad.

"We have a job to do Mr Bradley. That doesn't mean we are not human beings."

DC Grainger hurried into the room as the Inspector was speaking. He went directly to Richards and whispered urgently in his ear. Richards face went taut. He quickly strode out of the room with Cowan in pursuit.

A few minutes later he re-appeared.

"There's been a new development. There was a fire last night at your friend Blake's house – the fancy glass place. A team from the fire service was there most of the night. When they examined the site this morning they found a man's body. We think it might be Blake. I would like you to identify the body if you feel up to it. I have had a word with your Doctor.

He wants to examine you first. I'll leave DC Grainger here to bring you over."

"Why can't you leave him be!" Dad turned on him angrily. "You can see that he's not fit."

Richards remained unperturbed.

"I can understand your concern," he said steadily. "I don't like doing this, but a man is dead and this is now a possible murder enquiry."

Hospital routines, like Moses strictures are seemingly passed down from on high and set in stone. There is a timetable that governs each event of the day and cannot be changed. Due processes have to be followed and can in no circumstance be altered or hurried. Almost two hours elapsed before a doctor appeared and gave his approval. It took another painful ten minutes to get dressed and follow Grainger outside to his car.

We drove in silence until we were through the heaviest traffic. I took the opportunity to study my driver from the passenger seat. He must have been in his early twenties. Without the presence of the older and more senior Richards he seemed much more relaxed.

"You OK?" he finally asked. "Say if I am going too fast for you."

Taking my silence to mean yes, he continued driving as before. After a few moments, he turned and grinned at me.

"That was a choice crowd you were mixing with last night."

"They were not exactly there by invitation."

"Maybe not, but I don't think I would have done what you did."

"I didn't stop to think." I rejoined with an attempt at a smile. "When I saw the petrol cans I just reacted."

"It was lucky for you that we got there in time. Ronnie Bedford has form. Did time for re-arranging a bloke's face with a broken bottle. He's dangerous – a listed psychopath.

We are under orders never to tackle him solo. He pulled a knife on us last night. It took three of the uniformed lads to restrain him."

He chuckled at the recollection.

"I reckon his head was a bit sorer than yours this morning."

"Who was the other man with them?"

"Jackie Smith, another piece of low life. His mother is Billy's sister."

"Nice family business."

"Yes. Well now they will all be able to play happy families inside."

"What will they get?"

"Who knows. It's sure to be a long stretch. There's Breaking and Entering, Armed Trespass, Theft, Attempted Arson, GBH, Resisting Arrest." He paused. "Maybe attempted murder." He looked at me as he listed the final possibility. "Like I said, lucky for you we arrived in time."

I sat quietly for a few moments as it sank in how close a call it had been, but already another thought had arisen. I turned painfully in my seat, judging that he might be relaxed enough to provide an answer.

"I realize now just how lucky I was last night, but that is what's puzzling me. The fight only lasted a few minutes. How did you manage to get out to Eastonbury so quickly?"

Grainger stole a quick glace across at me and reflected for a moment.

"Look. I'm not supposed to tell you this, so make sure it doesn't go any further. It wasn't chance. We have been trying to tie others in with the corruption business, one in particular. We know he's involved, but he's clever. There's nothing we can pin on him. The chief won't allow us to put a tap on his phone – he's too well connected. We have just had to wait for a break. Yesterday we got lucky. Some of the lads have been keeping an eye on your friends the Bedfords for some time. Yesterday they followed them up to the water tower on the

Downs. It seems they had a meeting there with some well-dressed gent driving a Daimler. They took the registration number and checked it out."

"Fielding."

"Very good. Got it in one."

"So, you followed them here and let them break in and rip fireplaces out. They could have set fire to the place."

Grainger was unperturbed.

"I can see how it looks from your point of view," he said. "What you must realize is that we had to give them time to incriminate themselves. There is only one road in or out of that place of yours. It was the perfect trap. We had not anticipated that you would barge in and pick a fight with them."

I made no reply. We had reached the edge of the village. Up ahead I could see a group of vehicles clustered around the entrance to The Cascades' driveway. We had to park a little way off. As we walked towards the house, the full horror of the night's events revealed itself.

I had to stop to take it all in. The dark mirrored beauty of Rollo's creation was gone. Only the ground floor structure remained, its stonework blackened with soot and smoke. The whole of the upper floor had disappeared as a recognizable structure. Its great glass panels and the steelwork that had supported them had collapsed. Broken glass lay everywhere. In the centre, the cascade and its pools were hidden beneath a tangle of twisted metal where the great crown of the atrium had imploded. I felt sickened at the sight of this devastation. A feeling of nausea rose from the pit of my stomach and I had to swallow hard to suppress it. Beside me I heard Grainger's gasp of shock.

A small knot of figures was grouped in the remains of the atrium. Grainger gestured towards them.

"The boss is over there."

We walked past the small fire tender parked in the drive and made our way into the shattered building. Close up the destruction was even more sickening. The heat of the fire must have been intense. Metal framework had twisted into strange helix spirals and, what I had first thought were pools of dirty water, were revealed as the solidified remains of glass that had simply melted.

Richards led me over to the edge of the main cascade pool. Steel jacks had been used to shore up the fallen wreckage. Beside the pool lay a plumped-out body bag. Richards indicated the pool.

"The body was found in there. He must have climbed in to escape the fire. Ironic isn't it. The surgeon says that he thinks the man died as a result of a severed artery in his thigh. A chunk of glass must have fallen on him. Then he simply bled to death."

He gave a sigh of finality and turned to me.

"We know when he died and we know how he died. The fire service's preliminary investigations indicate that the fire was deliberately started, which raises the question 'why'. Before we can answer that we need to know who he is."

He indicated that I should approach the body bag. I moved forward slowly. My heart was in my throat as he drew back the zip.

"Is this Roland Blake?" he asked.

As he pulled back the side flap of the bag apprehension gave way to relief. Even in death there was no mistaking the arrogant urbanity of the face that had been revealed.

"No." I replied. "That's not Rollo. That is Francis Fielding."

He zipped up the bag, his face deep in thought.

"Fielding. Now what the devil was he doing here."

"Presumably he started the fire," I ventured.

"It looks very much like it," was Richards' thoughtful reply.

"Only he stayed on too long admiring his handiwork," Grainger added. "Perhaps he didn't have chance to get out."

Oliver Meadowes' graphic description of the difficulties

his men had encountered when constructing the crown had been running through my head since we had arrived at the site. Now another thought had arisen.

"Was this a petrol fire?"

Richards looked at me questioningly. "What are you thinking?" he asked.

"This part of the house was a huge atrium running up the full height of the building. Its roof was in the form of an intricate crystal crown. It was a very advanced design and by its nature relatively flimsy."

Grainger could see the way my thoughts were running.

"And petrol explodes when it ignites. So, if he had sloshed a fair bit around in a house that was shut up, you think there could have been a sort of shock wave."

"Exactly. The crown was designed for effect and to light the atrium. It didn't have to be strong. Its sections fitted together in a way that enabled them to hold themselves up and withstand external wind pressure. It was not designed to take pressure coming from underneath."

Richards stood cogitating for a moment.

"Interesting." He finally declared. "You may have something there Mr Bradley. We can check that out with the fire investigators."

His face immediately returned to its earlier puzzled expression.

"That still does not explain what he was up to. Why would he want to burn down an empty house?"

"Perhaps he was a pyromaniac," Grainger suggested.

"Pyromaniacs do this sort of thing regularly. They do not usually end up killing themselves." Richards replied acidly.

"You had some dealings with them," he continued turning to me. "Was there any grudge between Blake and Fielding? Had Blake crossed him in some way? Did Blake owe him money?"

"There was no enmity that I know of." I thought hard

before continuing. "In any case, I don't think that this was directed against Rollo. I think it was aimed at me."

Richards was looking at me in an interested way. He nodded to himself.

"It had crossed my mind that events here and at your property at Eastonbury might be connected. What makes you think that you were the target?"

"Fielding was paranoid and a control freak. He kept himself under tight control. His great passion was exercising control over other people. When I began to convert Eastonbury, I was in effect refusing to allow myself to be controlled by him. It spoiled a major scheme he had cooked up. I don't think he could handle being thwarted."

"Let me get this straight," Richards said. "Are you saying that he was a bad loser?"

I nodded my agreement.

"So how could he be getting at you by burning down Blake's house?"

I took a deep breath before replying.

"This house no longer belonged to Rollo. A few weeks ago, he made a legal gift of it to me from Brazil."

Richards face registered no change of expression. He sighed deeply.

"If you are feeling up to it Mr Bradley," he said. "I think you and I need to have a long talk back at the station."

It was approaching eight that evening when Grainger drove me back to Eastonbury. The easy attitude of the morning had gone. It had been a long day and he had reverted back to being a policeman. We had passed the trip in silence. Then as we pulled up in front of the house he turned to me.

"Your pal Blake," he said. "Do you think he is still alive?"

"Maybe. Who knows. Do you think your boss believed my story?"

"Probably. Most of it tallies with what we already know."

He gave a broad grin. "And we shall check out the rest. Now try and stay out of trouble."

I watched him drive away up the avenue. I was still thinking of his question. I remembered the dread I had felt as Richards had unzipped the body bag. I had wanted desperately for it not to be Rollo. I hoped he was alive. For all his faults, I thought, the world would be a less interesting place without him.

Across the parkland, behind the woods, the sun had almost disappeared. There was a distinct chill to the air that promised a late frost. I shivered in the cold air. Suddenly I felt very sore and tired.

I made my way through the gates into the walled garden. Dad was still at work in his greenhouse, probably fussing with the heaters. I went on into the house. There was a single letter for me lying on the hall table. I slipped it into my pocket without really looking at it and went to make myself a cup of tea.

I took the tea upstairs to the sitting-room. I was pleased to see that Dad had lit a fire. The letter came back to mind as I settled down by the fireside. It was from the bank manager, Gregory, reminding me that the next instalment of the loan repayment was due at the end of the next month. I made a quick mental calculation. The date was almost six weeks off. Either he was getting jittery or this was a manoeuvre of Fielding's to put pressure on me. On balance, I thought it more likely to be the latter. Either way it did not matter now.

I held letter and envelope over the fire and let them drop into the flames. The papers arched and curled in the heat and finally burst into flame. They burned with bright yellow flames that flared strongly for a few moments and then died, leaving only husks that glowed orange-red until they too began to lose their integrity. Piece by piece they broke up. Each fragment in turn fell between the burning logs until all were indistinguishable from the rest of the glowing embers.

www.ingramcontent.com/pod-product-compliance
Lightning Source LLC
Chambersburg PA
CBHW051441050726
47593CB00005B/1874